PRAISE FOR
VALERIE WOLZIEN
AND HER NOVELS

"Valerie Wolzien is a consummate crime writer. Her heroines sparkle as they sift through clues and stir up evidence in the darker, deadly side of suburbia."

— MARY DAHEIM

"Wit is Wolzien's strong suit. . . . Her portrayal of small-town life will prompt those of us in similar situations to agree that we too have been there and done that."

— *The Mystery Review*

By Valerie Wolzien
Published by Fawcett Books:

Susan Henshaw mysteries:
MURDER AT THE PTA LUNCHEON
THE FORTIETH BIRTHDAY BODY
WE WISH YOU A MERRY MURDER
AN OLD FAITHFUL MURDER
ALL HALLOWS' EVIL
A STAR-SPANGLED MURDER
A GOOD YEAR FOR A CORPSE
'TIS THE SEASON TO BE MURDERED
REMODELED TO DEATH
ELECTED FOR DEATH
WEDDINGS ARE MURDER
THE STUDENT BODY

Josie Pigeon mysteries:
SHORE TO DIE
PERMIT FOR MURDER
DECK THE HALLS WITH MURDER
THIS OLD MURDER

DEATH AT A DISCOUNT

VALERIE WOLZIEN

FAWCETT BOOKS • NEW YORK

A Fawcett Book
Published by The Ballantine Publishing Group
Copyright © 2000 by Valerie Wolzien

www.randomhouse.com/BB/

Library of Congress Catalog Card Number: 00-107301

ISBN 0-449-00630-1

Manufactured in the United States of America

First Ballantine Books Edition: December 2000

10 9 8 7 6 5 4 3 2 1

ONE

LIKE MANY COUPLES MARRIED FOR DECADES, THE WORTHS
had created little vignettes which they brought out on occasion to demonstrate exactly who they were. This evening the
Worths were attending a large party introducing potential
new members to the Hancock Field Club. Scott Worth, posed
with one elbow resting on an ornate marble mantel, a glass
of Scotch in hand, was repeating a favorite anecdote to an
attentive audience.

"The license plate on the BMW I gave her last Christmas
says it all. SHESHOPS. Get it? She shops. And, boy, does she.
My wife is the original shopaholic. Clothes, jewelry, furniture, imported appliances, art knickknacks, you name it. And
she can tell you the most expensive place to buy one—hell,
buy a dozen—of anything. The only thing Amanda hasn't
bought yet is a cemetery plot."

There were some appreciative chuckles. Amanda Worth
spent a fair amount of money to look younger than her fifty-odd years. It was hard for anyone to imagine her buying—or
needing—land in a cemetery.

"These days she's shopping for some sort of Oriental
temple to go in the backyard. Since I make sure she has
everything she wants, I don't know what she's going to pray

for—unless she wants to ask God to keep me making the big bucks!"

"Then your wife must be happy about that new outlet mall opening tomorrow," a young man, who had apparently never heard this story before, suggested.

"Are you kidding? Amanda doesn't know what an outlet is. The wastebaskets are stuffed with sale circulars from Bloomingdale's and Neiman Marcus. But does she go out in search of a bargain? No way! My wife, bless her, pays full price. That's right. Full price!" He repeated the words in case anyone had missed his point.

Susan Henshaw and Kathleen Gordon were sitting on the outskirts of the group gathered around Scott and, by mutual consent, they got up and drifted toward the bar in the corner.

"An Oriental temple? Could Amanda be thinking of practicing Buddhism?" Kathleen, a gorgeous blonde in her early forties asked, obviously amazed.

"Who knows? I'm sure we'll hear about it in time. We always hear about Amanda's latest outrageous purchase. You know, whenever Scott starts telling that story, I get an urge to dash out and buy a cemetery plot," Susan said. She was older than her friend, and she was pushing her shoulder-length brown hair off her face.

"Why? Because you're so bored you want to kill yourself?"

"That's a thought, but the reason is that it would be the first time I ever owned anything before Amanda did," Susan explained, reaching for a handful of salted nuts.

"Put those down," Kathleen ordered. "You're trying on swimsuits tomorrow, remember."

"How much difference could six peanuts and a filbert possibly make?" Susan asked, glancing down at the nuts lying in her palm.

"You won't stop there. No one stops with one handful. And there's temptation everywhere. Look around."

They were in the large reception room of the Hancock Field Club's clubhouse. Like many private clubs on the East Coast, the founding fathers (two bankers, two lawyers, and a manufacturer of a popular brand of health tonic made mostly from grain alcohol and sugar—and anything but healthy) had insisted the architects emulate the large Tudor manor houses of England—or, to be more accurate, had insisted the architects create the ambience they imagined would be found in the large Tudor manor houses of England. Walnut paneling, gray slate floors, and two massive marble fire-places flanked the room where dozens of little tables had been set up. Club members and their guests were drinking cocktails as they waited for the doors to the ballroom to open indicating that dinner was served. Each of the little tables was draped with a snowy linen tablecloth. A silver porringer filled with nuts was centered on each table.

"I did ask for the salmon entrée," Susan said, tightening her fingers around her snack. "It probably has less calories than the beef, so I deserve these."

"Fabulous Food is catering. They don't specialize in low calorie."

"Fabulous Food? Fantastic!" Susan tossed the nuts into the nearest ashtray.

"You're sticking to your diet?"

"Probably not. But I'm not going to spoil my appetite with junk when Fabulous Food is doing the cooking. Why don't we get another glass of wine and figure out a game plan for tomorrow? The new mall will be jammed, so we should prioritize our stops if we're going to find what we need. If only we knew which stores are there."

"We do! Wait until you see what I have!" Kathleen pulled a packet of papers from her purse and began to scrounge through it.

But Susan was still thinking about her shopping. "I need a new swimsuit, but I understand there's a Gucci outlet . . ."

"Are you going to the opening of the mall?"

"Wouldn't miss it." Susan looked up at the women who had joined them. "What about you two?"

"We can't. We were both on the committee that tried to keep that mall from being built. We think it would be . . . well, unseemly . . . if we were seen there on opening day."

"Yeah," her companion agreed. "My husband said this would happen and, much as I hate to admit it, I should have listened to him."

"But don't empty the stores. We figure in a few weeks everyone will have forgotten all about that damn petition and those town hearings, and we'll be there with the rest of Hancock!" one woman said.

"We sure will be," her friend agreed. "I'm going to get new everyday china and a travel raincoat and some suitcases. We're going to Lake Como for a few weeks in the fall and, if I save enough money on luggage, we'll be able to stay an extra day or two."

"You just got back from a week in Paris. Do you need new luggage?"

"Not really, but I'm tired of arriving at five star hotels looking like a couple of bums. My husband is still using the duffel bags he went off to college with—someone in the family has to add some class to our act."

"I remember hearing about a luggage outlet, but I don't know if it's Tumi or Hartmann," one of the women in the group said, emptying a cup of nuts into her hand and beginning to pick out the cashews and almonds.

"Vuitton!" Another woman spoke the word with awe. "I heard there was going to be a place that sells Vuitton at a discount."

That got everyone's attention. "Vuitton!" The name was repeated over and over.

"I don't give a damn what anyone says. If they're selling Vuitton at a discount, I'll be first in line!"

Susan responded to Kathleen's tug on her sleeve, and followed her friend toward the large French doors that led to a balcony overlooking the tennis courts. "What do you want?"

"Look what I have!" Kathleen flashed a sheet of light blue paper she had finally extracted from the mess in her purse.

"What is it?"

"Look!"

"It's some sort of . . ." Susan read the words across the top of the page. "It's a map of Once in a Blue Moon! How did you get it? Where did you get it? Those things have been the best kept secret in the entire state of Connecticut!"

"My cleaning lady's daughter works at the print shop where they were made. She grabbed this one for her mother and she duplicated it and passed it along to me."

"You could make a fortune selling this," Susan said, her eyes not leaving the sheet of paper for a minute.

"Right. You know, when Jerry heard that the stores at the mall were going to be kept a secret until opening day, he told me he thought the owners of the place were nuts. But even he's been admitting he was wrong."

"I know what you mean. Jed was the same way. It goes

against everything they were taught in college, and everything they've been doing down at the agency for years. Of course, it sure seems to be working. Everyone is curious." Susan was still examining the sheet of paper.

"There's a Calvin Klein store right between Ann Taylor and Anne Klein. He does some great swimsuits," Kathleen said.

"Yeah. I was just wondering . . ."

"What?"

"Did you look at this map?"

"Are you kidding? I wrote those little numbers all over it! See?" Kathleen pointed at the page. "That's the order I thought we could shop in. Unless, of course, you have different ideas."

"Uh huh."

"I have Calvin Klein at number one," Kathleen added when Susan didn't answer. "You know, for your swimsuit."

Susan had started to mutter, "Eddberg . . . lonex . . . liscla . . ."

"What?"

"Look." Susan pushed the map closer to Kathleen. "Eddie Bauer. Lennox. Liz Claiborne. Mikasa. Dansk. Joan and David. Nike."

"They're all there. So what?"

"They're also all in Maine and New Hampshire. And New Jersey. And Florida. And Pennsylvania. And Maryland. And most of the other large discount malls."

"So?"

"I thought Once in a Blue Moon was going to be different. The most deluxe of all the outlet malls."

"Sure. That's why they wanted it to be in this part of Connecticut, near a population with lots of disposable income and a taste for the finer things in life. At least that's what all the propaganda said."

"So where is it?"

"Where's what?"

"Where's Vuitton? Tiffany's? Armani? Or Prada?"

"Well, I think a Vuitton outlet would be in France. The company is French, isn't it?" Kathleen responded reasonably.

"I don't mean Vuitton specifically. I mean the luxury stores. Where are the luxury stores? I thought we were going to be able to buy from Madison Avenue boutiques at discount prices."

"I don't remember any mention of Madison Avenue," Kathleen said.

"Not specifically, of course. But the point of the name is that a 'blue moon' is rare—unusual—and the goods and stores at this mall are supposed to be rare and unusual. There's nothing less rare than a Liz Claiborne outfit. Not that I don't wear them myself, but, well, you have to admit it's not what we were led to expect."

"I guess not," Kathleen admitted.

"And you're not surprised?"

"Susan, what field are Jed and Jerry in?"

"Advertising, of course. Why do you ask?"

"And how many years have you and Jed been married?"

"Almost twenty-nine." Susan found this topic momentarily diverting. "Do you think we should go someplace special to celebrate our thirtieth or should we give a big party?"

"Both. But, Susan, pay attention. More attention to me than you've been paying to Jed all these years."

"I pay a lot of attention to Jed!" Her voice squeaked in protest.

"Then how did you miss the point that advertising exists

to cause people to buy things they don't know they want, and to believe those things are different than they are."

"I didn't miss the point. I just didn't think of Once in a Blue Moon in those terms. Naive of me, I suppose."

Kathleen didn't say anything.

"There is a Barneys' outlet," Susan muttered.

"And a Gucci and a Ferragamo shoe store," Kathleen added. "You can't say there aren't luxury stores here."

"But still . . ."

"It's a lot like a lot of other malls. Yes. I noticed that right away."

"But still . . ." Susan continued to study the map.

"Still. There's nothing like a bargain." Kathleen smiled.

Susan smiled back. "Nope, nothing at all."

"What are you two chuckling about? I hope you have some good gossip or something. I am so bored by these damn club parties. But when your husband's on the board . . ." Lauren Crone appeared by their side. "Is that a map of the new mall? Oh, my God, it is! Where did you get it? Where can I get one?"

"It's Kathleen's," Susan said, passing the buck.

"It was given to me," Kathleen said. "I don't believe there are any more available."

"But you will share it with the woman who may be going on the third-grade class trip with you next week, won't you?"

"I—"

"Is it the trip to the nature center?" Susan interrupted to ask.

"Yes, and I'm looking forward to it," Kathleen said, hanging on to the map.

"Would you take Kathleen's place on the trip for a look at this map?" Susan asked.

"Susan! I just told you . . ."

"Sure," Lauren held out her hand.

"Trust me and give it to her," Susan ordered her friend.

Kathleen paused for only a moment before, obviously reluctant, she gave it away.

"Oh, oh! Look at this! I can't believe it! I've got to show Amanda. You don't mind, do you?"

"No. Enjoy." Kathleen waited until Lauren was out of sight before continuing. "Why did you do that? Alex is expecting me to be on that class trip with him."

"Kathleen, the third grade class trip to the nature center is the worst. The bus trip is long. The nature center is heated by an inadequate wood stove. Part of the joy of the experience is the class mothers cook lunch on that stove—a lunch made up of natural ingredients found in the wild that half of the kids won't even consider tasting and will give the boys an excuse to make barfing noises for the rest of the day. And the highlight of the trip is an hour sitting silently in a bird blind waiting for migrating waterfowl to drift by—which they don't."

"But the kids . . ."

"The kids learn a lot. They should go. But other mothers should go with them—preferably someone you hate."

"Oh, well. I guess that was worth losing the map for."

"Believe me, it was." Susan leaned closer to her friend. "So, did you catch that?"

"What?"

"Lauren was anxious to show the map to Amanda."

"Amanda Worth?"

"She's the only Amanda at the Club," Susan answered, nodding.

Kathleen got it. "So Amanda *is* going to shop at a discount mall."

"That's what it sounds like," Susan said.

"I wonder if we'll see her at the opening tomorrow."

"Maybe," Susan said, and started to giggle. "She'll be the one wearing a wig and dark glasses."

TWO

Bᴜᴛ ᴡʜᴇɴ Aᴍᴀɴᴅᴀ ᴡᴀs ғᴏᴜɴᴅ ᴅᴇᴀᴅ ᴏɴ ᴛʜᴇ ᴅʀᴇssɪɴɢ
room floor, she was wearing a torn slip, a navy silk blouse,
French silk stockings, a Hermes silk scarf, and brand-new
red suede Ferragamos. Her purse and a navy silk skirt lay by
her side. The dress she was about to try on was still on its
hanger on the wall. It was late afternoon by then and Kathleen and Susan were tired, otherwise they might have recognized the one clue that would lead them to her killer.

It had been a long day. The friends had arrived at the mall
early in the Gordons' Range Rover (just in case they both
found large-size bargains, Kathleen had said). Expecting to
wait in the parking lot until opening time, they had come
prepared with cups of Starbucks coffee, a bag of Susan's
cream cheese pastries, and two copies of the day's *New York
Times*. All of which they had abandoned in the car when
they spied the large banner hanging over the mall's entrance.

Wᴇʟᴄᴏᴍᴇ ᴛᴏ Oɴᴄᴇ ɪɴ ᴀ Bʟᴜᴇ Mᴏᴏɴ—Eᴀʀʟʏ ʙɪʀᴅs ᴘʟᴇᴀsᴇ
ᴄᴏᴍᴇ ᴊᴏɪɴ ᴜs ғᴏʀ ᴀ ғʀᴇᴇ Iᴛᴀʟɪᴀɴ ʙʀᴇᴀᴋғᴀsᴛ.

"Are we early birds?" Susan asked.

"Not the earliest, by any means," Kathleen said. "Just
look around."

The large parking lot's freshly laid macadam was almost

11

covered with shiny Jaguars, Mercedes, and SUVs. A large group of well-dressed women wearing comfortable shoes marched toward the entrance. Hundreds of blue crescent-shaped balloons lined either side of their way.

"This is amazing," Susan said.

"Do you think we're too late for the food?" Kathleen, thin but always hungry, knew exactly where her priorities lay.

"Let's find out." They grabbed their purses and set out, moving into the flow of women toward the sky blue stucco walls of the new mall.

Breakfast consisted of paper cups of espresso and a selection of tiny Italian pastries. Kathleen and Susan didn't manage to sample either. But they didn't care. Many of the stores had opened early. They had shopping to do!

As planned, they began at Calvin Klein.

While Susan tried on swimsuits, vowing to begin a life of Slim•Fast and vigorous exercise, Kathleen tried on and bought two pair of beige slacks, a taupe cashmere jacket, two turtlenecks (black and gray), and a poncho in shades of beige, taupe, black, and gray.

"Well, you're set for the rest of the season," Susan said, opening the door for her package-laden friend.

"Anne Klein makes swimsuits," Kathleen replied, pointing to the store on their right.

"Lead on, champion shopper."

Susan found a swimsuit, but it was black. She already had two black suits. On the other hand, maybe black really did make her look thinner. If only the suits covered her thighs. She glanced over at Kathleen who was holding a pair of Lycra leggings up in front of her. "Too young?" Kathleen asked, raising her eyebrows.

"They will look fabulous on you."

"I think they have them in your size."

"I really don't need pants," Susan said. Especially not the type that would emphasize every lump, bump, and bulge from her hips to her ankles.

"Those jackets by the front door are your color," Kathleen called over her shoulder as she headed toward the curtain-covered dressing cubicles. "Did you see them?"

"No, I'll look." Susan spied the jackets in question—in a beautiful heathery rust colored wool—and hurried toward them. But every single jacket on display was either size two, four, or six. She sighed and glanced about. There was a selection of leather belts nearby that looked nice, but the large room was becoming increasingly crowded and it was getting more and more difficult to look around.

Kathleen came out of the dressing room with three garments over her arm and Susan hurried over to her. "Didn't you go in there with one pair of leggings?"

"Yes, but I found these hanging in the dressing room and I couldn't resist. What do you think?" Kathleen held out two sweaters sparkling with elegant beading. "I don't really need both, but . . . They're really different, don't you think?"

"They're both beautiful and . . ." Susan glanced at the tags hanging from their sleeves. "They're bargains. Go ahead. They must look gorgeous on you."

"Well . . . I think Jerry will like them. Let's hurry. There's a line forming at the cash register."

"Okay. Oh, look, there's a display of socks . . . I'll just glance at them while you check out." Susan hurried off. The display was a large one and Susan was still choosing between black socks with little golden retrievers running around the cuffs and a pair of white socks with tiny beach balls embroidered on the ankles when her friend joined her.

"For you?" Kathleen asked in disbelief.

"The black ones are. I thought Chrissy might get a kick out of the others. Tell me that isn't the line to the cash register."

"It sure is. There are three registers and two aren't working—What are you doing?"

"Putting the socks back. I'm not going to wait in a long line to save six dollars."

"Then are you ready for another store?"

"Sure."

"There's a discount shoe store . . ."

"Perfect!" Susan's mood improved immediately. Shopping for swimsuits made her feel fat and old, but her shoe size hadn't changed since high school!

The shoe store was wonderful. An hour after they entered, Susan left carrying almost as many packages as Kathleen—the store had carried one of her favorite brands of purses as well.

"How about a stop at the car to drop some of this stuff off?" Kathleen suggested.

"Good idea. And maybe we could pick up the pastry. I'm starving," Susan said. She'd start dieting tomorrow. She really would, she told herself, the image of the back of her thighs quite vivid in her mind.

"You know, there's a little restaurant out on the highway. It advertises authentic Mexican food—"

"And looks like a dive. It's been there for years, but I've never stopped in."

"Do you want to see if it's open for an early lunch? We could eat quickly and then we'd have more energy for the afternoon."

"Good idea."

With the thought of food as a reward, their pace quickened. But . . .

"I don't suppose you noticed where we parked," Kathleen said.

Susan looked at her friend. "You're kidding."

"No, I was thinking of breakfast and shopping and . . . and I just didn't think."

They both put down their packages and stared in front of them. The sun was shining and light gleamed off line after line of parked cars. Up and down the rows latecomers trawled for an empty spot. But where was Kathleen's white Range Rover?

"I think we came from that direction," Susan said hesitantly.

"It's as good a place to start as any," Kathleen replied, hiking suddenly heavy bags up in her arms.

They started off in the direction Susan had suggested and it was Susan who decided they were wrong. "When you turn around," she said, dropping two plastic bags as she did just that, "you can see that we walked from over there." She indicated the direction by bobbing her head to the left.

"Then let's try that way," Kathleen answered slowly. "But how far away were we? Do you have any idea how many cars we passed between my car and the entrance?"

Susan thought for a moment. "Maybe a couple of dozen? What do you think?"

"I think I hear a voice calling my name," she said. "And yours!"

"Someone's honking . . ." Susan spun around and another shoe box bit the dust. "I think . . . it's that navy Volvo . . . It's Kimberly and Lauren!"

They waited for the line of cars to pass and Lauren stuck her head out of the window on the passenger's side of the large sedan. "Hi, Susan. Hi, Kathleen. Did you leave any bargains for us?"

"I think so," Susan said.

"Are you done shopping already?"

"We can't find my car." Kathleen, who was sharing the responsibilities of class mother with Lauren, knew that it was frequently necessary to interrupt her to get a chance to speak.

The Volvo stopped so suddenly the tires squealed. "Are you just looking for it so you can dump those packages or are you leaving? Can we have the space when we find it?" Kimberly leaned across Lauren to ask the questions.

"Of course."

"Then get in and we'll comb the parking lot. There won't be an empty spot until someone moves and you seem to be the only people heading away from the mall," Kimberly explained while Susan and Kathleen were arranging themselves and their parcels in the backseat.

"So, in which direction shall we go?"

"Turn left when you get to the end of the row," Susan answered with more assurance than she felt. "We're looking for Kath's Range Rover."

"It's white, right?" Lauren asked.

"Yes, but it surely isn't the only white Range Rover here," Kathleen said as they passed two cars identical to her own lined up between a white Grand Cherokee and a white Lincoln Navigator.

"Did you finish shopping?" Kimberly asked, steering her car around an illegally parked Mercedes that was blocking the narrow turn at the end of a row.

"No, but we're starving. We're going to go someplace for lunch and come back."

"I thought there were places here to eat," Lauren said. "That's what we were planning on anyway."

"I saw a snack bar and a McDonald's, but nothing else."

"Not that we covered even a fraction of the mall," Kathleen added.

"Maybe we should look for someplace to eat here and not give up our parking spot," Susan said slowly.

"But then we won't get a chance to shop," Lauren wailed.

"We were planning to leave home earlier, but you know how it is," Kimberly said, speaking in the shorthand of mothers in suburbia. "How it is" could be a kid home from school with a cold, a cleaning woman who doesn't show up, or a husband discovered to be having an affair with the au pair, but the polite just accept the three words without question and nod knowingly.

"We were hoping Amanda would come with us."

"Amanda doesn't shop at discount malls," Kimberly said.

"But she seemed so interested in my map last night—that is, Kathleen's map that she was kind enough to share with me." Lauren smiled at Kathleen.

"She said she was going into New York City, looking for a spring coat," Kimberly said.

"Not a cemetery plot?" Susan said under her breath.

"Excuse me?"

"Nothing. I was just mumbling to myself. How do you know what she's doing today?" Susan asked, not really interested in the answer, but wanting to draw some attention away from herself. Kimberly and Amanda had been good friends for years; she didn't want to insult one of them in front of the other.

"We stopped by her house this morning on the way here. That's why we were so late," Lauren explained.

"Lauren insisted," Kimberly added. "I knew there was no way Amanda was going to get dressed in casual clothes and come grub through discount goods with the rest of us."

"She spent a lot of time last night looking at the map of the mall," Lauren repeated her point.

"She may have been interested, but this just isn't her type of place. Can you see Amanda here?" Kimberly waved the hand not on the car's steering wheel at the view through the windshield. Women trudged through the lot, most wearing designer jeans, cashmere sweaters, and shearling jackets with their walking shoes or aerobic sneakers.

Susan suddenly remembered running into Amanda on one of her trips into New York City. Susan had been rushing, meeting Jed for dinner with some colleagues, and, as she turned a corner, there was Amanda Worth peering up at one of the lavish window displays at Barneys. Amanda looked as good as the mannequins behind the glass. She had been wearing a red Chanel suit with matching purse and shoes. Everything bore the gold signature buckle of the line—except for the scarf around her neck, that had been unmistakably Hermes. She had looked both urban and urbane. Susan glanced out Lauren's car window, spying two young women pushing wailing preschoolers in strollers. No, she couldn't quite imagine Amanda shopping here. Amanda and Scott were childless and they seemed content with their state. Susan suspected—hell, knew—that children would have put more than a small crimp in their elegant lifestyle.

"You must have stopped there for a while," Kathleen commented.

"Amanda made us coffee and we had some fresh raspberry muffins before leaving. Amanda baked the muffins from a recipe she got from that new bakery up in Greenwich. If we have time we're going to stop in there on the way home. She said they make divine French baguettes. Amanda always knows where to get the best things," Lauren said yearningly.

"True—"

"There's my car," Kathleen interrupted Susan and pointed to a Range Rover near the end of the row.

"How can you tell from here? Can you read the license plate?"

"No, but I can see the hockey stick I bought for Alex yesterday afternoon sticking up in the back."

"Great. Now we'll just wait here for you to pull out."

Susan and Kathleen got out of the car, collecting their bags from the backseat and hurrying toward the Range Rover.

"Do you think we're making a mistake?" Susan asked as Kathleen turned the key in the ignition and looked over her shoulder to back out. "There might not be anyplace to park by the time we're done with lunch."

"Other people will be leaving. Women who have children in half-day nursery school will have to go home, right?"

"Besides, I think Kimberly and Lauren would kill us if we changed our minds now," Susan added as the Volvo squealed into the parking space they had just vacated.

"Truly."

"Do you ever think it's odd that women who already have almost everything anyone could possibly want would be so anxious to buy some more?" Susan asked, including herself in that group.

"Not just more stuff, stuff at bargain prices," Kathleen reminded her. "Almost everyone finds bargains hard to resist."

"Everyone but Amanda," Susan said, thinking wistfully of the heavy carpeting and quiet atmosphere of Barneys and Bergdorf Goodman. "Everyone but Amanda," she repeated.

THREE

EL TORO NERO WAS OPEN FOR BUSINESS. ACCORDING TO the sign falling off the door, it had been open since 6 A.M. and would remain so until 11 P.M.—except on Friday and Saturday. On those days it would close at 1 A.M.

Susan had been more than a little put off by the grubby entry and her first view of the interior wasn't encouraging. The restaurant was small and booths lined the walls. Tiny tables for two were set up in the middle of the room, dividing the space in half and creating a pair of inadequate, narrow aisles. Someone had attempted to brighten up the Formica and stainless steel decor with torn bullfighting posters and dusty paper flowers in chipped urns.

"Maybe there's another place in the area," Susan murmured to her friend.

"Good idea—Oh, Carla!" Kathleen interrupted herself to call out to a heavyset woman taking up most of a booth at the rear of the room. "Susan, look who's here. Is this the place you told me about?"

"Sí, El Toro Nero." The woman nodded her head vigorously, obviously pleased to see Kathleen. "And you bring your friend here to try our cactus mole. Yes?"

"Yes! Susan, you remember Carla. You've met her at my house."

"I . . ." Susan, a polite smile on her face, tried to remember when she had met this flamboyantly dressed woman. Possibly one of Kathleen's parties? Or was she a neighbor?

"Sí, Mrs. Henshaw remembers me. I clean suede love seat that she cover with chicken salad."

Oh, my goodness, this was Kathleen's cleaning woman! Thank goodness she hadn't said anything stupid. "I'm so glad to see you," Susan said sincerely. "Now I can thank you for giving Kathleen the map of Once in a Blue Moon."

"No need to thank me. My daughter get many copies. I give them to all my friends. You've been shopping this morning, sí?"

Kathleen answered. "Yes. And we're starved." She turned to Susan. "This place is owned by Carla's brother."

"Uncle," came the correction.

"Yes, of course, uncle. I've been wanting to try it."

"You leave the ordering to me. I get you the special. Today you eat the way the Mexicans eat. And if you spill, you spill only on plastic." She got up with surprising agility for such a large woman and headed for a door which, presumably, led to the kitchen. Susan and Kathleen exchanged glances and seated themselves at a large booth.

"Do you know anything about the food here?" Susan leaned across the table and whispered to her friend.

"Carla talks about it all the time and I've been promising her I would come down and try it out—only I had no idea this was the place."

"Well, I have that bottle of Tums that I take as a calcium supplement in my purse. I just hope the food isn't too hot."

Two huge steaming platters were placed before them almost before the words were out of Susan's mouth.

"We have everything ready for our special customers—but some of them wait a little longer today. Eat. Eat while it all hot."

Susan stuck her fork in the middle of a flour tortilla wrapped around an unknown and unrecognizable filling, broke off a piece, put it in her mouth, and chewed, gingerly at first and then . . . "Kathleen, this is wonderful!"

Kathleen emulated her friend and her response was equally enthusiastic. Soon they were so busy eating that they didn't take the time to comment on how few people were coming into the small restaurant.

The portions were huge, but the women were both wiping their plates when Carla reappeared with two generous helpings of quivering, creamy flan.

Kathleen reached eagerly for hers. Susan, aware of the meal's mounting calorie count, was slightly more hesitant. But, after the first bite, there was no stopping either of them. "That was wonderful," Susan said, putting down her spoon and taking a deep breath. "But I don't think I'll try on swimsuits this afternoon."

Kathleen glanced down at her wrist.

"What time do you have to be home?" Susan asked.

"Not until five. Both kids have play dates this afternoon, but I promised I'd pick up Alice before then."

"Then let's get our check and get going." Susan stood up. "What happened to our waitress?"

"I don't—Oh, here's Carla."

"How was your meal? Everything I promise, right?"

"Right!"

"It was wonderful," Susan said enthusiastically. "We were just looking for our waitress so we could pay our bill."

"No bill. You are both my guests today."

"But—"

"Thank you so much," Kathleen interrupted Susan. "It really was wonderful."

"Sí. See you tomorrow, Señora Gordon."

"Yes. 'Bye."

Susan and Kathleen thanked their benefactor profusely, squeezed through the narrow aisle, and out the door to the car.

"I'm stuffed," Kathleen said, pulling her car keys from her purse and beeping open the doors.

"Me, too. We should tell everyone we know to come here. The food is fabulous. But I felt guilty not paying."

"If we tell everyone we know to come here, and they do, and then the place becomes popular, we'll have helped them out more than by paying for lunch."

"Good point." Susan reached behind her and surreptitiously unbuttoned her wool slacks. Fortunately the cashmere sweater she wore was as long as a tunic. "So what do you want to look for this afternoon?"

"Well, we still haven't found a swimsuit for you. And I'd like to glance through the housewares outlet. Alex broke another salad plate. Maybe I can find a replacement."

"Sounds good to me," Susan said. "Now all we have to do is find a parking spot."

Amazingly enough, there was a car exiting right beside the entrance as they drove past. Kathleen used her Range Rover like a tank and grabbed the space.

"I think the blonde driving the navy Beemer over there is having very unkind thoughts about you."

"She should have known me when I was driving a police

cruiser." Kathleen laughed. "If I hadn't been a member of the force, I would have been arrested for reckless driving."

Susan joined in her laughter as they got out of the car and headed back into the mall. The crowd hadn't diminished; the walkways between the stores were still jammed with shoppers lugging around piles of packages. "I'm glad we ate," she commented, as they passed long lines of tired people waiting for seats in the mall restaurants.

"I'll say—hey, there's the Dansk store." Kathleen pointed.

"Good idea. They're sure to have salad plates."

"And they sent a coupon a few weeks ago. I put it in my purse."

Susan remembered receiving a coupon; it was stuck underneath a Cornell magnet on the front of her Sub-Zero. Oh, well, she didn't really need new china, she reminded herself, following Kathleen through the swinging door into the large, brightly lit store. A stand of shopping baskets was located nearby. Susan took one, thinking she could always help Kathleen carry her purchases. She turned down an aisle where hundreds of glasses were displayed on metal shelving.

When she caught up with Kathleen about a quarter of an hour later, the basket was full and she carried a large box as well.

"What did you find?" Kathleen asked as they moved into the checkout line.

"All sorts of things. Linen napkins—they're turquoise and white striped and will be perfect for meals by the pool next summer." She paused for a moment. The pool was at the back of their large landscaped yard and it was inconvenient to eat so far from the house—or the grill. But still . . . "And look at this great grill pan. Chrissy doesn't have one and I thought I'd send it to her."

"She can use it to grill dinner for the beasts." Kathleen referred to the bullmastiffs which, cute puppies when Chrissy's in-laws had given them to the couple as a wedding present, were now huge, drooling animals. Clue, Susan's golden retriever, went and stood guard by her food bowl whenever the animals were even mentioned. When the crew, dogs included, came for Thanksgiving weekend, Clue had lost two pounds. "What else did you buy?"

"These little frosted glass votive candleholders and these sets of tiny white vases. I thought it would be fun to scatter them around the house the next time we entertain."

"You have such good ideas," Kathleen said sincerely.

"Did you find your plates?"

"No. I'm just buying these plastic mugs. The kids will get a kick out of them."

They had reached the register and continued to chat as they passed over their credit cards. "So, what next?" Susan asked, once they were done.

"Our planning isn't working all that well. Why don't we just walk around and see what we run into?"

"Sounds good to me," Susan said, holding the door open for Kathleen. "You know what I always say—when in doubt, turn left."

"Then left it is."

Smiles on their faces, they continued their search for bargains, girded by the belief that if you can't buy happiness, you could at least buy many of its trappings.

They had a pleasant and productive afternoon. Susan found her swimsuit as well as a matching cover-up (interestingly enough it matched the napkins she had bought earlier); Kathleen bought salad plates, dessert plates, and a purse. The back of the Range Rover was full and they had promised themselves that the next stop would be their last.

"So what will it be?" Kathleen asked.

"The Saks outlet," Susan answered. "And I need to use the ladies' room when we get there."

"Lead on, oh fearless shopper."

The upscale store's outlet displayed almost none of the amenities that the customers at the regular store took for granted. Though well lit and well organized, missing were the elegant floor displays and the gleaming marble of its ladies' room. But Susan was just grateful for the lack of a line. She was washing her hands when Kimberly and Lauren entered the room.

". . . but that blouse is your color," Lauren was saying.

"But by the time I pay someone to alter it, I'd end up spending more than it's worth," Kimberly protested sounding, Susan thought, more than a bit irritated.

"Whatever happened to the little seamstresses who used to be everywhere?" Lauren mused. "My mother had a woman who did everything beautifully—and she was amazingly cheap."

"They all went to college, got degrees in computer programing, and are working for Microsoft," Kimberly said. "Oh hi, Susan."

"Hi. How's the shopping going?"

"Not great."

"Super."

"Lauren has found lots of stuff, but I just picked up some stockings and tights," Kimberly explained.

"Kimberly is too picky," Lauren insisted, pushing open the metal door to the toilet stall.

"I just want to use everything I buy." She lowered her

voice and moved over closer to Susan. "I can't believe the way Lauren spends money."

"Well, everyone's different," Susan replied, conscious of how small the room was.

"I'd heard they were rich, but, really she's ridiculous—"

"You're talking about Amanda, aren't you?" Lauren said, stepping out of the booth.

"She certainly does seem to have a lot of money," Susan said quickly.

"Hm." It was impossible to interpret Kimberly's response.

"I'd better get going. Don't want Kathleen to have snapped up all the bargains," Susan said, starting for the door. "See you."

Kathleen seemed to have disappeared. Susan wandered from department to department, picking up and putting down merchandise as she looked for her friend.

"May I help you?"

"Are you a saleswoman?" Susan asked, surprised by the offer. Most of the stores they had been in today had never, apparently, considered hiring more than a checker at the register.

"I work here, yes."

"I'm looking for my friend. She's tall, thin, and wearing a gorgeous tan sheepskin coat."

"Have you tried the dressing rooms?"

"Good idea. Where are they?"

"Right over there." She nodded toward a long line of women leaning against the wall, arms overflowing with clothing while they waited. "If she's not there, you might look in the small dressing area at the rear of the store. Right next to the rest rooms."

"Thank you." Susan tried her first suggestion, explaining

to some tired and quickly angered women that she was just looking for someone, not trying to cut in line. But Kathleen wasn't there so she hurried back toward the ladies' room, looking for the alternative dressing area.

The doorway was partially hidden by racks and racks of clothing discarded by shoppers. Susan squeezed through and was greeted by the sight of two small cubicles shielded by thin privacy curtains. "Kathleen! Are you there?" she called out.

"Susan. Is that you? I'm in here. The booth on the right. Wait till you see what I'm wearing. You won't believe it."

Susan followed the directions and pulled back the curtain.

The curtain behind her slid open and Kathleen appeared. "Susan? Oh, I'm sorry. I meant my right—your left—Susan?"

Susan, still staring down at the floor, said only one word. "Amanda."

"Amanda?" Kathleen repeated. "Is Amanda here? I thought she wouldn't be caught dead in a discount mall."

"She has," Susan said slowly. "She's been caught dead."

FOUR

Susan and Kathleen stared down at Amanda.

"She is dead, isn't she?"

Kathleen bent down and confirmed what they both knew. "I'll stay here. You find a salesperson and tell them to call mall security."

"What's up?"

Susan turned to find the saleswoman who had directed her here standing in the open doorway. "Call mall security," she ordered.

"I am mall security. What's up?"

"Really?" Susan was surprised. Then why hadn't she mentioned that earlier?

"What's up?" she repeated her question a third time.

"Oh, it's Amanda Worth. She's dead," Susan finally answered.

"Looks like we need an ambulance," the woman said, pulling a two-way radio from her belt and flipping it open.

Susan looked at Kathleen and shrugged.

Kathleen leaned over close to Susan. "What we need is the police," she insisted quietly. "She's not only dead, she's been murdered."

"Are you sure?" Susan asked, peering down.

"Look."

Susan looked. The scarf around Amanda's neck was pulled tightly—too tightly. "It looks like she was strangled. I . . . I don't suppose it could have been an accident."

"No."

"Who . . . ?" But she left the question unasked. With remarkably poor timing, Kimberly and Lauren were trying to get into the dressing room.

"Why can't we go in?" Lauren was asking plaintively. "You let other people in there. I see Susan Henshaw—"

"You cannot go in there." The security guard flashed what Susan assumed was a badge and Lauren squealed.

"Oh, no! Don't tell me you're arresting Susan for shoplifting."

"I am not at liberty to say anything at this time."

"And I'm not being arrested for shoplifting—or for anything else," Susan protested loudly.

"Ladies, there's a small problem here. Why don't you just return to your shopping and let us settle it?"

"Susan, is there anything we can do?" Kimberly called out.

"No. I think—"

But Lauren had pushed herself into position to see the floor. "Oh, my God, it's Amanda. And she's unconscious. What happened? Did she fall? Did someone hit her? Was she . . . oh, my God, was she assaulted?"

"Have you called for an ambulance?" Kimberly asked.

"Lauren—" Susan began.

But she was cut off by the arrival of emergency personnel, carrying bags of equipment and a portable stretcher, knocking over piles of clothing and one or two garment racks.

"Excuse us."

"Let us by, everyone. Please move."

"Excuse us. Excuse us."

"Out of the way, ladies. Let us do our jobs."

There were three uniformed people and, certainly, no-where near enough room for them to get into the tiny dressing area. Susan and Kathleen instinctively moved out of the way.

"You two should stay around. The police will be here soon."

The EMS men finally got close enough to look at Amanda. "Hey, what the hell did you call us for? This broad is dead!"

As a comment, it was, Susan thought, at least as effective as yelling "Fire" in a crowded theater.

"Dead? Dead? Did you say Amanda is dead?" Lauren leapt backward.

"Susan? Kathleen? Is she? Is Amanda dead?" Kimberly asked.

"She is," Susan answered, moving toward Kimberly as she spoke. She knew how close the two women were. Kimberly would be saddened as well as shocked by this tragedy.

"How? How did it happen? Were you with her?" Kimberly asked another question.

"No, I was looking for Kathleen and I found her." The women moved away from the dressing room while they spoke. It was apparent to Susan that Kimberly was near tears. "I mean, I was looking for Kathleen when I found Amanda. And Kathleen, I found Kathleen as well."

Kimberly was apparently not interested in anything other than the crisis at hand. "How did she die? What happened? She was healthy. Was it an accident? Did she slip on some-thing and hit her head?"

"She was—"

"It's really much too early to know what happened,"

Kathleen interrupted. "Maybe you should find someplace to sit down?"

Susan looked closely at Kimberly. "You should. You're so pale. Do you feel faint?"

"Maybe. I'm tired. Shopping and all. And it's been a shock. Are you sure it's Amanda in there?"

"We are, Kimberly," Susan said gently. "I was as close to her as I am to you."

Kimberly bit her bottom lip, but seemed determined not to cry. "Shouldn't we call somebody? Scott?"

"Let's wait and see what the authorities say," Susan answered slowly. She really had no idea what they should do. The woman who claimed to be mall security was talking quietly to the emergency people, but nothing seemed to be happening. Susan knew no one should touch anything, that the police should be called, but if she said anything she would upset Kimberly even more. She looked over her shoulder back at the dressing room. On the other hand . . . "You might not want to walk about in there like that," she found herself saying.

"She's dead. What damage can we do now?" The single emergency person who had not apologized for breaking through the crowd answered back.

"You're destroying the crime scene," Kathleen answered.

"A crime scene? What happened to Amanda? I thought she'd had an accident . . ."

"Kimberly, we—Kathleen and I—think that she was strangled," Susan answered quietly.

"Strangled? Oh, how horrible. Who would want to strangle Amanda?" The last words were barely distinguishable through Kimberly's tears.

"We're never going to find out if those idiots keep moving

things in the dressing room," Kathleen muttered as she walked toward the front of the store. "I'm going to make a call. . . ."

"You'd better call Scott." Kimberly raised her tear-stained face. "He'll be devastated, but he should know right away, shouldn't he?"

"I'm sure Kathleen knows what to do," Susan murmured. She hoped the police would arrive quickly.

The thought had barely had time to occur when Kathleen reappeared with a good-looking man at her side.

"Brett! Thank goodness you're here," Susan cried. "Where . . . ?"

"Brett was shopping with Erika when he heard someone say something about an accident," Kathleen explained.

"Actually, I heard someone say something about a body and Susan Henshaw. When Susan and a body are mentioned in the same breath, I know it's time to move," Brett said over his shoulder, heading straight into the midst of the emergency personnel.

"We're not needed here right now," Susan said. "Why don't we find someplace to sit down and get out of the way?"

"Good idea. Come with us," Kathleen added, putting an arm around Kimberly's shoulder. "There's nothing we can do."

They turned and discovered the store had been cleared of customers. Three young women, apparently the sales staff, hovered around nervously. An older woman, pink with fury, was arguing with someone on the phone. "Dead customers are not my problem. I was promised. . . ." Her voice was shrill and Kathleen and Susan instinctively moved away.

"I think I saw a small seating area near the other dressing rooms," Kathleen said.

"Let's go there." Susan glanced at the window-lined store-front as she spoke. A crowd had gathered. The chairs Kathleen had suggested (five hard plastic seats provided a bit grudgingly by the management for unhappy husbands or tired shoppers) were sufficiently far away from the window so they couldn't be stared at by curious onlookers.

Kimberly allowed herself to be led, sniffling, to the chairs. The three women sat down with their backs to the room.

"I wonder where Lauren went?"

Kimberly stopped crying long enough to answer Susan's question. "She said she had some phone calls to make."

"Probably called the police," Susan suggested.

Kathleen, who knew Lauren a bit better, looked skeptical. "I hope so. Did she tell you who she was going to call?" she asked Kimberly.

"No . . . I don't think . . . Maybe she said something about Annie Nelson. . . ."

"Annie Nelson? Why was she going to call her?"

"I don't know. She and Amanda are good friends . . . Were good friends. I guess Lauren thought Annie should be one of the first to . . . to know about Amanda."

"Oh." Susan leaned back in the chair and closed her eyes.

"Are you saying that Lauren is . . . is spreading the news about Amanda's murder?" Kathleen asked.

Kimberly looked up, stopped crying, and asked three questions. "I—who said anything about murder? Was Amanda killed by someone? I thought you said it was an accident!"

"We didn't say that," Susan protested gently.

"But why? Who would murder Amanda?"

Susan and Kathleen didn't even try to answer her question. "I wonder if we should go find Lauren," Susan suggested.

"How was she going to make her calls?" Kathleen asked.

"She had her cell phone," Kimberly answered. "She always has her cell phone."

"She does. And much of the time she's talking on it," Kathleen explained to Susan.

Susan was quiet a moment, wondering exactly what Lauren had told Annie. Had Lauren, unlike Kimberly, understood that Amanda had been murdered? Had she passed along that information to Annie? Then she had another thought. "Did you talk to Erika?" she asked Kathleen.

"No, I didn't even see her. Brett was coming in the door as I left the dressing room. He said he had been shopping with Erika and had heard that there had been a death. He just came along to see if he could help out. He doesn't have any authority here. We're not in Hancock, remember."

Susan remembered. The original plan for the outlet mall had actually been within Hancock city limits although well away from the downtown area, and the protests that had engendered had astounded her. Not that she wanted her downtown merchants competing with chain stores and discount outlets. And she certainly agreed that the traffic resulting from a mall would be undesirable. But the petitions, the outrage, the town meetings, the phone calls from parties pro and con—well, she had told Jed, you would have thought they had been talking about building a prison right next to the library. Anyway, the protests worked and now, two years later, Once in a Blue Moon had opened a respectable twelve miles from Hancock.

"The police are going to be involved in this, aren't they?" Kimberly looked up. "Amanda would have hated that. She probably would have thought it was tacky."

Susan nodded. "Probably."

Suddenly, there was a loud crash and the three women stood up. One of the doors had broken open and curious shoppers flooded the room.

"Oh, this is bad," Kathleen said.

"It's worse than bad," Susan commented. "Do you realize how many of these people we know? And how many of them knew Amanda?"

"That's Lauren. She can make more phone calls in a few minutes than anyone I've ever met."

Susan glanced at Kathleen, hoping to verify Kimberly's statement. And realized, for the first time, what her friend was wearing. "Kathleen . . ." She pointed, having no idea what more to say.

Kathleen looked down at her attire and then up at Susan. "I told you, when I was in the dressing room. I told you you'd never believe what I had tried on."

FIVE

"SO WHAT WAS SHE WEARING?"

Susan took a moment to concentrate on Erika's attire before she answered her question. As always, Erika looked wonderful. Today she was wearing a camel hair tunic over slightly darker wool slacks. Chunks of amber hung from her ears and circled both wrists. Her cap of dark hair was shiny, her makeup perfect. "She had on a red suede mini skirt and a red and yellow flowered blouse—cut sort of like a Western shirt, you know? Her waist was encircled with a turquoise belt and there was a matching bandana around her hair."

"Why?"

"Why what?"

"Why was she wearing such odd clothing?"

"Apparently some hotshot designer thinks that's the way for women to look. Kathleen thought it would be fun to try on the entire outfit."

Erika changed the subject. "You're sure Amanda Worth was murdered?"

"Oh, yes. There's no way it could have been an accident—or suicide. Someone grabbed the scarf around her neck and pulled it tight until she was dead."

"Sounds like an awful way to die."

"It probably was." Susan was silent for a moment.

"How well did you know Amanda?" Erika asked.

"We've known each other for years. She and Scott are very active down at the Club. In fact, I think Scott was head of the admissions committee the year we applied for membership."

"Is that how you met her?"

"Boy, you don't know anything about the Field Club admissions process, do you? At least, the way it used to be. Things have changed."

"How was it when you joined?"

"Two members had to nominate the entire family. And then the husband—the husband alone—was interviewed by the admissions committee."

"Sexist."

"It hasn't been done that way for years," Susan explained quickly. "But the truth is that the Hancock Field Club was more than a bit behind the times back then."

"So that's when Jed met Scott, but when did you meet Amanda?"

"Oh, there was a luncheon for the wives of new members. Amanda was the hostess."

"Where was it held? At the Club?"

"Yes. It was an official Club function. But later Jed and I were invited over to the Worths' house for drinks. I remember how impressed I was with what Amanda served—Kir and some kind of pâté. I know it sounds like nothing now, but thirty years ago, it was very sophisticated dining. And she had done all the cooking herself."

"How che—" Erika stopped speaking as Brett returned. "Brett, what's happening?"

"You wouldn't believe it," he answered. Susan and Erika had left the shopping floor and were sitting around a table in the tiny employees' lounge. "I don't believe it and I've been watching for the last half an hour."

"What?"

"Incompetence. The security system here is completely incompetent. What am I saying? There is no system. Security is a bunch of inexperienced and apparently untrained people who have no idea how to handle a real emergency. They don't know what to do and they're too stupid to call in the people who do."

Susan looked up. "They haven't called the local police?"

"I called them myself and they arrived a few minutes ago. I wouldn't have dared leave the crime scene before they got here. The security people were not only walking all over any evidence that might have been left, they were moving things."

"They're not trained to deal with murder," Erika suggested.

"Then they should leave it alone!" Brett exploded. "I've never seen anything like them. One moment they're in a panic because they have no idea what to do. The next moment, they're going to band together and catch the killer single-handedly. One of them actually suggested that there might be a reward for the person who caught the murderer of 'this rich broad'—his term, not mine, I must add. God, I hate it when amateurs get involved. . . ." Suddenly he grinned. "Present company excepted, of course."

Susan smiled back. "Of course."

"But the police have arrived." Erika insisted on getting back to the point. "Doesn't that mean we can leave?"

"I'd sort of like to hang around for a while," Brett answered. "I know some of the guys on the local force here. I think it might be a good idea if I had a few words with them. Perhaps you could get a ride home with Susan?"

"Sounds good to me. I came with Kathleen, but my car is at her house. If you don't mind a little detour—because I know Kath has to be home for Alex and Alice—we could stop there and then I could drop you off."

"I'd appreciate it—if it wouldn't be too much trouble," Erika said.

"I'll come by your house later and drop off your packages," Brett added. "Unless you want to get them now."

"I can . . ."

"I think you'd better do as Brett suggests," Susan said. "There's hardly room in Kathleen's car for you—I don't think we'll be able to squeeze in your purchases, too." She was puzzled. Brett and Erika had been dating for over almost two years, but here they were acting as though barely acquainted.

"I'd better drop her stuff off. Erika was a great bargain hunter today."

So that was it! Brett was miffed about all the time Erika had spent shopping. Just like an old married couple, Susan thought contentedly.

"But right now I think I'd better get going," he said, turning to leave.

"Why don't we go find Kathleen?" Susan suggested.

"Aren't the police going to want to question you? You did find Amanda, didn't you?" Erika asked.

"Yes . . ."

"Don't worry about it. I gave them your name and address—they'll get hold of you. Probably soon," Brett added.

"Then let's get going," Susan said.

They found Kathleen, dressed in her own clothes, waiting for them by the front door.

"Look at the crowd!"

Kathleen nodded. "Incredible, isn't it? I've been standing here wondering how they all know that something has happened. Can we leave now?"

"Yup. Brett gave our names to the police. He says they'll be calling."

"Then let's get going. I have less than twenty minutes to get home before the kids arrive."

"Erika's coming along," Susan said. "Brett's going to stay here and I'll give her a ride home."

"If you don't mind . . . ?" Erika spoke up.

"Not at all."

The uniformed officer at the door allowed them to pass, but they had to work to push through the crowd peering in the large windows. Susan saw more than a few women she knew, but this wasn't the time to stop and chat.

"Whew! I guess even bargains aren't as interesting as murder," Susan said. "I couldn't believe how many people were there. I'll bet a third of the Club members were hanging around outside that store."

"How did they find out about the murder so quickly?" Erika asked.

"They probably didn't. They probably saw the police and the ambulance and just came over to see what was going on. I guess," Susan added uncertainly.

"I don't think that's it," Kathleen said.

"Huh?"

"Well, while I was waiting for you two, I could hear some of what was being said outside, and a lot of the women seemed not only to know that a murder had been committed, but the identity of the dead woman."

"How would anyone know that?" Susan asked, staring at the signboard that had been placed at the corner of the mall.

"I haven't the foggiest."

"Do either of you know where we're going?" Erika asked.

"We parked just outside the main entrance," Kathleen explained.

"And that's where?"

"I think it's to our right," Susan said slowly. "If I'm reading the signs correctly . . ."

"I thought left . . ."

"I'd heard that malls were designed so people got lost in them, but I'd thought that was just an urban myth. After today, I'll believe it. Brett and I have had to stop and think each time we needed to go to the car."

"Well, men—" Kathleen began, but Susan interrupted.

"I don't believe it."

"What?"

"Susan, even if it's the bargain of a lifetime we're going to have to pass it up," Kathleen insisted. "I really have to get home to the kids."

"It's Lauren," Susan said. "Look. She's on the bench. By the bead shop. See?"

"Yes. So what? She's just making a phone call. Maybe she has kids that she's worrying about, too."

"Come on, if she sees us, we'll have to stop and chat—and you know how long that can take."

"Do you think she's been making phone calls for the last—what? Has it been half an hour since we found Amanda?" Susan asked as they trotted away.

"About that. Why?"

"How many phone calls do you think she's made in that time?"

"I don't know. . . ." Kathleen looked over her shoulder at

the women surrounding the Saks outlet. "You don't think she's been telling everyone about Amanda's murder?"

"It's possible."

Erika was intrigued. "I'm dying to know what the two of you are talking about. How does Lauren know about the murder?"

"Lauren Crone and Kimberly Critchley came into the dressing room right after we found Amanda," Susan explained.

"What does that have to do with Lauren sitting on a bench half an hour later talking on the phone?"

"She said she was going out to make a phone call. . . ."

"Possibly more than one," Kathleen added.

"Definitely more than one if she's still at it," Susan said. "Hey, we're at Mikasa. I think I know the way back to the car from here."

"Thank goodness."

Susan was thrilled to discover that in fact, she did know the way and, in just a few minutes, they were busy moving things around in the Range Rover to make room for a third passenger.

"I'm making a lot of trouble for you. I hope you don't mind," Erika said as she slid into the narrow empty spot the women had created.

"Not at all. Besides, now that I have you trapped back there," Kathleen said, getting into the driver's seat, "I can ask you for a donation for Alex's holiday fair at school. I'm in charge of the raffle."

"Twigs and Stems would be thrilled to make a donation. What do you need? We do some beautiful big wreaths—or maybe some handmade candelabra." Erika referred to the company she ran from Hancock. Twigs and Stems had begun as a small natural flower and accessories shop and had morphed over the years into a chain of boutiques from Portland, Maine, to Atlanta, Georgia.

"We would be grateful for anything, believe me. It seems like all the stores in the area have donated so often they're tired of the very idea."

"Have you considered raffling off services? There's a party planner I work with who would probably be glad to offer to do a party just for the publicity."

"What a good idea! Do you know anyone else?"

"Well . . ."

Susan sat in the passenger's seat feeling like a third wheel. Erika had her thriving business. Kathleen was involved in her children's lives as Susan had once been. Truth was, she felt left out. A semester of college had taught her many things, but hadn't provided a permanent solution to her empty nest. She frowned. She had just bought a lot of new clothes, but she had fewer and fewer places to wear them.

She had no idea what she was going to do with the rest of her life. On the other hand, someone was going to have to discover who killed Amanda Worth.

SIX

ALEX AND ALICE ARRIVED HOME BEFORE THEIR MOTHER, so Kathleen had had no time for long good-byes. Erika had helped Susan load her packages into the back of Susan's Cherokee and they had headed to Erika's.

"I'd like to buy one of those cute new VWs," Susan said as they passed one on the road, "but how would I manage to fit all this stuff in that small space?" She looked back over her shoulder at the bags and boxes filling her car.

"I know what you mean. I haven't the foggiest how I'm going to squeeze one more thing into my apartment. I suppose it's time to move, but I love that place and it's always suited me." Erika lived in a small remodeled carriage house behind one of the large Victorians in the oldest and most exclusive part of town. On days when the idea of deserting her family was more than a little appealing, Susan entertained fantasies of living in a similar setting.

She envisioned long, leisurely days spent reading favorite novels, stopping only to sip tea from a transparent porcelain cup and nibble on elegant meals consisting of salads, baguettes, butter, and meltingly soft French cheeses. She would stay up late, listening to music as she lounged on a pillow-strewn bed covered with flowered sheets. Sometimes there was an elegant, unknown, mysterious man in the background pouring champagne into stemmed crystal. Usually she was completely alone. But as fast as the fantasies came, they vanished. She realized she would miss walking Clue, and Susan really loved her big Colonial house with its familiar gardens, and, well, the truth was she couldn't imagine life without Jed.

". . . some way to add more closets without knocking out walls."

Susan returned to reality and realized Erika was still talking about her storage problems.

"Will your landlord let you remodel?" she asked.

"Susan, I own my house."

"I thought you rented."

"I did, but two years ago the Harpers found out that the property the carriage house sits on could be subdivided and, when they offered it to me, I snapped it up."

The Harpers, Susan knew, were the owners of the large Victorian the carriage house belonged to. "Good for you . . . but—" Susan stopped, not wanting to pry into things that weren't her business.

"They never said anything specifically, but I think they needed the money."

Susan was surprised. Of course, these big houses required lots of upkeep and property taxes had increased enormously over the years, but the Harpers had never seemed to need money.

"They have three kids in college," Erika reminded her.

Susan got the impression that Erika was uncomfortable talking about it. "Whatever the reason, it's great you were given an opportunity to own your home," she said tactfully.

"It was. And that's part of the reason I feel uncomfortable

about possibly enlarging the building. I can. My lawyer insisted on checking that out before I bought the house. But to know I can do it is different from doing it."

"Why?"

"Well, it's not like I have a lot of land and there's less than twenty feet between my house and theirs, so anything I do will impact the big house."

"And you don't want to do that."

"Exactly. The Harpers were great landlords and now they're great neighbors. That's important to me."

"Maybe there's an alternative. Have you called any of those storage companies? They claim to be able to work wonders."

They were turning into the long, circular driveway which led to Erika's home. Erika laughed at Susan's suggestion. "Come on in and have a glass of wine and I'll show you my problem."

Susan had been hoping for just such an invitation. She loved Erika's house. The ground floor consisted of a living, dining, and cooking area with five French doors leading to a small deck. A circular stairway wound its way to the second-floor bedroom. Although she saw Erika socially and considered her a friend, Susan rarely got up to the second floor. And she was, she admitted, hopelessly nosy.

It took only a moment for Erika to unlock the front door. "Come on in. Just toss your coat on the couch. Red or white?"

"White," Susan said. "You have new furniture!"

"Some. You like?"

But Susan had crossed the room and was examining the large cherry armoire that had replaced the low sideboard and abstract oil which had hung above it. "It's a gorgeous piece of furniture."

"It is, isn't it? Thomas Moser. But, to be honest, I miss

the painting that hung there. It's practically the only serious piece of art I've ever owned and it sort of defined this room."

"Where is it?"

"At the office looking hopelessly out of place among the potpourri and dried flowers."

"But this is elegant." Susan ran her hand across the satiny wood as she spoke.

"And it holds about three times the amount of stuff as the piece that was there before." Erika poured wine into the skinniest stemmed goblets Susan had ever seen and passed her a glass.

"These are beautiful, too."

"Thanks. Brett hates them. He says—"

"That he's afraid he'll break them." Susan finished Erika's sentence and then laughed at the expression on her face. "Jed would say exactly the same thing. I think he's happiest using old jelly glasses."

"Has he ever broken a wineglass?"

"All the time. But not because they're fragile and some-how fall apart in his hands—he has the oddest habit of put-ting the glasses down on the floor by the side of his chair and then, of course, when he gets up he smashes them to smithereens. Men."

Erika just nodded. "Bring your glass. Come see my closets."

"Closets? How many do you have?"

"This one." Erika opened the door to a small entryway closet by the stairway.

The space was barely big enough for the six coats stuffed within. Susan noted a new fur jacket and wondered if Brett could make enough as chief of police to afford to give such gifts. Of course, there was no reason a woman couldn't buy herself a fur coat.

"And this one, which I use for brooms and kitchen overflow."

Susan peered into an identical closet on the other side of the room. It was so full that Erika had to grab a heart-shaped Le Creuset casserole before it hit the floor.

"A Valentine's Day present from Brett," she explained, pushing it onto an overflowing shelf and slamming the door before anything else could fall.

"Brett gave you cooking utensils for Valentine's Day?" Susan asked, hoping, immediately, that she didn't sound as horrified as she felt. If a man gave gifts like that before you married him what could you expect afterwards? Bed socks? Hot water bottles shaped like animals from children's books? Tires for your car? She shook her head. She had always thought Brett was one great guy, but . . .

"He filled it with my favorite French chocolates," Erika explained. "He says you can't give flowers to a woman whose business is flowers and he was looking for something original."

"That's wonderful!" Susan enthused just a bit too loudly.

"It is, isn't it? Of course, he—"

"Ate most of the chocolates." Susan finished that sentence, too. "They always do," she continued as Erika raised her eyebrows.

"How long have you and Jed been married?" Erika asked, starting up the stairs.

"Too long," Susan answered automatically before realizing she wasn't speaking with one of her married women friends. "I mean . . ."

"I know, Susan. No one can be friends with you and Jed for long without realizing how healthy your marriage is."

"Healthy?"

"Sorry. I've been seeing a therapist for a while. I guess I'm beginning to talk like her."

"A bit," Susan agreed. "Is anything wrong? I mean, is there anything I can do?"

Erika laughed. "Just don't tell anyone. I don't want Brett to know I'm seeing someone—at least not yet."

"Are you and he having problems?"

"Not really. It's just that I can't seem to make up my mind about . . . about marrying him."

Susan's grip tightened on her glass and she suddenly understood Jed's worries about fine crystal. She didn't know what to say. But, apparently, Erika wanted to chat.

"This is what I'm talking about," Erika said as Susan joined her in the bedroom.

Susan said nothing for a few minutes. Erika had always been one of the most organized women she knew and her home had reflected that. The closets downstairs came as a surprise, but nothing like this. The bedroom was small and had, as she recalled, been immaculately organized.

But things had changed. There seemed to be more furniture. There definitely were fewer ruffles. And there was an odd metal box sitting in the middle of the dresser. But Erika ignored all that and led the way to the closet and pulled open its door.

"Oh. Wow." Susan had no idea what else to say. As a defense against destructive moths, the closet was perfect. There wasn't enough space for a fly. "I hope . . . I hope you didn't buy anything big today."

Erika sipped her wine. "You see my problem."

Susan nodded. "You've changed things around in here, haven't you?"

"Hmm. Brett needed some space. For his clothes and his gun and all." She nodded her head to indicate the metal box. "He keeps it locked up there when he's here. Not that he thinks I'd shoot him—at least that's what he claims—but he's a big believer in better safe than sorry."

"You must appreciate that." Again, Susan didn't know what to say.

"We're not living together. At least, not officially. He still has his apartment, of course. But he sleeps over and needs his things here. I won't show you the medicine cabinet. Every time I open it, something falls into the sink and breaks."

"If you're going to stay here, you'll have to expand—or break up with Brett." It was said casually, but Susan noticed the expression on Erika's face. "Oh, Erika, you're not going to break up with Brett. Not over closet space."

"No, if we break up it won't be over closet space, not exactly."

"What do you mean?"

"Money. It sounds stupid, but if we break up it will be over money."

"But surely you have enough money to remodel. Oh, that's not what you mean, is it?"

"No. I have more than enough money to remodel, or buy another place, or even two, for that matter. The problem is that Brett doesn't."

Susan sat down on the edge of the bed, a serious expression on her face. "To be honest, I've wondered about that. Brett is a sweet guy, and as liberated as they come, but . . . but I've wondered if your success bothered him."

"Has he ever said anything?"

"No. In fact, he's incredibly proud of you and your business as far as I can tell."

"He says he is and I think he's sincere about it, but, of course, a policeman doesn't make the type of money the CEO of a corporation makes. You know I took the company public last month."

"I heard. Congratulations." Susan didn't actually know what it meant, but she knew it was significant. And, from the gossip she'd heard around town, she gathered Erika had made a lot of money in the deal.

"Thanks. But I think my success may keep Brett and me apart."

"And that's why you're seeing the therapist?"

"Yes. I love Brett. I don't want to make a mistake that will affect both our lives."

"You're not thinking of Ivan Deakins, are you?" Susan and Erika had met after her first husband had been murdered.

"No. I was so young then. I'm a different person now. I just . . . I just don't want to hurt Brett." She picked up her wineglass and drank. Susan got the impression that their conversation had come to an end.

She was sure of it when loud knocking on the front door preceded Brett's voice calling up the stairs. "Erika? It's me."

"In the bedroom," Erika called back.

Susan stood up. "I'd better get going. Jed will wonder if I got lost at Once in a Blue Moon. Hi, Brett," she greeted him.

"Hi, hon." Erika gave Brett a quick kiss. "Want some wine?"

"I hate to say it, but I have to get back down to the station. Scott Worth is there and, apparently, having a fit. I figured I'd stop here and drop off your packages. Using a police cruiser for a shopping basket isn't all that professional."

"Poor Scott. He must be terribly upset over Amanda's death," Erika said.

"I'm sure he is, but according to the call I got, his main concern is that his wife was found at a discount mall instead of Bloomingdale's—and what the publicity will mean to him."

SEVEN

Susan DECIDED SHE NEEDED A REASON TO VISIT THE PO-
lice station. Clue, she remembered, had lost her dog tags and
this was as good a time as any to apply for a replacement.
And, if she found out what was happening with Scott Worth
at the same time, all the better. She called home on her cell
phone as she turned out of Erika's driveway. But there was
no answer. She glanced at her watch; Jed was probably out
walking Clue. She left a message on the answering machine
and drove on.

The Hancock Police Station was part of an attractive municipal complex. The large parking lot was almost as full as
the one at Once in a Blue Moon. Feeling she had already
spent more than enough time driving up and down rows of
cars, Susan was becoming impatient by the time she finally
found a spot far away from the building near two overflowing Dumpsters.

She got out, locked the car, and pulled her sheepskin coat
tightly around her shoulders. It was freezing! All the promotion for Once in a Blue Moon had mentioned its spring opening. The person who wrote that copy must live in California.
March in Connecticut was cold, cold, cold. She hurried over
to the well-lit building.

The lobby was crowded with people. Reporters, she realized, as she tried to push through the group. They completely ignored her polite requests to move aside and she was becoming more than a little annoyed when a young man in the crowd recognized her.

"Hey, that's Mrs. Henshaw! Mrs. Henshaw found the body!"

Susan recognized the enthusiastic voice of Tom Davidson. She had met Tom when he was covering Ivan Deakin's murder for a local cable television station. She was surprised to hear his voice here in Hancock. The last she'd heard, he was reporting for one of the network affiliates in New York City.

"Mrs. Henshaw!"

"Mrs. Henshaw!"

"Over here."

"Hey, lady, look in my direction!"

Susan was stunned by flashbulbs, cameras clicking, and the hum of videotape. "I—" Someone grabbed her hand.

"Come with me. This way."

It was Tom Davidson, and Susan allowed herself to be pulled through the crowd, only once banging her head on a protruding camera lens. Microphones were shoved in her face and lights blinded her. It was a relief to be pulled through a doorway, away from the crowd. "Now I know what Madonna feels like," she said, looking around. "This is the bathroom," she said, glancing at her reflection in a duo of mirrors over the sinks. She sure didn't look anything like Madonna. She looked like a middle-aged woman who had been shopping all day—pretty terrible.

Tom Davidson was staring at her.

"I look awful," she insisted, always willing to state the obvious.

"You do look a bit tired," he conceded. "Of course, you must be distressed over finding your friend murdered," he added in a voice which sounded just a bit less sincere to her.

"Why are all those people out there?" Susan asked, ignoring his comment.

He brushed his thick dark hair off his forehead and looked at her more closely. "Because of the murder. Why did you think?"

"Tom, there have been murders before in Hancock. I don't remember—in fact, I'm sure the press have never been particularly interested. And, even if there wasn't much news and some young reporter thought he could make a name for himself doing an investigative report on mysterious deaths in the affluent suburbs—why no place is safe to live or some such garbage—it's never been anything at all like this."

"Yes, but the identity of the victim creates interest. Or, in this case, the identity of her husband."

"Amanda and Scott Worth? Why would either one of them be of interest outside of Hancock?"

"Susan, Scott Worth is famous in his own field. Surely you know that."

"I know he works on Wall Street. . . ."

"Susan, he's the manager of one of the biggest hedge funds in the country."

"I don't know much about that type of thing. I usually use the business section of the *Times* to pick up after Clue in the yard," she explained.

"Oh, you still have the big golden retriever."

"Yes." Susan spared a moment to hope, again, that Clue was getting a much needed walk after her long day alone.

"But, Mrs. Henshaw . . ."

"Susan . . ." she suggested.

"Thanks, Susan. Stories about Scott Worth have been on the front page of the *Times*. He's news. His fund is being investigated by the Securities and Exchange Commission. There are rumors that he's been involved in money laundering for various groups and individuals who need that type of thing."

Susan frowned. "I guess I've seen stories about money laundering. I don't remember Scott Worth being mentioned though."

"How about Worthington Securities?"

"Maybe . . ." She didn't want to admit that she rushed through much of the hard news and almost all of the financial news to get to the things that interested her—fashion, style, food, art, music, and, to be honest, the obituaries. "Is Scott Worth an important person at Worthington Securities?"

"Scott Worth is Worthington Securities."

"I had no idea . . . but Scott wasn't killed. His wife was," Susan protested and then realized there was another possibility. "Unless he killed her."

"No."

"He's a suspect. The husband is always the first suspect."

"Not in this case. Apparently Scott Worth was being interviewed by one of the large cable business stations—CNBC or CNNFN or something similar—much of the afternoon. He has about as good an alibi as anyone is going to get—he's on videotape. No, Scott Worth did not kill his wife."

"Then why is this such a big deal?"

"Because he's a big deal. The Worths are celebrities in financial circles. And when something happens to a celebrity—"

"We hear about it over and over for months," Susan said.

"It is covered by the media."

"Yeah, and in a few months, it will be rehashed about a million times on various supposed news shows and, probably, the Worths will be the subjects of about a dozen television biographies for the next decade." She had an awful thought. "You don't suppose the shots of me . . . just now, without makeup and without my hair combed and . . . and all . . . will be on those shows."

"Could be," Tom Davidson said cheerfully. "So, will you help me?"

"What can I do?"

"Give me an exclusive story. You know the Worths—at least I thought you did—and you did find the body," he added more cheerfully.

"I do know the Worths. We've socialized with them for years and years. But how did you know I found Amanda?"

"It was in the press release the police handed out."

"Oh, no, does that mean there's going to be a lot of publicity about this and I'll be getting calls at home and all?"

"Maybe." He seemed completely disinterested in that aspect of the situation. "So, will you help me? I'm one of the junior guys at the station and it would really mean a lot to me."

She had forgotten his appealing hangdog smile and light blue eyes. "Sure, why not? If I say I'm only going to talk to you, maybe the other reporters will leave me alone, right?"

"I wouldn't bank on it," he answered honestly. "So, tell me about your discovery of the body."

"What do you want to know?"

"Where was she? How did you happen to be there? Was she already dead? When did you realize it was murder and not an accident?" He flipped a few switches and stuck a microphone in her face.

"Well, I found her—that is, she was in a dressing room, but I thought she was Kathleen. Not that I expected to find Kathleen on the floor or anything, but, at first, it just didn't register."

"Was she naked?"

"Excuse me?"

"There's a rumor going around that she was naked when you found her."

"She was not naked. She was fully covered."

"In her own clothing?"

"Well, of course, whose clothing would you expect her to be wearing? Oh, you mean was she wearing the store's clothing. Was she trying on something . . ."

"That's what people usually do in dressing rooms, isn't it?"

"Of course. I hadn't thought of that. And you're right. She was getting ready to try on clothing. She was half-undressed and there was an outfit hanging on the wall of the room. But I don't see what that might have to do with anything."

"You never know. Besides, the more details the better the story."

"Oh, okay. Well, she was lying on the floor when I pulled back the curtain. Because I thought she was Kathleen—that Kathleen was in the dressing room—I wouldn't have pulled back the curtain on just anybody," she assured him.

"Of course not. So, there she was. Lying on the floor. Did you notice if she was breathing?"

"No, she wasn't. I'm sure of that. She had been strangled, you know."

"No, that wasn't in the police report. With what?"

"Her scarf. It was Hermes," Susan explained.

"That's a scarf company?"

"That's the scarf company of all time."

"Is there a store at Once in a Blue Moon?"

"A Hermes outlet? Not that I noticed. But Amanda was always wearing Hermes scarves. She had a whole collection of them."

"Is that significant?"

"Only if you consider the fact that they cost a small fortune. Hundreds of dollars apiece."

"You're kidding! What the hell are they made of?"

"Silk. But they're the best," Susan assured him.

"They better be. So, go on. She was strangled with this insanely expensive silk scarf."

"And that's it. She was dead. I screamed or yelled or something and Kathleen—who was trying on clothing in the other little dressing room—dashed right over. Then a security person came."

"Why? Did one of you go out for him or did he just happen to arrive?"

"He was a she and she just happened to arrive, I guess. I mean, we didn't call for her. We may have been making more noise than she expected to hear in the dressing room—I guess."

"So she arrived and called for the police."

"So she arrived and called for an ambulance and then the police. At least I think that's what happened." Susan frowned. "Brett showed up before anyone else."

"Who decided to call the Hancock Police?"

"No one. No one called them."

"So how did Chief Fortesque know about the murder?"

"Brett just happened to be at the mall."

"Hmm."

Susan wondered what that meant. And then realized something else. "Why is the press here in Hancock?"

"Because Scott Worth is here."

"I wonder why."

"Why?"

"Well, the murder didn't happen here. The investigating police department isn't in Hancock. The body isn't here—I assume—so why is Scott here?"

Tom Davidson looked at her with respect. "A very, very interesting question. And I don't think anyone has asked about that yet. Excuse me, I'd better be going." Without another word, he spun around on one heel and, after knocking very gently into the doorframe, left the room.

Susan stood and stared at the door as it swung closed behind him. Then she shrugged and entered one of the booths. She was here; she might as well use the facilities. The door opened and closed and she hoped it wasn't another reporter but she was busy and decided not to call attention to herself by yelling out.

But she couldn't stay inside forever and she left the privacy of her booth a bit hesitantly. And gasped. There was a man. . . . She looked around. Oh no! She hadn't seen the row of urinals on the wall when Tom Davidson was interviewing her. Maybe, she thought, she could just tiptoe out and he—whoever he was—wouldn't notice.

Unfortunately, she smashed her purse against the wall.

Even more unfortunate was his identity: the man was Scott Worth.

EIGHT

LIKE QUEEN VICTORIA, SCOTT WORTH WAS NOT AMUSED. In fact, he appeared to be furious. Not that Susan blamed him. He hadn't expected to find a woman in the room when he turned from the urinal, zipping his fly. But Susan got the impression that who she was was bothering him more than her sex.

"Susan Henshaw! What the hell are you doing here?"

"I didn't know. . . . I thought this was the ladies' room."

"Why are you here?"

"I . . . I had to use the bathroom."

"I don't give a damn about your . . . your physical needs. I want to know why you're here . . . at the police station."

Susan suspected the excuse about Clue's lost dog tags wouldn't work. "I . . . um, I wanted to talk to Brett about something."

"What do you know?"

The question came as a surprise. "I . . . I don't know anything." She had a terrible feeling that, on some days at least, this was a true statement.

"They told me you found her."

Susan interpreted this to mean that the police had told him of Susan's discovery of his wife's body. "Yes."

"You know what I think?"

"Not really."

"I think you should mind your own business."

Susan had no idea what to say. But, as she had frequently admonished her children, manners are important. And, after all, this man's wife had just died. "I'm sorry about Amanda—it was . . . it was terrible finding her there like that."

She thought she had said, if not the perfect thing, as least something innocuous, but, much to her surprise, Scott Worth became even angrier.

"You . . . you choose to attack me at a time like this?"

"I . . ."

"Amanda, the love of my life, is dead, and you insult her . . . insult me . . . insult us—our marriage, our lives together. I . . . I cannot speak with you anymore." He turned to leave, but, hand on the doorknob, appeared to think better of it. "Mind your own business, Susan Henshaw. Hear what I said? Mind your own business."

He left Susan alone, her mouth hanging open, her heart beating rapidly. She had no idea what to do. . . . Except get out of the men's room, she realized as the door began to open. She looked down at the floor and rushed by the man entering, hoping he wouldn't recognize her.

But this particular man was almost as familiar with the back of her head as with her face.

"Susan?"

"Jed?"

"What are you doing here?"

"What are you doing here?"

"Tell you what." Her husband grabbed her hand. "Why don't I stay here and do what I need to do and you go out there and meet me. . . ."

"I'll wait just outside the door," she announced, getting the idea. "But hurry. I don't want to be interviewed by the press anymore."

"Don't worry. There's an official press briefing going on in the auditorium at the library. There's no one out there to bother you."

She opened the door slowly, relieved to discover what her husband said was true. The lobby was deserted. She ran a hand through her hair, wishing she'd taken a moment to freshen up. By the time her husband reappeared, she had another worry.

"Jed! What about Clue? I told you I might be late this evening and you said—"

"That I would be home early and walk her. Which is close to what I did. I actually took her down to the track to run with me."

"Dogs aren't allowed on the high school track," Susan protested.

"I know that now—I saw the sign as I was parking the car. So I tied her up to a tree and planned to do my three miles."

Susan realized he was leaving something out. "And?"

"I guess I should have paid more attention to knot tying when I was a Boy Scout."

"She ran away!"

"Ran, dashed, fled, sped. You name it, she did it." He smiled. "She had a wonderful time. The junior high and senior high track teams were working out. And there was a meeting of the Little League coaches on one of the fields. Cheerleaders were in the bandstands and some sort of Tai Chi class was going through their paces under a tree. Clue dashed around, interrupted every group, and then jumped right in the stream that runs along the parking lot there. She was the filthiest golden retriever in the world. And one of the happiest."

"But . . ."

"Don't worry about the house. I closed her in the garage with an old army blanket, her dinner, and a large bowl of water. She's probably asleep right now."

Susan, who knew Clue's habits better than her husband did, doubted it. "I guess we'll have to give her a bath when we get home." She looked up at her husband. "But why are you here?"

"Kathleen called. When I explained that you weren't home yet, she told me what happened this afternoon. She thought you would be at Erika's house, but Erika said you'd already left—right after Brett. I thought you might be here when I saw all the cars in the parking lot. I found a place to park so I stopped in to check it out. The meeting in the men's room was fortuitous—I didn't go in there looking for you."

"You stopped in? Are you going somewhere tonight?"

"Membership committee meeting down at the Club, remember?"

"Oh, that's right!" She didn't, in fact, remember at all, but she also didn't want to admit that she might not have been paying attention when he told her about it.

"So what about you?"

"Me?"

"Are you going to explain to me what you were doing in the men's room?"

"Ah . . . Tom Davidson pulled me in there."

"Tom Davidson? The kid who used to be a reporter for

the local cable show? The one Chrissy dated a few years ago?"

"Yes. He's working in New York City now."

"Does that have anything to do with why he pulls middle-aged ladies into men's rooms?"

"Jed!"

"You're not answering my question, Susan."

"Tom Davidson wanted to interview me in a private place and the men's room was the most private place around—I guess."

"What about?"

"About Amanda Scott's murder."

"What about it?"

"I found her body—didn't Kathleen tell you?"

"Kathleen was trying to keep her children from killing each other when I called. She didn't explain anything."

"Well, we were at the mall—" Susan began.

Jed was more interested in his watch. "Susan, I'm already fifteen minutes late."

"Oh . . . well, I guess I can tell you all about it when you get home."

"Great!" Her husband gave her a quick, husbandlike kiss and was off.

Susan frowned and then realized that she was exhausted and hungry. An evening alone at home might be just the thing. She could put away her new clothes, check out her closet to see what went with what. Have a glass or two of wine and a salad and not have to worry about feeding any-one else. . . . And she could wash the dog. Alone, she realized, watching her husband walk away. Damn. Damn. Damn. She cursed all the way home.

But it was nothing compared with what she said when she entered her garage.

Clue had discovered the bag of dog biscuits that Susan stored out there. It was huge and it had been half-full. Now it was empty; there wasn't a crumb to be seen. Clue was lying on the cement floor, a grin on her golden retriever face, surrounded by dried caked mud. Unfortunately there was even more mud still attached to her fur. Susan stopped to pet the dog and then headed straight for the bottle of Chardonnay chilling in the refrigerator.

Clue followed her into the house. Susan sighed and stopped. The wine would have to wait. She either bathed Clue now or washed down the entire house later.

"Come on, sweetie." The downstairs bathroom was reserved for two groups—guests, and the dog and whoever was washing the dog. The expensive Italian tile that lined the room was for the guests. The walk-in shower stall with handheld sprayer was for Clue and Clue's bather.

The next half an hour was awful and, by the time it was over, Susan was cranky and soaked, the bathroom was filthy beyond belief, and Clue, clean and fresh smelling, was making known her need to go outside.

"Okay. But make it quick. We're both wet and it's cold out there."

It really was cold and only one of them was wearing a fur coat—Clue. In the five minutes it took the dog to find an appropriate location to do her thing, Susan practically froze to death. She headed back into the house as interested in a hot bath as in a glass of wine.

"Or maybe a nice hot toddy," she said aloud, stopping on her way through the kitchen. Clue went to her water dish and Susan pulled open the refrigerator door and found a fresh lemon.

When the phone rang, a few minutes later, she was stirring hot lemon juice, brown sugar, and water into a few ounces of Kentucky bourbon. She took a sip before answering.

"Hello?"

"Susan. Thank goodness you're home. Are you alone?"

"Who is this?"

"Lauren. Are you alone?"

"Yes, but—"

"I'll be right over."

Susan put down the receiver and picked up her drink. She had time for one more relaxing sip before the doorbell pealed. "Who the hell could that be?" she asked her dog.

Clue ran to the door, tail wagging, to find out.

"Coming," Susan called, forgetting that it might be the press and she might prefer to pretend to be out.

It was Lauren.

"Lauren . . ." She opened the door, perplexed. "Someone just called on the phone claiming to be you."

"It was me. Cell phone," she added, patting her large Fendi bag. "We need to talk."

"Come on in," Susan said, although in reality Lauren was already in. "Would you like a drink? I was just having a hot toddy. Bourbon," she added.

"Heavens no! Nothing hard." Lauren protested as though Susan had suggested a little arsenic in her tea. "Maybe some bottled water—bubbly—with just a splash of white wine?"

Susan regretted her offer. "I'll just go into the kitchen and get it. We could sit in there—or in the living room," she offered.

"I'll wait for you in the living room."

Susan hurried back to the kitchen. She thought there was a bottle of Pellegrino in the refrigerator and she could open that wine. Although it was a rather good bottle to water down.

But Susan's hospitable instincts won and, in a few minutes, she entered her living room, tray in her hands. "I thought you might be hungry after shopping and . . . and all, so I brought us a snack as well."

Lauren looked down at the selection of cheeses, water crackers, and olives with a strange expression on her face. "I . . . I don't think so. After what happened to Amanda . . . well, I find it difficult to believe I'll ever want to eat again." She looked more closely at the food. "Amanda used to offer olives—she marinated them herself using herbs from her garden."

The food Susan offered had come from the best gourmet grocery in the state. She had nothing to be ashamed of—and she, at least, was starving. She spread some Gorgonzola on a cracker, popped it in her mouth, and picked up her now tepid toddy. "Why are you here?"

Lauren put down her drink and looked at Susan. "I need your help. Amanda needs your help."

"Amanda? Amanda is dead. What could she possibly need me to do?"

"Find out who murdered her," Lauren said dramatically.

"I . . . That's for the police to do."

"You've done it in the past. Everyone in town knows that."

"But there's always been a reason for me to get involved in those murders." Perhaps not a very good one, she admitted to herself, but said nothing out loud.

"But there is a reason!" Lauren insisted.

"What?"

"You have to protect Amanda."

Susan sipped from her mug. Lauren and Amanda had been friends. Was it possible that Amanda's death had unhinged her mind in some way? Or perhaps she had had a breakdown and . . . and was the murderer. Susan hoped the bulge in the sleek Fendi bag was only a phone and not a gun. . . .

"Susan, Amanda was your friend. She was our friend. She was one of us. We have to do what we can to protect her reputation now that she can't do it herself."

"Lauren, as far as I know Amanda's reputation is intact."

"But what is going to happen when the police start looking for her murderer?"

"What do you mean?"

"They will start asking questions, right?"

"Of course, but—"

"And they'll look into Amanda's life."

"I suppose so. That's one of the places I always start. The more you know about the victim, the easier it is to find a motive for murder," Susan explained, feeling more than a little like a character in a PBS drama.

"And what will happen if they find out things that are . . . are damaging . . . to Amanda?"

"Like what?"

"Like the fact that she was having an affair!"

NINE

NOTHING LIKE A GOOD BIT OF GOSSIP TO PERK YOU UP AT the end of a long day. Susan sat up straight. "Amanda Worth was having an affair? How do you know about it? Who is the man?"

"I don't know who—she wouldn't tell me."

"She told you she was having an affair, but she wouldn't tell you who she was involved with?"

"No—I would never have asked either. If . . . if she had wanted to tell me what she was doing she would have told me."

Susan reached out for more cheese. "I'm sorry. I just don't understand." And sometimes a little extra cholesterol helped.

"You must have noticed how close Amanda and I have become in the last year or so." Lauren paused and took a deep breath.

Susan hadn't, in fact, but that didn't matter. She nodded and chewed, and Lauren continued.

"We were very much alike—Amanda and I," she added in case Susan didn't get the point.

"You're having an affair, too?"

"Heavens! No! Never! Albert and I are happy together. Very happy," she added in case Susan had missed her point.

"I would have said the same was true of Amanda and Scott," Susan suggested.

"Well, yes, I would have too—until recently."

"That's when Amanda told you about the other man."

"She didn't exactly tell me." Lauren seemed to find the food interesting after all.

"Then other people know about it?"

"Susan, I don't think that's possible. If Amanda chose not to confide in me, I don't think she would tell anyone else."

Susan stopped chewing long enough to make a confession. "I don't understand. If Amanda didn't tell you she was having an affair, why are you telling me she did—did her lover tell you?" Susan was uncomfortable asking the question. Somehow a lover and Amanda didn't "go" together.

"No, Susan, you just don't understand. I guess I'm tired and not explaining too well."

"It's been a long and horrible day, don't worry about it. Go on."

"You won't repeat what I'm going to tell you?"

"No, of course not."

"Well, Amanda and I have become such good friends in the past year, I probably notice things about her that other people might not." Lauren looked as though she expected an answer.

Susan just nodded. It had occurred to her that, while Lauren was talking a lot, she was saying very little.

"Naturally, we've spent tons of time together—shopping, and lunching, and stuff like that."

Lauren stopped again and Susan began to wonder what she was so afraid to say. "Go on," she repeated.

"But suddenly everything stopped. Every time I called to

set up something, she was busy. After a while, of course, I began to get suspicious."

"Why? Maybe she *was* just busy."

"No, she never gave me a reason. In fact, sometimes I thought she was going out of her way not to give me a reason. And then one day after this had happened about a million times . . ." Lauren noticed the expression on Susan's face and changed her story. "Okay, probably only about a dozen times—but it really wasn't like Amanda—really! And then this one day I saw her. . . ."

"Who was she with?"

"I don't really know—but it was a man and . . . and they must have been having an affair. There was certainly no other reason for anyone to be in that place."

"What place?'

"You know that motel out on Route 95?"

"The Omni?"

"No. The place I'm talking about is nothing like the Omni. It's called the Nutmeg Motel. Do you know it?"

Susan did. It was a small place right on the road. Built in the early fifties when suburban motels were a new idea, it had probably been cute at one time with cutouts of squirrels on the screen doors of each of its two dozen or so rooms. But the screens were now torn or completely missing, the paint was peeling and, from the outside, it looked as though the roof was letting in more of the elements each year.

"There's a restaurant there."

"Really? Where?"

"Right next to the office—well, it's really part of the office. Or, I should say, the office is in the restaurant—which is a . . . a what do you call it? You know, little . . . rundown. . . ."

"A luncheonette?"

"No, it starts with *d* . . . A dive. That's it! The place is a dive. I can't imagine anyone we know eating in a place like that, can you?"

"Some of these little out-of-the-way places have wonderful food," Susan suggested.

"Yeah?" Lauren looked skeptical.

"Really. Why, just today Kathleen and I ate in a spot I'd been passing for years and our lunch turned out to be excellent."

"Oh, you must tell me where it is sometime." Lauren's lack of interest was so apparent that Susan decided she wouldn't bother. "Anyway, I just happened to stop in there one morning. I needed to use the bathroom frankly, but there was one of those tacky signs that says something like 'restrooms for customers only' so I ordered a cup of coffee. Which meant I had to sit down for a minute, and guess who was sitting on the other side of the room."

"Amanda."

Lauren opened her mascara-framed eyes wide. "How did you know?"

"That's who we're talking about, right?"

"Oh, yes, of course. Anyway, she was there *and* with a man."

"Who?"

"I could only see the back of his head and I didn't hang around to look more carefully, I can tell you."

"You figured she didn't want to be seen."

"Why else would she—would they—be eating in a place like that?"

"It's near the road. Maybe she and this man were just hungry and stopped in for a bite."

"Susan, the Hancock Inn is less than ten minutes from

there. And there's a McDonald's and a Friendly's even closer than that if all she and this man wanted was a quick cup of coffee or some fast food. That doesn't sound like Amanda to me, anyway."

Susan agreed, but it was obvious where this story was going so she thought she would hurry it along a bit. "So you think the only reason she and this man could possibly have been eating at the Nutmeg Motel is if they were having an affair there."

"Yes."

"Did you ask her about it? Tell her that you had seen her and this man at the Nutmeg Motel?"

"Not in so many words."

"What did you do?"

"I . . . I asked her if she had ever been there. You know, in conversation, sort of casually."

"I gather she said she hadn't been."

"She claimed not to even know that there was such a place."

"And you're sure you didn't make a mistake. You're sure it was Amanda?"

"Susan, we were good friends! Besides, the sun was coming in the window and shining off that huge emerald Scott gave her for their twenty-fifth anniversary. I couldn't mistake that ring."

Susan tended to agree. Amanda's two-carat clear emerald had, in the few short years since she'd been given it, become part of the lore of Hancock, a benchmark in husbandly love that many a man found himself wishing he wasn't judged by. Jed, ordinarily the best of husbands, had given Susan a new sewing machine for their twenty-fifth. "It is odd, though, don't you think? I mean, if the inside of the motel rooms are anything like the outside suggests, I wouldn't think they're appropriate for an illicit tryst, would you?"

"No, but where else would they go?"

"Someplace in New York City? The Plaza or the Pierre? Or maybe the Griswold Inn? I mean, there are dozens of places. . . ."

"But none as inappropriate as the Nutmeg Motel. That's what's so brilliant! No one would ever expect to find Amanda there—it's as safe a place as she could find."

"I suppose. But what does all this have to do with me getting involved in the investigation of her murder? Do you think this strange man killed her?"

"Well, naturally, I have no idea if that is true or not, but don't you think the person running the investigation should know about Amanda and this man? It certainly could have something to do with her death."

"Makes sense to me. So why don't you just tell the police?"

"That's exactly what I don't want to do! I want to keep Amanda's reputation intact. That's why you have to figure out who murdered her. Because I'm not going to tell anyone about that strange man and that awful motel—it would destroy Amanda's good name."

"But . . ."

"And, if they don't know all the facts, the police aren't very likely to arrest the right person, are they?" Lauren continued.

"That's the reason you should tell them," Susan said.

"I'm only going to tell you."

"I could tell them."

"No, Susan, you can't possibly do that."

"But . . ."

"The only option—the only one, believe me—is for you to solve this murder yourself. Otherwise you'll destroy Amanda's reputation and something terrible may happen."

"What?" Susan asked, suspicious of Lauren's sudden reticence.

"Susan, think! If the police don't know about Amanda's affair, they won't have important information about her life and that might cause them to arrest the wrong person."

"So you're saying that, since I'm the only person you've told about Amanda's affair, I'm the only person who is likely to discover the identity of the guilty party."

"Exactly."

Susan, uncharacteristically forgetting her duties as host, gulped down the last piece of cheese as she pondered the problem.

But Lauren wasn't one to sit around unoccupied. "I have to go," she announced, standing up. "Albert and I are going to go see Scott this evening and I want to shower and change first."

"You're going to go to his house?"

"Yes. As one of Amanda's best friends, I think my place is at his side. He will have so many decisions to make—about the funeral and all—and Albert and I feel that we should offer him our assistance."

"That's very nice of you." Susan stood also and led her guest to the door.

"I'll call you in the morning. Then you can tell me what you're going to do first."

"I . . ."

"Thanks so much for doing this, Susan. I'm sure Amanda would be relieved to know her . . . uh, her murder investigation is in such capable and understanding hands."

"I didn't say I would investigate anything," Susan insisted.

"You will." Lauren spoke with confidence. "When you think about it, you'll see that it's the only answer. 'Bye."

"The only answer to what?" Susan said, closing the door and looking down at Clue.

Clue wagged her plumy tail, turned, and trotted back to the living room. Susan, realizing what was going on, dashed after her to rescue the leftovers. The dog had managed to finish up all the crackers before she arrived, but Susan was in time to grab her sticky mug, still half-full of bourbon and lemonade, before Clue spilled it on the rug in her attempt to lick up every last drop.

"Let's see what's in the kitchen for dinner," she suggested.

Dinner was one of Clue's favorite words and the two of them walked down the hallway toward the back of the large Colonial house.

Susan had filled Clue's bowl with one of those oddly named health foods for overweight dogs and was rummaging in the freezer for a Lean Cuisine for herself when the phone rang.

She wasn't surprised. When the news of Amanda's death got out, her social group would be buzzing. She picked up the receiver, wondering if she was going to learn something else about Amanda's life.

"Hello?"

But the voice on the other end of the line wasn't concerned with Amanda's life. The voice was muffled and almost too low for Susan to make out exactly what was being said—for a moment. Then she realized that someone was threatening her life.

"What the . . . Who are . . ." She was too shocked and too upset to finish a sentence.

But that was all right; with a final insult, the caller hung up.

TEN

"HE CALLED ME A BITCH! CAN YOU BELIEVE THAT? FIRST
he threatened me, then he called me a bitch and then, without giving me time to say a word, he hung up. I couldn't believe it! I still can't believe it!" Susan, home alone and more
shocked than scared, had dialed Kathleen's number almost
without thinking.

"Are you sure it was a man?"

"A man?"

"You've been saying he," Kathleen said gently.

"I . . . I have no idea why I said that." She thought for a
moment and then continued. "Maybe the voice did sound a
bit more male then female, but the words were whispered or
muffled in some way. I'm really not sure. Kathleen, what
should I do? Aren't you supposed to report this type of thing
to the phone company? When I got obscene calls in college
that's what I did."

"I think the world was a bit different back then. There was
only one phone company and it tended to be—well, paternal.
If you call now, someone will probably listen to what you have
to say and then try to sell you a cheaper long distance carrier."

Susan chuckled. "Only if I call them during the dinner
hour."

"You should call Brett."

"I guess I should, but he's probably still busy at the press briefing down at the civic center. . . . Kathleen, do you have a few minutes to talk?"

"Of course. Jerry's finally home so, if Alex and Alice need something, he can take care of it."

"Great, because I had a strange conversation with Lauren this afternoon."

"What about?"

"She wants me to look into Amanda's death. To find out who murdered her."

"What does Lauren have to do with it?"

"She claims to be worried about Amanda's reputation," Susan answered. "You won't believe the story she told me about seeing Amanda at the Nutmeg Motel. . . ."

"Amanda? At the hovel out on the highway?"

"Yes. Apparently she's been having an affair and meeting her lover out there."

"You are kidding, aren't you?"

"No."

"Susan, that place is awful. What sort of man takes his lover there?"

"Someone who doesn't want to be seen by all the people we know who would never go there," Susan suggested.

"Well, maybe, but there are lots of places you can go for privacy where you aren't going to end up with lice as well."

"Lauren said she saw Amanda and a strange man—she didn't see his face so she really can't identify him—at the Nutmeg Motel early one morning."

"Coming out of a room?"

"Eating breakfast in the luncheonette. Lauren seems to

think no one would eat there except that it is convenient to the motel."

"Why?"

"Apparently it's a dump."

"You probably thought that about the place where we had lunch today, right?"

"That's exactly what I was thinking."

"And now that you've eaten there, would you go back?"

"Of course. Our meal was wonderful."

"So maybe the food at the Nutmeg Motel is something special."

"That's easy enough to find out. What are you doing for lunch tomorrow?"

"Meeting my friend at the Nutmeg Motel," Kathleen answered promptly.

"Great!"

"So tell me why Lauren thinks you should involve yourself in the investigation?"

"To preserve her best friend's reputation apparently."

"But Lauren isn't Amanda's best friend. If anyone is, it's Kimberly."

"Well, she's putting herself in the position of being best friend. She was on her way over to the Worths' home tonight to help Scott plan the funeral. Wait a minute. I just had a thought. If Lauren isn't Amanda's best friend and is on her way to see Scott tonight, why can't I do the same?"

"I don't see why you can't. In the neighborhood where I grew up a bereaved family was never alone. The amount of food that was given to some of these people . . ."

"That's a good idea. I could bring something for Scott to eat. Or maybe something for him to serve if he has people over to the house after the funeral—unless he has that catered."

"Scott and Amanda never had anything catered. She always cooked everything and he always bragged about it," Kathleen reminded her.

"Yes. But unless Scott has been secretly helping Amanda out, I think we can be pretty sure that, without a wife, all that work will be done by someone else. Anyway, I have a large casserole of beef carbonara in the freezer. I'll take that to him and ask if I can help out in any way."

"And nose around a bit?" Kathleen suggested.

"You bet."

"But, Susan, you did get a threatening phone call and Amanda was murdered. Promise me you'll call Brett and tell him about it before you head over to see Scott."

"I will . . ."

"Right away!" Kathleen insisted.

"Just as soon as I wash my face and change."

"Okay. See you at lunch tomorrow. Noon?"

"I'll be there," Susan assured her and hung up. She stood and stretched, realizing for the first time how exhausted she was. Well, perhaps a quick shower would help, she decided, and headed up to the bathroom. And she should wear something a little less casual, but not formal. . . .

Forty-five minutes later she was showered and changed. The dog was walked. She had written a note to Jed and left it where he would find it (on the bottle of wine sitting in the middle of the kitchen table). There was a dark red Le Creuset casserole propped between pillows on the floor of her car and she was setting the burglar alarm when she remembered her promise to Kathleen. She reached for the phone and dialed the number of Brett's office at the police station. She smiled when she realized she had gotten his voice mail. If she could only leave a message, she wouldn't have to answer any questions.

"Brett, this is Susan Henshaw. I got a threatening phone call this evening. I think it was from a man. He said I should forget everything I saw today or I would be in big trouble. And he called me a bitch. 'Bye."

She drove across town, feeling that she had handled her obligations satisfactorily.

The Worth house was lit up as if for one of their famous parties. Cars lined the street and Susan had to park around the corner. By the time she arrived at the house, she was wishing that her cookware was a bit smaller and a whole lot lighter. Walking up the sidewalk, she realized her first impression—that neighbors and friends had flocked to Scott Worth's side in this crisis—was incorrect. The press had arrived here, too, kept on one side of the lawn by four uniformed police officers. Susan tucked down her head. She didn't want to be recognized. She didn't want to be questioned. Fortunately, one of the officers recognized her before anyone else, and escorted her through the crowd and up to the door.

"Susan, we were just talking about you," Lauren said, opening the door for her. "And you brought a casserole. How nice. Why don't I just take it back to the kitchen and you can go speak to Scott. He's in the living room. Do you know the way?"

"Of course." Susan resisted the urge to remind Lauren that she had known the Worths for over a decade before Lauren and her husband arrived in Hancock. She walked through the well-lit hallway, noticing that someone had already sent a massive bouquet of Easter lilies, and entered the living room.

The Worth home was decorated with what Amanda always

referred to as "cherished family antiques" inherited from both her parents and Scott's. Susan had spent many a long evening listening to the antecedents of each and every piece of furniture in this room, so she knew that the Victorian settee that Scott was sitting on had traveled across the plains when Amanda's great-grandmother followed her gold mining husband to Central City, Colorado. Amanda sometimes referred to it as one of her most cherished possessions. But Susan had heard this said about numerous things in the house—most of them a damn sight more comfortable than the settee. Susan suspected that whichever relative had given it to the newlyweds had been thrilled to get rid of it. And as for the wobbly cobbler's bench that was used as a coffee table . . .

"Scott . . ." She walked toward him quickly, with both hands out. "We're . . . I'm so sorry about Amanda. Jed would have been here, but he had a . . . an important meeting," she ended, thinking that Jed's commitment would sound frivolous under these circumstances.

Apparently Scott didn't agree. "Of course, he's on the membership committee down at the Club this year, isn't he? Glad to know there are good people guarding the gates, so to speak."

"Ah, yes." Susan knew, in fact, that Jed didn't think of his position as a guard at the gate to keep undesirable people out, but as a welcoming committee hoping to bring in members of the more diverse community that Hancock had become over the past decade or so. "I brought a casserole," she said, changing the subject.

"I can't say that I'm hungry. . . ."

"Of course not!" Susan felt she had been insensitive. "In fact, it's frozen. I thought . . . well, I didn't know, but . . .

many people have everyone over to their home after the funeral . . . I thought . . . Well, it could be heated up and offered then." She was, she felt, handling this poorly.

Scott almost perked up at her suggestion. "Yes, in fact, Lauren and I were talking about just that thing a few minutes ago. Right before you arrived. Did you see her when you came in?"

"Yes, in fact, she opened the door for me. We spoke—"

"Then it's been all taken care of. How can I thank you?"

She had no idea what to say. This seemed inappropriately effusive for a casserole, although her beef carbonara was excellent, if she did say so herself. "It's nothing."

"Nothing! Susan, you amaze me. How can you call it nothing? You know at least half the town will be here. This could be the biggest event ever held in this house. Your task will be enormous. Why you won't have a spare moment in the next three days."

"I—"

"I'm sure Susan can handle it. She's known for her entertaining." Lauren had returned.

Scott's face fell. "As was my dear Amanda."

"Of course—" A phone rang and Susan stopped speaking.

"No need to worry. Amanda had so many dear friends and some of them have come to help me in my time of need—as have you, my dear Susan, as have you."

Kimberly Critchley entered the room, phone in hand. "Scott, it's the funeral director. He has some questions about the service. . . ."

"I'll take it in the library."

Susan was relieved when Scott left the room. "What's going on?" she asked Kimberly. "Scott seems to think I'm going to be doing something to help him out—and I'm sure

I'm glad to do anything at all that I can, but I do need to know what."

"I've been in the library calling a list of friends and colleagues he thought needed to know about Amanda's death. It's been dreadful. Of course, we have a lot of friends in common, but some of the names on the list he gave me mean absolutely nothing to me. I felt a bit uncomfortable being the one to give them the news, frankly. But, anything I can do to help—besides, you're the one who has volunteered for the big task."

"Actually, I don't—"

"Well, that was horrible." Scott Worth was back with them. "The funeral director wanted me to pick out the clothing that Amanda is to be laid out in and bring it to the home."

"Oh, I could do that," Susan said quickly.

"That would be very helpful. He . . . he reminded me to choose something with a high neck. . . ."

"I'll do that."

"They don't need the outfit until tomorrow night. We've decided the funeral will be Friday morning. Viewing at the Hancock Mortuary Wednesday and Thursday afternoon and evening. I hope that schedule will give you enough time."

"I . . ." Susan suspected that Amanda had closets full of clothing, but still, how long could it take to pick out one outfit? "That's plenty of time," she assured him.

"Excellent. I know there's no way to replicate Amanda's style and flair, but I do want everything to be as nice as possible."

"Of course." And it wasn't as though she was going to be shopping for the clothes; she would only be choosing from what Amanda had already chosen, so to speak.

The doorbell rang. "That must be my lawyer. I am going to make a statement to the press this evening and he suggested we go over it together beforehand."

"Of course. I should be getting home," Susan said, edging toward the door. Was Scott Worth going to be accused of his wife's murder? Is that why he needed a lawyer? Or was he merely being cautious? But his next words drove those questions out of her mind.

"I think you should plan on food and drink for at least three hundred. Sort of a cocktail affair, but Amanda always said that when you invite people over for drinks, you really should offer them something substantial—and warm. It is still cool this time of the year. And the church might be chilly. Our . . . my . . . guests might have to warm up."

What could she do? she asked, going over the events of the day in bed with her husband a few hours later. She had asked if there was anything she could do to help. How was she to know that the help Scott Worth required was a volunteer to prepare a substantial buffet for three hundred guests in three days?

ELEVEN

THE NEXT MORNING, SUSAN'S HAND WAS ON THE PHONE AS her feet touched the floor. When she talked over the problem with Jed the night before, he had come up with the obvious answer—the only answer—find someone to cater the party. That must have been what Scott Worth was asking her to do. She would hire a caterer, plan the food and decorations (merely a flower arrangement or two), and turn the bill over to him. Surely no one could expect more.

By 9:45 she realized it wasn't going to be so easy. She had only used one caterer herself, but after years of attending parties, she knew of many others. But after making a dozen phone calls, she had heard eleven no's and one voice mail message—the company she knew and loved was closed for two weeks for a well-deserved vacation. She pulled on black leggings and a gray thermal tunic. Yanking her hair back off her face with a fluorescent purple scrunchie, she took a moment to wonder when was she finally going to throw away all her daughter's abandoned accessories and buy some more appropriate for a middle-aged woman, and headed to the kitchen and coffee.

When the caffeine hit, her brain cells began to work and she realized she knew someone who might know how to solve her problem. Erika had probably worked with every caterer in the tristate area. And Erika was probably a woman who got to work early. Susan reached for the phone book.

Susan's call was answered by a secretary who put her through to Erika immediately. Susan didn't waste any time getting down to her problem. "Erika, I'm desperate and I can't think of anyone else who can help me. Somehow I ended up in charge of the reception taking place at the Worth house after Amanda's funeral and all the caterers I know in the area can't seem to take on the job at the last minute."

There was silence on the other end of the line. Susan thought she should explain a bit more.

"Erika? I really wouldn't bother you at work if it weren't important. I brought a casserole from my freezer over to the Worths last night and volunteered to help out. You know how you do in a crisis. Anyway, somehow I ended up being in charge of the reception. Things could be worse, I guess. For a while there, I actually thought Scott expected me to do all the cooking for his guests." She poured coffee into a mug decorated with the face of the host of a popular morning show on NPR and took a sip. After hearing Erika's reply, she was relieved that she had already swallowed.

"He probably does," Erika said.

"You're kidding!"

"Or else he expects you to pay for any caterer you hire."

"What? That's impossible! In the first place, we're not very close friends and expecting me to do all that cooking for something happening at his house is completely nuts. In the second place, the Worths are rich—well, at least, they have more money than we do. Why would he ever expect me to pay for . . . It just doesn't make any sense."

"How well do you know the Worths?" Erika's question surprised Susan.

"We've known them for years and years."

"But how well?"

"Not very, which is exactly why they would never expect us to pay for anything as expensive as a catered meal for their friends at their house. . . ."

"If you knew them well, it wouldn't surprise you at all."

"What?"

"Sorry, that's not true. I should have said that if you had ever *worked* for them, you wouldn't be at all surprised. They've probably stiffed most of the small business people in the area."

"I can't believe that."

"Think for a second. When you were calling up all those caterers, did you explain that you were calling for Scott Worth?"

"Of course. It's going to be at his house."

"Well, that's your answer."

"You're telling me that no one is willing to accept the job because they're afraid Scott won't pay the bill?"

"Exactly."

"Shit. What the hell am I going to do?"

"You could—you should—call Scott and tell him that you can't take on this task."

"Erika, the man's wife just died and I volunteered to help. I can't turn around less than twelve hours later and tell him I'm sorry that I can't help because he has a reputation for being cheap."

"What will Jed say if you get a bill for thousands of dollars for a catered affair that wasn't even held in his own home?"

"I can't do that. Period."

"Do you have another solution?"

"I . . ." She couldn't think of anything. "Well, I can't just call Scott on the phone and tell him I'm backing out. I'm going to pick out the clothing Amanda is going to be buried in and take it over to the funeral home this morning. I'll talk to Scott then and explain that I just can't help out. I'll make up some reason."

"Good luck. You might want to know that the reason all these people end up stiffed by Scott and Amanda is that the Worths always—always, Susan—have some good excuse for not paying."

"Like wh—"

"Susan, I have to go. I'm having trouble getting an order through customs out at Kennedy and someone from there is on the other line. See you."

There was a click and Susan was left alone with her thoughts. Well, not actually: when you have a golden retriever, you're never alone. "Okay, sweetie, let's go for a walk." She'd get some exercise and it would give her time to think of a way out of this predicament.

Walking to the street, she considered claiming to have the flu. There had been an especially virulent strain around last month, surely no one would want her to have anything to do with food while she was contagious. But how would she explain about all the caterers in the area claiming to be busy? Of course, she thought, turning a corner and spending a few minutes examining Clue's favorite fire hydrant, she could say that she felt unworthy, that, because of the style in which Amanda and Scott had always entertained, she was going to turn down his request. She didn't believe it was true, but Scott always claimed that no one could put together a party as well as his wife could. Susan would just explain that she didn't feel that she was even qualified to make the attempt.

She only hoped Scott would buy the excuse. She urged Clue back home and headed straight to her car, deciding that there was little reason to change. Maybe she'd stop at the track later this morning and begin to run again. Her sneakers were waiting in her gym bag in the back of her car. She hoped they were comfortable—they'd been there for seven months.

But today was the day, she decided, pounding on her steering wheel. First she would select an outfit for Amanda to be buried in, then she'd explain to Scott that she wasn't qualified to cater an affair at his home, then she'd get off her butt and back on the track.

It was quiet at the Worth house. No press, no police, no cars in the driveway. She parked on the street, not wanting to block the entrance to their shingle style garage, and climbed out of her car. As she walked up the blue slate path to the front door, she wondered, for the first time, if Erika could possibly have her information wrong. The Worth home was large and old—and, from here, it looked impeccably maintained. That took money and lots of it.

Susan walked onto the porch, noting a stenciled border that she hadn't seen before and knocked on the shiny door. It slid open.

"Oh!" She took a step inside. "Anyone home? Scott? It's Susan Henshaw."

No answer. She moved farther into the foyer and, wanting to preserve the heat, closed the door behind her. "Scott? It's Susan . . . Susan Henshaw. I'm here to pick out an outfit for . . . for the funeral home. Scott?"

Still nothing, but she noticed a note on the table next to the phone. She had told Scott she would be here this morning. Maybe he'd written her a note. . . .

Yes, and in what Susan thought of as typically male fashion, it said almost nothing.

Had to go out. Be back soon. Please go ahead with your task.

Susan reread the words and then, smiling, started upstairs. She still didn't know how to explain to Scott that she couldn't possibly be in charge of the reception at his house. But, on the plus side, she had been left alone to scrounge around in Amanda Worth's famous closet.

Susan had never seen Amanda's closet, but she had heard about it innumerable times over the years. While Scott bragged about Amanda, Amanda bragged about Scott—he was, in her words, the only man in the world who would never, ever question her need for an entire room to house her extensive wardrobe. Susan had no idea where the closet was located. There were four bedrooms on the second floor, all with open doors. Two bathrooms were there as well as three doors which were closed. Susan reached out for the first one. A well-stocked linen closet. A pile of heavy embroidered sheets fell to the floor and Susan stooped down quickly to pick it up. She fingered the stiff material as she returned it to the only shelf with any space available at all. The pillowcases were embroidered with flamboyant *F*s—perhaps Amanda's maiden name?—whatever it might be, Susan thought. She closed the door and hurried to open the next one. That door hid steep stairs and Susan peered up at the unfinished ceiling of a dark and dank smelling attic. Well, she thought, going down the hall, this last door must be it. And it was a closet, but stuffed with odds and ends—suitcases, games, stadium blankets, brown boxes, some labeled and some not.

Well, apparently Amanda stored her clothing in some other location.

The master bedroom was easy to find. It took up almost the entire front of the house. Here there were three doors also—one led to a large, old-fashioned bathroom, the other to a good sized closet full of men's suits and shirts from the best stores in New York and, when she opened the third door, she realized her search had ended. The closet was really a good-sized room, probably once used as a nursery or sewing room by the original owner, but now lined with dark wood paneling, shelving, drawers, and lots of rails for hanging up clothes. Located in the center of the space was a beautiful walnut dressing table and a delicate French papier-mâché stool. A bentwood rack hung from the ceiling displaying hats of all types and appropriate for all seasons. Susan, who couldn't remember seeing Amanda in any hat other than a knit cloche in the middle of a snowstorm, ran her hand over an elegant feathered extravaganza from the thirties or forties. She adored antique clothes and would have loved to take the time to try these on. But, she reminded herself, the owner of these hats was dead and she had a job to do.

The closet, she realized, circling slowly, was fabulously well organized. Wool suits hung together, dresses likewise. One wall was devoted to separates, pants hanging beside two tiers of shirts and tunics. There was pullout shelving for shoes, and drawers with glass set in the fronts through which she could see packages of stockings and neatly rolled socks and folded scarves. Heavy, elegant silk scarves hung from specially made racks. Some had been well loved and well worn; frayed ends betrayed repeated use. Susan remembered, suddenly, the Hermes silk encircling Amanda's swollen neck. She shivered and got to work.

What did one wear to be buried in? Her grandmother, she remembered, had always talked about being buried in her wedding gown. When the time came, though, no one could find the dress and something else had been used. Had Amanda ever expressed a similar wish, she wondered, fingering a gorgeous deep purple silk jacket. The price tag, she noticed, was still attached. Neiman Marcus—sixteen hundred and ninety-five dollars! Wow. No wonder the fabric felt so fabulous. Could it be taken back for a refund or was this the perfect, as well as last, opportunity for Amanda to wear it? She kept strolling around the room.

Amanda must have gone on a fabulous shopping binge recently. She noticed a half dozen or more tags still attached to outfits. She had pulled two dresses off the rod and was trying to decide whether or not black was too clichéd for a woman with as much style as Amanda, when she heard someone walking up the stairs. Not wanting to startle anyone, she carried the dresses back into the master bedroom. And met Scott coming in the doorway.

She didn't startle him—apparently she scared him to death. He turned pale, then pink, and put both hands up in front of his face as if to ward off a blow.

Susan knew she looked messy, but she hadn't even considered the possibility that she wouldn't be recognized.

"Scott, it's me. Susan Henshaw."

"What are you doing here? With my wife's clothes?" Now that he knew who she was, his fear turned into anger.

"You . . . you asked me to pick out an outfit to take to the funeral home. Remember?" she added gently, reminding herself that this man was suffering and bereaved.

"I . . . I don't doubt that. But I never, ever gave you permission to walk into my house."

"The note—"

"What note? I never wrote you a note!" Scott, obviously furious, pulled the dresses from Susan's hands.

"The note on the phone table. It said for me to come on in." She paused for a minute and looked into Scott's face. "Unless the note wasn't for me. I . . . I never thought. . . ."

Her admission didn't seem to make him feel any better, but his attention was turned to Amanda's dresses. "This is what you picked?"

"I . . ." Susan realized one of the dresses she had chosen had intact labels. "Not that one," she said, pointing to the dangling bit of cardboard. "You . . . you could probably take that one back to the store. . . ." She bit her tongue, resisting the urge to volunteer for this task.

"Why would I want to do that? What exactly are you getting at?"

Apparently she couldn't say anything right. "Nothing. It's just that . . . Amanda never . . . the dress has never been worn. You can get your money back."

"I . . . You . . ." Scott tossed the dresses on the unmade bed, sat down next to them, put his head in his hands and began to sob.

"Oh, Scott, I'm so sorry." She reached out her hand, feeling some human touch might help, but he looked up and she pulled back before contact had been made.

"Susan. I am sorry. I know I'm acting irrationally. I can't seem to help myself. You're doing so much for me. I have no idea how I'm going to thank you."

"I . . ."

He took a deep breath and, apparently, pulled himself together. Susan waited quietly for him to speak.

"How are your plans coming for the reception?"

TWELVE

"WHAT COULD I SAY? THE MAN WAS CRYING! IT WAS NOT the time to tell him that I couldn't help him."

"Susan, I understand, but what are you going to do?"

"I have no idea. I was thinking about it on the way over here. Years ago when I was involved in the schools, I'd just call down the class list and ask for donations." Susan stopped talking, put down the mug of coffee the waitress had just handed her, and looked across the sticky table of the Nutmeg Motel's restaurant to her friend. "Do you think that might be possible?"

"You're going to call a class list?"

"No, of course not. But what if I call all of Amanda's friends and ask them to bring something to her house the morning of the funeral?"

"And then serve it to them when they come over after the service?"

"Exactly."

Kathleen thought for a moment. "Who's going to serve? Set everything up? And what about drinks? You have to offer wine and coffee. . . ."

"We ain't got wine. Lost our liquor license about a decade ago." Their waitress had returned.

"No. We don't want any wine. We were talking about . . . about something else."

"So what do you want to eat?"

Susan glanced at the grease-stained menu again. What looked safe?

"I'll have the Greek salad and a tuna sandwich," Kathleen ordered quickly.

"And I'll have the cream of tomato soup and a grilled cheese sandwich—on rye. . . ."

"We got white and whole wheat."

"Then whole wheat would be fine."

Apparently in a hurry to return to the kitchen where loud heavy metal music was playing, their waitress hurried off.

"You were talking about what drinks to offer the Worths' guests," Kathleen reminded her.

"Do you think the food is any good here?"

"Not if the coffee is anything to judge by," Kathleen answered, putting down her mug.

"So Amanda probably didn't come here for the food."

"Probably not. But that doesn't mean she and that man were having an affair. Maybe they were checking out the place for some other reason—as an investment or something."

"I suppose that's possible."

"So let's get back to work on the reception. What about drinks? Who's going to pay for them?"

"I'll worry about that after I get enough donations of food. Do you have any paper?"

Kathleen rummaged through the large Dooney and Bourke purse by her side. "Will this do?" she asked handing Susan a notebook displaying a garish Pokémon on its cover.

"Perfect." Susan flipped it open and started to write.

"What are you doing?"

"Making lists. What we need first—I have to know exactly what to ask people to bring. Let's see, Scott said three hundred guests. What do you think?"

"I think more than that. In fact, I wouldn't be surprised if there was standing room only in the church—what church did the Worths attend?"

"I have no idea—what are you looking for?"

"I ripped out the information about the funeral from the paper and stuffed it in here before I left this morning."

"Good thinking." Susan continued to write.

"The paper says interment will be private, a memorial service at St. Anne's at three o'clock followed immediately by a reception at the Worth home. Too bad. Usually a lot of people don't go to the cemetery and so fewer attend whatever follows, but this way everyone who goes to the service will stop by the house. Susan, I think it could be more than three hundred. Most of the town knew the Worths and even more people will be curious about the way she died."

Susan sighed deeply. "You're probably right. It's going to be a challenge, wining and dining three hundred people and solving a murder at the same time."

"If anyone can do it, you can," Kathleen said.

Susan glanced up at her friend. Was that sarcasm she heard? "And you'll help?"

"Why not? In fact, if you get us organized—figure out how much of what we need and stuff—I'll make the calls for you. I did it for the school fair last spring. It wasn't all that bad."

"That's great."

"But there's one problem."

"What?"

"Who are we going to call? And where are we going to

get their phone numbers? I mean, it should be the Worths' friends helping out, not ours."

"Good point. I—You know, we could use the Club's membership list. Most of their friends are members, don't you think?"

"Probably . . . but, to tell the truth, I have no idea where ours is. The only lists I use a lot are the kids' class lists."

Susan chuckled. She remembered those days. And, when it came to the seemingly endless hours she had spent on the phone back then, she didn't miss them one bit. "No problem. Jed's on a committee down at the Club. He has everything— membership lists, rules, whatever—in a large folder in his desk drawer at home. I'll just borrow the phone list for the afternoon."

"If you give it to me, I can call them."

"I have to admit, I was hoping you would offer," Susan said, looking down at the meal the waitress had just placed in front of her.

"Look, you've got a huge job getting this all together. Let me go home, pull some stuff from the freezer for dinner, and make sure the kids are cared for until Jerry comes home. Then I'll be free to do whatever needs doing. You go on home and I'll come over as soon as possible." Kathleen picked up her fork and prodded a wilted leaf of romaine lettuce.

"Great." Susan sipped her soup from a bent spoon. It reminded her of when her children were young and she had fed them can after can of Campbell's soup on cold winter afternoons.

"What do you think?"

"It's canned. How's your salad?"

"Not great. But I'm starving."

The two women ate quickly, paid their bill, and left, driving off in different directions.

Susan reviewed the plans she'd made so far as she drove. Years and years of entertaining at school and at home were paying off. She knew how to organize an event—but she had never imagined that she would be asked to do one in only two days. She stamped on the accelerator. With luck, the police were too busy to set up speed traps.

Susan had expected to sit down and get to work as soon as she got home. She released Clue into the expensive dog run that the animal hated and then, a few minutes later, let the once again muddy dog back into the house. She made herself a cup of tea which she carried to the large walnut desk in Jed's study, pulled open the desk drawer and found the folder containing membership lists and other information. She was still studying the papers when Kathleen arrived.

"I brought my cell phone. That way we can both call at once," Kathleen said, tossing her coat across a chair and flopping down on the couch.

"Good idea," Susan said, sounding as if she didn't mean it.

"You haven't finished calling already, have you?" Kathleen asked.

"I haven't even started."

"Susan . . ."

"Kathleen, look at this." Susan pointed to the stapled sheets of paper on the desk before her.

Kathleen got up and did as Susan requested. "What is this?"

"I wasn't sure at first, but I think it's a list of club members who are behind in their dues payments."

"Where did you get it?"

"It was in the back of the file Jed is keeping on club activities. I was looking for the membership list and found this."

"Boy, look at all the people. . . ."

"The check mark just means that the dues are late," Susan explained. "But look at this," she added pointing.

"The Worths are two years late," Kathleen said slowly as she read. "And they're still charging everything. Heavens, they owe a lot of money!"

"And, if you look at the list carefully—they're the only members who are so late."

"The amounts are different. . . ."

"Interest. There's interest charged as well as late fees."

"Some of these seem to have been excused by someone. . . ."

"I noticed that, too. But everywhere you see that some amount has been excused, there's been a good reason. Like the Clarks. They were nine months late and owed some interest on top of the late fee. But it was excused."

"I don't think I know the Clarks. Why should they have been excused?"

"Arnie Clark was in an auto accident while on a business trip in Minnesota. He was in the hospital and then in a rehabilitation clinic out there for months. I'll bet the second notice of their dues wasn't even sent to them until he was back on his feet and functioning. That is, if Edgar Finch had anything to do with it."

"I know Edgar. He's club treasurer, right?"

"Yes."

"And can he—would he—do that?"

"Oh, yes. In fact, I'd always heard that he was known as a compassionate treasurer. I just hadn't understood what that meant before."

"I suppose that's why he's always elected to that office," Kathleen muttered, still busy going through the papers on Jed's desk.

Susan chuckled. "The truth is that no one wants to be club officer anymore."

"Those jobs must be a lot of work," Kathleen said.

"Thankless work," Susan said. "I think at one time there was a lot of status involved in being elected. But now things have changed. According to Jed, the Club is actually worried about having enough members to remain financially viable."

"You're kidding. Jerry told me that when he moved here, he had to wait three years to join."

"Times have changed. At one time, the Hancock Field Club was pretty much the only game in town. Now people join gyms and work out instead of playing tennis or swimming."

"Hmm. I suppose. When you have kids, it's great. They're safe and they learn to swim. . . . I was worried about it being—you know, snobbish—but it hasn't turned out to be like that at all."

"And people like Edgar Finch keep it the way it is," Susan said.

"But, you know, it's one thing to carry a member who's been in an auto accident, but why were the Worths allowed to owe so much money?"

"I don't know, but maybe it has something to do with Amanda's murder," Susan suggested.

"Could be—How well do you know Edgar Finch?"

"Well enough to know that he wouldn't like me seeing this list," Susan said, pointing at it. "He's always made a big deal about keeping club financial affairs private. Of course, now I know why," she added.

"Could you go see him, or call him on the phone, and ask him about the Worths—without letting him know you were asking?"

"I could try." Susan brightened when she realized what Kathleen was suggesting. "Does that mean you really are willing to make all the phone calls asking for food?"

"If we go through the list together and mark the people to be called."

"You got it."

That project took less than fifteen minutes and Susan, using her cell phone, called Edgar Finch and told him that she needed to talk with him. She hoped Edgar's gentlemanly instincts would cause him to agree to see her and she was granted her wish.

"Why don't you call from here," she suggested to Kathleen. "This can't take very long and, when I return, we can go over everything together. Okay?"

"Great." Kathleen was picking up the phone as Susan left the room.

Edgar Finch was a widower. A conservative man in his early sixties, he did all his entertaining at the Field Club. Susan had never been inside his home, but she had read about it in such illustrious places as *The New York Times* and *Architectural Digest*. Designed by a man who had followed in the footsteps of Frank Lloyd Wright until he died young, the house was one of the only examples of what architectural critics were fond of referring to as his "unfulfilled promise." Set in a heavily wooded section of town, only a corner of the home could be spied from the road. Susan, always curious, turned into the long driveway between rows of small Japanese maples, momentarily diverted by the opportunity she was getting.

The house turned out to be stunning. Built from natural Connecticut limestone, copper, and glass, it denied its heritage, looking as though something from the Orient had fallen in the woods. It was large, set slightly above ground level, and surrounded by an ample deck. The tiled roof tilted up at its edges like those of a Buddhist temple. There were round windows set into stone walls. Susan, hearing tinkling, looked for wind chimes and spied small metal bells hanging from the soffits. The front door appeared to have been fashioned from burnished metal and, as it opened, Susan found herself expecting the person standing there to be wearing a silk kimono.

But Edgar Finch had on navy wool slacks, a white Izod polo shirt, a deep ruby cashmere cardigan, and worn Docksiders. He looked much the same as he always did at club functions. And he appeared pleased to see her.

"Susan, welcome to my home. I don't believe you've been here before. I imagine you would like the grand tour."

"I'd love it!" She resisted looking down at her watch. It would take Kathleen at least an hour to make all the calls. Surely she could see the house as well as ask a few questions in that time.

"Then come on in."

Susan followed him across the threshold into one of the messiest rooms she'd ever seen. (Including her own the day after her daughter's wedding and that really was saying something.) There was an elegant leather settee right inside the door; it was literally covered with coats, gloves, and scarves, as well as magazines, unopened mail, and assorted newspapers still wrapped in the plastic bags they'd been delivered in.

"Sorry about that. I just returned from vacation. I've been in Australia for five weeks and I'm afraid everything just piled up. Come on into the living room and you'll see things the way they usually look. I'm not much of a housekeeper myself, but I have a wonderful service that comes in twice a week."

"When did you get home?"

"About two hours ago. I'm feeling a bit jet-lagged actually."

"Two hours—then you don't know about Amanda Worth."

Edgar Finch narrowed his eyes. "What about Amanda? Has something happened? An accident?" he asked quickly.

"She's dead. She was murdered."

"When did this happen?"

"Yesterday."

"Who . . ." He paused and Susan got the impression that he hardly dared ask the question.

"No one knows who did it," she explained quickly.

"Her husband . . . Scott Worth . . ."

"Oh, there's no way Scott can be implicated in the murder. He was in New York City all day—apparently there were a lot of witnesses."

"Well, thank heavens for that, at least."

"I . . ."

"Susan, we're going to have to put this off until another day . . . I . . . this news . . . there are many things I must do. You'll have to excuse me, my dear."

And Susan found herself outside again, with only the tinkling of the little bells to keep her company.

THIRTEEN

SUSAN ARRIVED HOME FEELING DISCOURAGED. OVER-
hearing Kathleen's spiel on the phone didn't help any either.

"I'm sure Susan will thank you in person as soon as she
can. . . ."

"Tell me you haven't been saying that to everyone," Susan insisted, flopping down on the couch and plopping her
feet up on the same coffee table she had yelled at her children for using as a footstool over the years.

"Only the people who know you well," Kathleen said.
"And it's worked! Everyone has been very generous. On the
other hand . . ."

"What?"

"No one said they weren't coming. It's possible that Scott
might need more food than we're planning on. And I still
can't figure out what he's going to offer people to drink. I
can't imagine a BYOB reception after a funeral, can you?"

"No, I think the only thing to do is just go down to the
liquor store, order some cases of wine and have them charged
to Scott. If he doesn't pay his bills, that's not my fault."

"I thought exactly the same thing—until I called Hancock
Fine Wines. The man who answered the phone said he

couldn't take my order unless I charged it to someone who pays their bills. He was starting to tell me how much money the Worths owed the store when the owner grabbed the phone and censored him."

"The owner? Don Hooper?"

"Yup. He was more discreet, but the message was the same. No more credit for the Worths. And, Susan, it's going to be a large order. I can't just pick up the cost."

"Of course not. You shouldn't even consider it. You know, I may not have gotten what I wanted from Ethan Finch, but it wasn't a complete waste of time. I did some thinking on the way home. Where's the phone book?"

"Oh, I dumped it on the floor somewhere." Kathleen bent down and retrieved the large book. "Here it is. Why?"

"Why don't we try that new liquor store out at Once in a Blue Moon? What's its name? Something odd . . ."

"Salubrious Libations."

"Really?"

"I think so . . . Why not?"

"Doesn't salubrious mean healthful?"

Kathleen shrugged her slim shoulders. "Perhaps they only sell red wine? And you know what people say about red wine."

"That it gives you a headache if you drink too much?"

"That it lowers your cholesterol. Did you find the number?"

"No, it isn't listed yet. I'll call information." There was a pause while she did just that and Kathleen went over her lists. "Now let's just see if this works. Hello, I'm Susan Henshaw and I'm in the middle of planning a reception to be held the day after tomorrow and I'm wondering if you could help me. . . ."

Kathleen picked up her empty coffee mug and headed for

the kitchen. When she returned, Susan was hanging up, a broad smile on her face. "You look happy. I gather you found someone who is willing to give Scott Worth credit."

"Yup. I ordered four cases of Chardonnay, four cases of Merlot, two cases of beer, and six bottles of dry sherry—I think I read too many English mystery novels," she added, noticing Kathleen's surprised expression at the last item.

"You may be right. I gather the store is willing to bill Scott Worth?"

"Yup. They were thrilled to get such a large order. And I figure getting paid for it is their problem. The man on the other end of the line acted like I was the maid or something—so I don't feel bad about any problem he may have when it comes to getting paid."

"So we're set."

"Almost. What time did you ask everyone to deliver the food to the house?"

"Early morning. Before the service. Are you going to be there?"

"I'd rather not be. I don't know Scott that well and I certainly don't know Amanda's kitchen—I was thinking about asking Kimberly Critchley to help out."

"Good idea." Kathleen looked at her watch. "I'd better get going. If you need anything else, just yell."

"I will." Susan glanced at the desk covered with lists and paper. "You know, it's time for Amanda's close friends to take over planning the reception."

"Actually, they should have been doing this already."

"You know, that's true. Kimberly was at the house last night. I wonder why Scott didn't ask her to arrange the reception and choose Amanda's clothing. I mean, if I died, you'd be here helping out Jed, wouldn't you?"

"Of course."

"And Jed wouldn't ask people we know only casually to pick out clothing for me to be buried in or to help him entertain guests after my funeral. . . ." She shivered. "It's creepy talking about my own funeral."

"But you're making an excellent point. Where the hell has Kimberly been all this time? She and Amanda were always together. Why would she suddenly be less important after Amanda's death?"

"Good question. I'll ask her when I see her."

"You're going over to her house?"

"Yes." She glanced down at her Rolex. "If I leave now maybe she'll offer me a glass of wine and a bite to eat. That lunch was pretty awful."

Kimberly Critchley did offer Susan a glass of wine and a full platter of crackers and cheese. But she almost had to—they were sitting on the coffee table in the middle of the living room when Susan walked in the door.

"It's just possible that someone is coming over this evening," Kimberly explained.

Susan realized her hostess was wearing rather a lot of makeup for a woman spending an evening alone at home. She hadn't noticed earlier because she had been so busy looking around. Kimberly had gotten divorced a few years ago. The Critchleys' large split-level where they had brought up their daughter had been sold and Kimberly had moved into a new riverside apartment complex. Susan had never been here before and she was quite impressed with what she found. The apartment was spacious and cheerful.

The women sat together on a small sofa which just fit into the bay window jutting out over the river.

"This is lovely," Susan commented, sipping wine and wondering how to start.

"It is. It's also drafty and creaky. This complex was built with an eye for style and not much substance. Jon says that one day it's all going to fall right into the water. Frankly, since I'm renting, I don't care all that much."

"Jon's the man you brought to the Valentine's Day dance at the Club?"

"Jon took me. My membership lapsed in December and I didn't—well, actually couldn't—renew."

"But you've always been so active in the Club . . ." Susan began automatically before realizing that she was being rude and, very likely, insensitive.

"I can't afford it anymore, Susan."

"But I thought—you said your divorce settlement was very generous."

"I lied."

"Why?"

"Because I know how much money means in this lovely, quaint, little New England coastal town."

"But I don't think—"

"You probably don't. I know I didn't. Not until I didn't have any."

"But your friends wouldn't care."

"Some of them wouldn't. Maybe. But they'd be living their own extremely expensive lives and that can cause problems. I've seen it happen. Remember Cynthia Myredal?"

"Sure. But she left Hancock over a year ago. I heard she was living in California."

"Yeah. And I hope she's happy there because her last year here was miserable."

"Really? I had no idea. Her oldest son was in Chad's

class. I remember him at graduation. He was an excellent student—one of the speakers."

"Yes. Good thing, because he needed a scholarship to go to college."

"And I heard he got one."

"Yes. And he spent the summer between high school and college working three jobs to take care of expenses."

"Chad has had summer jobs," Susan protested.

"Susan, your kids get jobs for experience, not money. They're like most of the kids in this town. They have piles of great stuff—from shoes to cars. They think nothing of asking their parents to send them on expensive trips and their parents don't think anything of saying yes. They have little jobs, but they're also interns whose parents actually pay for the privilege of their little darlings working in classy fields—you know, things like government and media."

Susan nodded. Her son had done just that last summer. As far as she could tell, he'd learned a little about television production, a lot about construction, and even more about a young female carpenter. "But what does that have to do with Cynthia moving to California—or you living here?"

"We're both trying to accomplish the same thing—in different ways."

"What?"

"Saving face. We're both acting like the fact that we used to live in huge houses, take expensive annual vacations, and buy our children whatever their hearts desired wasn't that important. We're both pretending that the lives we're living now are just fine, thank you. Not diminished, only different."

"And they're not."

"I won't speak for anyone else, but mine is seriously diminished. The move from that house to here is more than symbolic, if you're really interested. And now that Amanda is gone, you're the only person who knows. I tell everyone else that I was ready for a change to bijou living. It's a complete lie, of course. I'd do most anything to get back in a big house on the other side of town. I'd even marry Jon Ericksen—if I can get him to ask me."

"You would marry someone for his money." Susan was shocked.

"Damn right." Kimberly took a sip of her wine and seemed to decide that her statement called for an explanation. "I wouldn't have when I was younger, of course. I was romantic. Idealistic. Although, I guess, I always knew Marc would make a good living. He was doing his second surgical residency when I met him."

"That's right. You were a nurse, weren't you?"

"Nursing student. I never completed my training. Marc and I were married the day after he finished his residency. I got pregnant almost immediately. We moved to Hancock that year. Into one of those small three-bedroom Colonials near town. Then, when Mimsie entered kindergarten, we moved out to our dream home on Wisteria Lane."

"You built that house, didn't you?"

"We bought it from the builder. He went bankrupt. There was a big scandal about it. You might remember."

"Not actually."

"Well, we got a good deal. But we really didn't need it. Marc was making a fortune by then. Somehow I was stupid enough to think some of that money was automatically mine."

"But you must have gotten a settlement. . . ."

"I did. I got a pittance. And one third of the house."

"Who—?"

"It's being kept in a trust for Mimsie. Which is fine with

me. And I'm living on the other third. It's a nice chunk of money, but it's not going to keep me forever. Marc got a third which he probably uses to buy shoes and handmade suits. He couldn't care less how I live, but he's obsessed with his appearance. Of course, he has to impress his twenty-nine-year-old chickie."

"I'd heard that he was involved with someone," Susan lied tactfully. Actually everyone had been talking about it at the Club the week after Marc appeared with a gorgeous blonde for the tennis mixed doubles tournament over the Fourth of July. Their whirlwind romance led to marriage before Labor Day. "She has something to do with the hospital, right? Is she a nurse?"

"That bitch runs the neurologic research department. Not only is she beautiful and young, she's rich and smart."

Susan was beginning to understand why Kimberly was so depressed.

"And he bought her an even bigger house—on three acres of land."

"Three acres!" Susan was impressed. Three acres in this part of Connecticut cost a fortune—both in initial cost and in taxes.

"Yeah. I guess it's true love—" The phone rang and Kimberly jumped and grabbed the receiver. "Hello?"

Kimberly's voice had dropped an octave into "sexy" range. "Oh, hi, Jon . . ."

Apparently the voice wasn't enough.

"Oh . . . well, maybe some other time." Kimberly's shoulders sagged as she hung up. "Why are you here?" she asked, apparently—and suddenly—realizing Susan wasn't one of her usual guests.

"I wanted to talk to you about Amanda's funeral. And the reception afterwards. At the house," Susan added when Kimberly didn't respond.

Kimberly seemed interested in something other than her limited social life. "You're holding a reception at your house after Amanda's funeral?"

"I . . . No, I'm not. But Scott asked me to arrange for one to be held at his—well, at their house."

"And what have you done?"

"Oh, it's all organized," Susan said quickly, hoping Kimberly didn't think she had come over to ask her to do all that work. "Kathleen—you know Kathleen Gordon, don't you? Well, we organized everything this afternoon. Everyone was very generous."

Kimberly shook her head. "What do you mean?"

"We decided what was needed to feed the guests and asked a lot of the Worths' friends to donate food. You know, either prepare a dish or pick up something and bring it to the house the morning of the funeral. Then—"

"What? Susan, this isn't some sort of PTA party. It's Amanda's funeral! Why didn't you just call a caterer? Why didn't you just call the best caterer in town?"

Susan decided there was no reason to be less than frank. After all, Kimberly was a friend of the family. "Well, you know that Scott owes money to everyone in town. . . ."

"I . . . No, I didn't know that. In fact, I can't believe it."

"Well, I'm not making it up," Susan insisted, responding to the indignation in Kimberly's voice.

"Then you are seriously misinformed. Amanda spent much of the winter shopping for a fur coat. She was just making up her mind between an imported chinchilla from Fendi and a sable at Saks. Does that sound like something she would do if Scott owed money to everyone in town? Really, Susan, I know you think you're a hotshot sleuth. But this time you've got it all wrong!"

FOURTEEN

SUSAN DROVE HOME, TIRED AND PUZZLED. AN HOUR AGO, if anyone had asked her who knew the most about Amanda she would have unhesitatingly replied Kimberly. If Kimberly had no idea that the Worths were well known among the businesses owners in town for not paying their bills, it seemed likely that no one knew.

Of course, she realized, she had been so surprised that she had forgotten to ask Kimberly to act as hostess for the reception following the funeral. She'd also forgotten to ask why Scott wasn't depending on his wife's closest friend in his hour of need.

But it was late, she was tired and hungry. She turned the corner to her street, hoping Jed was home.

And there he was, walking Clue. Susan pressed the gas pedal. Lunch had been awful, she hadn't had the time or inclination to eat any of the appetizers that Kimberly had obviously prepared for someone else. She had a vision of a glass of chilled white wine next to a plate of roast lamb accompanied by wild mushroom and truffle risotto, a specialty of the new chef down at the Hancock Inn. It had been a long day. Perhaps she'd even treat herself to a gooey dessert and a cappuccino.

She pulled into the garage, got out of her car, and hurried into the house, only to discover dirty plates and an empty glass on the kitchen table. She looked up as Jed entered the room through another door. "You've eaten."

"Yes, it was late and I didn't think you would want to cook."

"You were right about that." She sighed. "What did you have?"

"I found a casserole on the second shelf of the freezer and dug out a helping of stew."

"Jed . . ."

"I put the rest of it back in the refrigerator. It really was delicious," he said.

"I was going to thaw that casserole and take it over to the Worths' house for after the funeral."

"Can't you just make another pot of stew?"

"Beef Bourguignonne. And, no, I cannot just make another pot of stew. It takes an entire day to make that! I'm sorry. I'm tired and hungry, and I was looking forward to a meal at the Hancock Inn."

"We could . . ."

"No, you've eaten. There's no reason to go anywhere. I'll just make a small salad and heat up some of the beef."

"Would you like a glass of Merlot?"

"A large one, thanks," she answered, opening the Sub-Zero and pulling out a humongous Tupperware. "You know what? There's lots in here. I can still take this to the Worths' house. I'll just pick up some bread and cheese and take it along, too." She pushed it back into the refrigerator to thaw. "I'll have crackers," she decided, looking deeper into the refrigerator. She had been on a diet recently so the pickings were slimmer than usual. "Well, there's always a can of soup," she decided, closing the door and opening a cupboard.

"Ah, Chickarina—one of Chad's favorites. With a salad, this will be a good dinner. Where are you going?"

"I was thinking of lying down and watching some TV."

"I know you're tired, but I had something to talk about."

Jed rarely failed her. "Sure. What's up?" He sat down at the table as though he'd never planned on spending the evening resting.

"I was looking at the financial records of the Club," she began.

"Susan, those are absolutely confidential. I hope you didn't show them to anyone else."

"Just Kathleen and you know she'd never gossip."

Jed took a sip of his wine. "I can guess what interested you. The Worths' bills, right?"

"Yes. I didn't examine the list carefully, but it seemed to me that the Club wasn't carrying anyone else—although maybe most members pay their dues on time."

"Not as true as you might think. But it is true that no one else has been allowed to remain a member like the Worths without paying for the privilege. And you want to know why."

Susan, busy ripping up romaine leaves, just nodded.

"Things have changed. When you and I moved out here from the city one of the first things we did was look for a place where the kids could learn to swim and would be safely cared for during the long summer. Right?"

"Yes."

"Now with fathers and mothers both working—and many of them commuting to New York City each day—they hire live-in nannies and sign their kids up for more classes and activities than we ever dreamed of for Chrissy and Chad."

"And that was more than enough," Susan muttered, remembering years filled with carpooling to and from all sorts of lessons, clubs, and athletic teams.

"And we wanted some place to play golf and tennis, and swim," he added.

Susan smiled. They both knew which one of them had been interested in those sports.

"But, in fact, I play more during lunch in the city than here—and that's true of a lot of people. When we moved in it was hard to get into the Club. There was a waiting list and a very discriminating membership committee. Now much of the membership committee's job is to make sure enough people apply for the empty spots."

"Is that what you're doing?"

"No, that's what Scott Worth is doing. And has been doing for years."

"Which is why he doesn't pay his membership dues?"

"It's why we don't push him to pay. Scott has done a lot for the Club. If he's fallen on hard times . . ."

Susan realized what her husband was saying. "If? Are you telling me you don't know if he's not paying because he can't or because he doesn't want to?"

"I'm telling you I don't know. There are probably a few people who do."

"Like Edgar Finch?"

"It's more than likely that Edgar knows as much about what is going on as anyone. He would probably be very upset if he knew you and Kathleen had seen that sheet of paper. It's an accident that I have it, actually. I had misplaced the members list that was sent to us in January and asked the club secretary for another one. She mailed this out to me. I didn't even open it for a few weeks, but with the membership committee meeting looming, I pulled it out and discovered what she had sent. I suppose I should have returned it, but it never occurred to me that anyone would see it."

"I would never have looked in that folder if Amanda hadn't been killed."

"What does Amanda's death have to do with it?"

"Kathleen and I used it to arrange the reception. We needed a list of the club members to call for donations."

"I thought you were just going to hire a caterer."

"It turned out to be more difficult than I imagined. So we came up with an alternate plan."

If this struck her husband as unusual, he didn't mention it.

"I was so curious that I went over to see Edgar Finch," Susan continued. "But . . . well, we didn't get a chance to talk."

"Why not?"

"He had something to do. He didn't know Amanda had been killed. He seemed awfully upset when I told him. He—his first reaction was that Scott had killed her. Strange, isn't it?"

"Not necessarily. The husband is usually the first suspect, isn't he?"

"I suppose. But it was more than that."

"Well, you know, it's possible that Edgar's been doing business with Scott."

"I thought Edgar was retired. In fact, I'm sure of it. His retirement party was held at the Club. We were invited."

"What does that have to do with it? Just because he's retired doesn't mean that he doesn't have to manage his money—or have someone manage his money."

Susan took a wild guess. "And Scott Worth manages his."

"It's possible. Scott manages his own money fund. You didn't know that?"

"I did, but . . ."

"I once talked to you about investing some of our savings with him. You don't remember?"

Susan tried. But every time the subject of investing came up, whether it was the stock market, the bank, or the bond market (was there a bond market?), her brain shut down. The problem was percentages. Susan had done just fine in math until her fourth grade teacher had introduced percentages. She'd never really learned them, and still didn't feel comfortable figuring them out. Thus, when people started talking profit and loss, she was left behind. "We didn't invest with him, did we?"

"No. We don't have enough money."

"Jed! We do very well. Heavens, you've been a partner at your firm for almost fifteen years. You—"

"You have to be rich. And I mean really rich to have Scott Worth investing your money for you."

"I don't understand."

"He only accepts people who have a minimum of a million dollars to invest—and that money is put in very high risk stocks."

"You mean you have to be able to afford to lose a million dollars."

"Exactly. Although I don't think anyone has ever lost money investing with Scott. That's why he attracts the big bucks."

"Is that possible?"

"What? That he limits investors to those with a million or more?"

"No, that it's possible to invest in the stock market and never, ever lose money."

"To be honest, I don't know that much about how he does it. But, from what I've heard, he invests in all sorts of things—foreign currency, futures, options. You know."

She didn't, but she also knew that Jed didn't either. They had been lucky financially. They had enough money for a wonderful life in a lovely part of Connecticut. But neither of them particularly cared about money in and of itself. Their investments were conservative and, to someone knowledge-able in investing, probably uninteresting.

"But what does that have to do with Scott not paying his bills?"

Jed frowned. "I—This is going to sound more like something you would say. It's entirely speculation—and I didn't really think about it at all before Amanda died. . . ."

"So tell me!"

"Well, what if members of the Club are allowing Scott to get away without paying his bills—to protect their own investments with him?"

"That sounds like something I would say?"

Jed chuckled. "Now you know how I feel. But listen. Suppose you're someone who has a considerable amount of money invested with Scott. And suppose it gets out that he doesn't pay his bills."

"I really don't sound like this," Susan insisted.

"You do. And, as you're always telling me, just listen for a minute."

"Okay."

"So there are people who invest with Scott who know that he doesn't pay his bills. But part of what you're buying when you buy into a fund is the expertise of the fund manager. If you're invested with Scott, you want everyone to believe he's doing well. It is to the benefit of the investors that nothing negative about Worth becomes public knowledge."

"I hope I explain things better than this."

"Susan!"

"What you're saying is that Scott doesn't have to pay his bills. His numerous investors will cover up for him to protect their own money."

"Or that Scott can't pay his bills. The investors will have the same response."

Susan thought for a moment. "What you're saying makes sense—what do you think it has to do with Amanda's death?"

"I have no idea. I wasn't thinking of Amanda."

Susan speared a large chunk of lettuce. Kimberly had insisted that Scott was buying Amanda an expensive fur coat. And just the other night, Scott had said that Amanda was shopping for some sort of chapel . . . or temple . . . or something.

Jed yawned.

"You really are tired."

"Exhausted. If you don't mind, I'll just walk Clue one last time and go up to bed."

Susan knew a hint when she heard one. "I'll clean up in here and walk Clue. You go ahead."

"You're sure?"

"I am." She kissed him good-night and returned to her meal. There was a newspaper on the table and she reached out for it. Reading while she ate combined two of her favorite activities.

It was the *Hancock Herald* and, not surprisingly, Amanda's murder was front-page news. Susan read through the story, noting one bit of incorrect information (the reporter had written that Susan was trying on clothing when she discovered Amanda, not that she had been looking for Kathleen), two typos, and three grammatical errors. But what was interesting was on page three: Amanda's obituary. Including five photographs, the obituary covered the entire page. And it was fascinating.

Amanda's father had been a developer of such renown that even Susan had heard of his name. Entire blocks of New York City had been built, then sold or rented, by him.

Amanda's mother had been a house model for a New York dress designer. Apparently she had retired at the birth of her daughter. It also appeared that Amanda was an only child. There was no mention of any other family.

Amanda had attended a prestigious private girls' school and been further educated in Europe. (The article was so vague about this aspect of her life that Susan suspected low SAT scores at the very least.) She had worked for the designer who had employed her mother, but in what capacity the article didn't mention. Apparently any career she had planned vanished when she met Scott Worth. It took three paragraphs to describe their wedding and there were two photos of the bride and her wedding party. Three prominent families were represented in the twelve attendants. The guest list included musicians, artists, and politicians. An international elite attended and were wined and dined by Amanda's parents. Susan wondered, rather cynically, whether or not Scott Worth's first investors had been culled from this list.

The next bit of information took Susan by surprise. "After a honeymoon in Capri, the happy couple moved into the family home in Hancock, Connecticut." Whose family home? Susan wondered. The Worth family home? Or had Amanda been raised in that large shingle style house where, supposedly, her husband was now mourning her?

The rest of the page was about Amanda's time in Hancock. It listed her various club and charitable activities, ending with the type of tribute Susan had come to expect from the local paper. Susan picked up her wineglass. Why hadn't she known about Amanda's interesting parents? And, since Amanda had no siblings, where was her parents' money?

FIFTEEN

DESPITE A LONG WALK WITH CLUE AND AN EVEN LONGER bubble bath, Susan found it difficult to sleep that night. She had a lot on her mind, but what was bothering her the most was how little she had known about a woman who, in fact, she had known for years. Why hadn't she heard even a hint about Amanda's family? Why, after hearing so much about the heritage of Amanda and Scott's furniture, hadn't she known that their house had belonged to someone in their family? She dozed off and then an idea struck that made her sit up, pulling the blanket off Jed, and pushing Clue onto the floor.

Would Amanda's parents be at the funeral? Were they still alive? The obituary, which had seemed so complete when she read it through the first time, had one glaring omission. There was no list of surviving family members. Did that mean Amanda's parents were dead? That would be easy enough to find out, she realized, glancing at the clock.

Five A.M.! She'd thought it was around two.... Oh well, she might as well get up early. At least she could make some coffee. Too bad it was too early for the library to be open. She sure would like to be able to do some research.

Except that she didn't need the library, she realized. She was living in the information age. The paperless information age. She could find out about Amanda's parents—or anything else—on the computer. Chad and Chrissy had gone off to college leaving behind computers that were, Jed had assured her, obsolete. So he had bought a new model last fall and, determined to join the information age, she'd taken a course down at the library in January. So far, she had used the Internet to look up recipes, check out hotels, and research airline fares. She got dressed quickly and hurried down to the kitchen.

Fifteen minutes later, a steaming mug of coffee by the keyboard, she had started her search.

An hour and fifteen minutes later, Jed found his wife lying on the floor under his desk. "Susan? Hon? What are you doing?"

"The printer was jammed and when I fixed that, I must have pulled one of these wires because something is disconnected and I can't . . . wait, I think I have it. Press the print icon on the tool bar . . . Hey, it works!" She sat up so quickly that she smacked her head against an open drawer. "Ouch!"

"Are you okay?"

"Just fine." Susan pulled sheets of paper from the printer.

"What is all this?"

"Mostly recipes for Easter breads."

"You got up in the middle of the night to look up recipes?"

"Of course not. I was trying to find out if Amanda's parents are still alive."

"Amanda Worth's parents?"

"Yes. Jed, did you know her father was—or is—one of the men who developed the upper west side of New York?"

"I had no idea."

"Amazing, isn't it?"

"That Amanda's father is famous or that I had never heard about it?"

Susan thought for a moment before answering. "Mostly that you had never heard about it. I mean, think about it, most of our friends have heard about your mother and about my parents. . . ."

"Well, they all visit from time to time."

"Exactly. But Amanda's father is famous! There are buildings named after him. How come we've never heard a word about that?"

"Maybe . . ."

"And did you know that the house Amanda and Scott are living in belonged to her family?"

"I—Are you sure about that? I read the obituary in the paper and it just said that the happy couple moved into the family home in Hancock."

"Because I found an old biography of her father and it said that he grew up in . . ." She looked through the pile of papers. "Wait, here it is. The exact quote is 'an exclusive community on the coast of Connecticut.' That sounds like Hancock, doesn't it?"

"It could be. . . ."

"I really think it is, Jed. But why don't we know about it?"

"I gather you think this is significant? That it might have something to do with her murder?"

"It could."

"Then, to be honest, it does seem a little strange. We do know something about the parents of most of the people we've known over the years."

"True." Susan took a sip from her husband's mug and thought for a minute. "But, you know, Scott and Amanda didn't spend much time schmoozing about the normal problems of life. They were more likely to be talking about their last trip to Paris than what to do with an elderly parent."

Jed turned around. "That's true."

"Where are you going?"

"To get more coffee."

Susan hurried after him. "Save some for me."

"I'd suggest that we eat breakfast, but the table seems to be covered with papers," Jed said as they met at the coffeepot.

"I was going over plans for Amanda's reception while waiting for the coffee," she explained, starting to straighten up.

"Hon . . ."

"I know. I'm doing too much."

"That isn't what I was going to say. If you can handle it, fine. But I need some help. I was wondering if you would go over the list of prospective club members and see if any of the names are familiar. One of them actually put your name down as a reference."

"Who?"

"Sorry, I don't remember the name. It's on the top of the list, but I left it up on my dresser." He glanced up at the copper-framed clock on the wall. "I'm going to miss the train and I have an early meeting, hon . . ."

"You better get going then."

"Sue . . . about that list . . ."

She knew him well. "You want me to look at it right away."

"If you could. I know you're busy." He glanced at the table. "But we have another committee meeting tonight and we're going to consider these people again."

"Don't worry. I can manage."

"Thanks. You're the best."

"And don't you forget it," she said, kissing him good-bye and turning back to the coffeepot.

She'd have more coffee, walk Clue, and figure out which of the three piles of paper to attack first.

Almost an hour later, she entered the house, chilled to the bone. March had come in like a lion and that feline hadn't given way for the lamb yet. It was windy, cold, and the sky looked like snow.

And she had no idea what to do first. She still didn't know if Amanda's parents were alive. She needed someone to set up the reception at the Worth house on Saturday. But it was still a bit early to call anyone for help. On the other hand, she wondered who had used her as a reference for club membership. She headed for the bedroom.

But Jed's dresser, while piled high with coins, papers, business cards, and the flotsam and jetsam of his life at the ad agency, didn't reveal anything like a list of prospective members for anything. She did, however, find a garage door key they had accused Chad of taking off to Cornell with him at the end of winter break. Susan nagged and nagged at Jed to straighten up, but . . .

She put down the key and turned slowly. There had been a noise and she was almost positive that her front door had opened and closed. She glanced at Clue lying in the middle of her unmade bed. The dog was dozing peacefully. Jed was always saying that as a watch dog, Clue was a complete washout. Apparently he had been right.

Another clank . . . There was someone in the house. . . .

Grabbing the portable phone off the nightstand, Susan tiptoed out the door. Clue opened one eye and then closed it again. Realizing she was on her own, Susan took a deep breath and started downstairs.

There were sounds coming from her kitchen—someone opening and closing her cupboards. Looking for valuables—not that she stored many things of value in the kitchen. Except for her copper pans—the French mandoline she'd paid almost two hundred dollars for—the Italian espresso machine she really was going to master one of these days. . . . Determined to protect her valuables, she pushed gently on the swinging door.

The burglar seemed to be filling her dishwasher!

"Mary!"

"Susan." A redheaded woman with a scarf wound through her long hair spun around and smiled. "You're going to have to take that stuff off the table if you want me to wash it."

Susan smiled at her cleaning woman. "I'll do it right away. I wasn't thinking. In fact, I forgot you were coming today."

"Then you must have been surprised to open the door and find me here."

"Yes. . . ."

"You've got a lot on your mind. With Mrs. Worth murdered out at the mall."

Susan wondered, as she had before, why she was on a first name basis with every employee she'd ever had, when it was obvious most of them were more formal with other employers. "It was a shock," she admitted.

"I heard that you found her." Mary squinted at Susan then returned to her task.

"Yes. I did." Susan paused. "You worked for the Worths at one time, didn't you?" Mary was an excellent cleaning woman, hardworking, reliable, honest, and as Susan knew, she was uncomfortable carrying tales of her employers from one house to another.

"Yeah. Twice."

"You cleaned their house twice?"

"No, I worked for them. For two stretches I guess you'd say."

"When?"

"The first time was about ten years ago. Worked for them for over a year. Then they went on that around the world cruise and I left. When they came home I didn't go back. Heard they had hired one of those cleaning companies. Not that that ever works out."

"Is that why you went back again?"

"I guess."

Susan realized Mary didn't want to elaborate. But Susan was interested. "How long did you work for them the second time?"

Mary turned off the faucet and turned to Susan. "Four weeks. And, before you ask, that was almost two years ago. They still owe me money."

"They didn't pay you?"

"They paid some." Mary placed her sponge on the back of the sink and turned to Susan. "But there was always a reason why they couldn't pay up exactly what they owed."

"What do you mean?"

"The first week, they paid me five dollars less than they owed me. Mrs. Worth said she would add it to the next week's wages." Mary shrugged. "That was fine with me. People do that all the time."

Susan found herself wondering if she had the proper change in her purse or if she was going to have to cash a check before Mary left for the day so she missed the next part of the story. "You mean you didn't get paid at all the next week?"

"Yup. It seems to me that her excuse was something about not having any cash in the house and Mr. Worth had their checkbook with him in the city."

"Why didn't she go to a cash machine?"

"I didn't see her. She wrote me all this in a note, so I couldn't ask any questions. I was pretty upset. I'd never dealt with anything like that before. Everyone always pays me—on the day that I work and in cash usually."

Susan nodded. That was how she did it. "Well, did you say something the next week? Or did she pay up?"

"She paid me, but not enough. She always gave me my money in an envelope and I didn't open it until I got home. She'd stiffed me by almost fifty dollars. I did the math more than once thinking I might have made a mistake. But I hadn't and she did. I shouldn't have gone back the next week. Should have just taken my losses and gone on. I don't have any trouble getting work in Hancock."

"But you went back."

"Yeah. And she didn't pay me that day either. I lost more than a hundred dollars on that deal."

Mary had turned back to the sink and Susan realized that she didn't want to tell her any more.

"You investigating her murder?" Mary asked.

"Yes."

"Who have you talked to so far?"

"Just a few of her friends—Lauren and Kimberly—and Scott, but he wasn't exactly helpful."

"I heard that he has an alibi." It was a statement rather than a question.

"Yes. He was being taped for a television show in New York City. Apparently there's no way he could have been the murderer. I don't suppose you've heard a rumor about Amanda and another man," Susan added, remembering the meeting at the Nutmeg Motel.

"Amanda Worth and another man? Who told you about that?"

"It's true!"

"It's not something I ever heard."

Susan glanced over at Mary's back. There was something she wasn't saying. And Susan got the impression that she wasn't going to say it.

"You talked with the Worths' neighbors?"

"Their neighbors? No, which ones?"

"Well, seems to me Mr. and Mrs. Clayton have known the Worths for an awfully long time. . . ."

"Brooke and Hamilton . . . That's right, they've been next-door neighbors of the Worths for almost two decades. . . . Did you work for the Claytons?"

"Did and do." The scrubbing increased and Susan decided to leave her kitchen while the sink still had some of its factory finish left.

SIXTEEN

BROOKE CLAYTON WAS JUST LEAVING HER HOME WHEN Susan drove into her driveway. Brooke was the product of the most traditional prep schools on the East Coast. There was no way she could ignore a guest—even though that guest had shown up before eight in the morning. Fixing a smile on her face, Brooke walked over to Susan's car.

"Good morning, Susan."

"Hi, Brooke, are you going out?"

"I . . . I was, but . . ." She looked at the navy Mercedes waiting in her driveway and back to Susan and seemed to make up her mind. "But it's not important. Would you like to come in for coffee?"

Susan silently blessed the person responsible for teaching Brooke such wonderful manners. "Yes. Thank you." As Susan followed Brooke in through the door, their attention was attracted by a nearby screech. Both women looked toward the sound—that just happened to be coming from the house next door.

"Poor Scott," Brooke commented. "He's never really learned to drive a stick."

"Then why . . . ?"

"Amanda preferred it."

Susan saw the license plate—SHESHOPS—and realized Scott Worth was driving his wife's BMW. "Why would he be driving her car?"

Brooke shrugged her slender mink-covered shoulders. "I have no idea. He's been acting a little strangely since her death. But who can blame him? Not only to lose your wife, but for her actually to have been murdered . . ."

Brooke didn't finish her sentence, but Susan got the impression that she thought the method of Amanda's death had lowered the tone of the neighborhood. "Of course, they were so close," Susan muttered.

Brooke gave her a sharp look. "You think so?"

"I gather you don't," Susan answered as the door swung closed behind them.

"Why don't we sit in the morning room?"

Susan followed her hostess through the pastel decorated foyer, down a long gold and white hallway to her cheerful "morning room." She had always envied Brooke this room. Like the famous morning room at Manderley, it was elegant, decorated with English antiques and special pieces of imported porcelain. Susan found herself wondering if Mrs. Danvers would appear with a menu for the approval of the lady of the house. Instead the figure in the doorway was male, wearing a pinstriped business suit, and scowling.

Hamilton Clayton had excellent manners, too. The smile that he put on his face may have been a bit insincere, but he said the right thing. "Susan Henshaw. How wonderful to see you. And so early in the day."

"Hi, Ham. I'm sorry it's so early. I needed to see your wife about something and . . ." Inspiration struck. "And you are both so busy that I just thought it would be easier to find her at home now."

"Brooke is one of the women who keeps the town running—and it keeps her running, too."

Susan smiled. She'd heard this before.

"Aren't you going to be late for work, dear?"

"Wall Street will have to do without me today. I have a client meeting in New Haven at ten, but you're right. I'd better say good-bye and leave." He rather ostentatiously walked across the room to kiss his wife. " 'Bye, Susan. Give my best to Jed."

"I will. Have a good day."

"Call if you're going to be late for dinner," Brooke trilled as her husband left the room.

"Don't I always?"

He was out of view, but from the tone of his voice, Susan would have guessed that the frown had returned to his face.

"Ham is worried about some sort of IPO in the market." Like a good wife, Brooke made excuses for her husband's mood.

"He's a stockbroker, isn't he?"

"No, he's a stock analyst."

"Does he work with Scott Worth?"

"For Worthington Securities? Heavens no."

Susan was immediately curious. "Why not?"

"Oh, Scott Worth is well known for working alone. If he gets advice from analysts, he keeps quiet about it."

"Is that unusual in his business?"

"Very. Well, very for someone who is in a legitimate business. Some of the day traders or penny stockbrokers work completely alone. No one legit would work for many of them frankly."

"You seem to know a lot about it."

"I've picked up a bit during long, boring dinner parties with Ham and his colleagues."

Susan nodded. She knew what Brooke meant.

"Is that why you're here? To ask me questions about Scott?"

Susan knew she'd never convince this woman that she had dropped in for a casual visit so early in the day. "I'm sort of investigating Amanda's murder."

"Good for you. I hope you catch the bastard who did this and they hang him."

The vehemence of her response caught Susan off guard. "Why?" she asked quickly.

"I always felt sorry for Amanda. She never seemed to have much of a life."

"Amanda?" Susan wondered if they were talking about the same person.

"I always think compulsive shopping is just an attempt to fill up a large void in an unsatisfactory life."

"I never actually thought of Amanda as a compulsive shopper."

"Oh, Susan, she was always at it. And why? How many objects can any person buy?" Brooke glanced around her well-furnished room with the satisfied air of a woman who has shopped—and shopped well enough to feel that there was nothing more to be sought—or desired.

"I suppose you could be right. . . . But what do you think was wrong with her life?"

"Everything. Her house. Her husband. Her lack of children. The fact that she had no career. Amanda Worth always seemed to me to be an unhappy woman."

"Living next door to her, you probably saw things that I didn't," Susan suggested.

"Of course." Brooke surprised Susan by suddenly standing up. "Coffee. I invited you in for some coffee. I'd better go get it."

"But . . ."

"Cream and sugar. Right?" Brooke swept from the room without waiting for Susan to reply.

Susan, more than a little surprised by her hostess's departure, got up and looked out the window. This house sat on one of the large two-acre lots common in this area of town, but they were near the water where the land was rocky. Basements were difficult to dig in some places, and no one had even considered dividing up the land in nice, neat rectangles. For that reason, this corner of the Clayton house was very close to what must have been a small stable or carriage house when the Worth home had been built. The first floor had been converted into a three-car garage and Susan remembered that Scott and Amanda had once collected classic Pierce Arrow roadsters, and guests to their home would be treated to rides in these large autos. But Amanda's BMW and Scott's Jaguar sedan were the only cars housed there now.

Susan moved closer to the window. From this side of the building, it was evident that the second floor was a living space—a good-sized living space. Susan was reminded of Erika's apartment, and wondered if the Worths rented it out or if they had found some other use for it. She was still wondering when Brooke returned with coffee.

Susan wasn't surprised to see the silver coffee set or the English bone china. She was, however, surprised by the expression on her hostess's face. Brooke looked worried—very worried. Susan hurried back to the couch and sat quietly, waiting for Brooke to explain what was causing her distress.

But Brooke was of the stiff-upper-lip tradition. She might

look distressed but she didn't seem inclined to talk about it. Susan, however, was too busy to wait all morning. "What's wrong?" she asked, picking up the cup of very light coffee that Brooke handed her.

Brooke answered her question with a question. "You said you were investigating Amanda's murder."

"Yes."

"Everyone says that Scott couldn't be the killer."

"That's true. He was in the city being interviewed for a television show. There's absolutely no way he could have left there, gotten to the mall, killed Amanda, and returned to the city without anyone noticing."

"But he could have hired someone to do it."

Susan hadn't thought of that before. "I suppose so." And then she realized what Brooke was saying. "Do you know a reason why Scott would have wanted Amanda dead? We thought—I thought—Most people seem to think that they were such a close and devoted couple."

"Of course, they worked hard to give that impression." Brooke put down her coffee cup untouched. "Maybe I shouldn't say anything. If Scott isn't a suspect."

"But you just suggested that he might have hired someone to kill her," Susan reminded her.

"I really don't believe that. I really don't believe that Scott wanted Amanda dead. It's just that . . . Well, that they didn't get along. Their marriage was a sham. In some ways they acted more like business partners than loving mates. If you're investigating, you probably know that already though."

"I've heard various things," Susan answered, trying not to lie. "But it's important that I hear everything—especially from someone who knew them as well as you and Ham."

"Well . . ."

"How long have you been neighbors?" Susan asked quickly.

"We moved in here almost fifteen years ago. Amanda and Scott appeared at the door as the moving van was leaving. They brought a loaf of French bread that Amanda had baked. It was still warm from the oven. I was terribly impressed at the time. Ham found some cheese and we opened a few bottles of wine and sat in here—on unopened cartons of books— and got acquainted. At the time, I thought we were terribly lucky to have moved next door to such a wonderful couple."

"So you became friends."

"We got along for a few years. Scott got us in the Field Club almost right away and we were thrilled. That was in the days when there was always a waiting list of people wanting to be considered for membership. And Amanda got me involved in a bunch of her charitable activities. They took a lot of time, but the kids were all going to school by then, and it helped me find a place in the community."

She stopped speaking and Susan got the impression that there was more to this.

"I know you're involved in fund-raising for the hospital. Did you begin that then?"

"I'm on the board at Community Hospital, Planned Parenthood, and St. Swithun's Nursing Home. But those activities are more recent. I was a surgical scrub nurse when Ham and I were married."

"I didn't know that."

"Yes, I worked for one of the best plastic surgeons in New York City."

And, from what Susan had heard, one of the best plastic surgeons in New York City had worked on Brooke. "So the medical charities had nothing to do with Amanda?"

"No."

"What did you help her with?"

"Heavens, there were so many things back then. Let me think for a bit. I collected for about a dozen different charities over the years from the American Cancer Society to some home for unwed Indian mothers in the hills outside of Santa Fe. And I helped her organize the Hancock Annual Charity Ball for more years than I can count. I did it all—hired caterers, arranged for dance bands. Three years in a row I organized the silent auction. . . ."

"Three years!" That job had been known to send its organizer to Canyon Ranch for a month, trying to restore both energy and sanity.

"Yes. I must have been nuts back then."

"Why did you do it?"

"I just told you. I was nuts. Oh, not really," she added seeing the puzzled expression on Susan's face. "I guess a better explanation was that I was in over my head."

"I'm sorry . . ."

"You don't understand because you believe the myth of Brooke Clayton's life."

"What myth?"

"That I'm the quintessential rich WASP." Brooke looked at the stunned expression on Susan's face and continued. "Well, part of it is true. I am a WASP. My parents may have been unemployed—and unemployable—drunks, but they were Protestant, white, and their background was Anglo-Saxon."

"You didn't go to prep schools. . . ."

"I did. On scholarship. I arrived at school a poor kid with scraggly hair, dirty nails, no manners, and no polish. My name was Barbara, so I was known as Barbie—like the doll.

Only I was tackier. But I was smart and I used my brains for more than academics. Six years later I went off to college with a new name, a new hairstyle, and a determination to move permanently into the economic group of my wealthier classmates. And I was anxious to start. I was smart enough to go to med school, but I headed into a nursing program, planning to get myself married to a rich doctor. But I met Ham and he was what I was looking for—a rich WASP. We got married, moved to Hancock, and I left my childhood behind. I never lied about my past, I just let people assume that this polish was inborn rather than carefully applied."

"I don't think anyone would have cared about how much money your parents had . . ." Susan began.

"You're right. Most people wouldn't have. But *I* did. I was desperate to fit in. And Amanda and Scott seemed to recognize that. So they helped me—only I ended up working my ass off to prove just how much of a WASP I was. Until I realized that Amanda and Scott were taking much of the credit for my work. Besides, I was miserable—always working to be accepted. So, after more than a few years of therapy, I stopped doing what my popular, community-minded next-door neighbors thought I should be doing and got involved in things I cared about. I think Amanda understood, but Scott hasn't said a nice word to me in years. He is not a man who appreciates independence."

"And do you think that's true of his feelings for Amanda?"

"No one could live next door to them and doubt that."

SEVENTEEN

SUSAN WOULD HAVE LIKED TO KILL THE PERSON WHO chose that moment to call and remind Brooke that she was going to be late for a hospital board meeting if she didn't hurry. Susan worried that Brooke would regret her openness and it would be difficult—if not impossible—to regain that mood. But Brooke had offered one hint. If the Worths' next-door neighbors knew things no one else did, well, then Susan should speak to whoever lived on the other side of them.

But who lived on the other side? Susan wondered, staring at the name on the mailbox before the other house. Newman. She knew a Newman family down at the Club, but she wasn't sure where they lived.

She was still puzzling over how to knock on the door of this house and ask whoever was inside about their next-door neighbors when the problem solved itself. The front door opened and a young woman smiled and waved at her.

"Hi! Can I help you?"

"I . . . I hope so." Susan started up the sidewalk toward the extraordinary creature standing in the open doorway. She was young and had short hair dyed a bright, unnatural red. The bright pink glasses perched on her freckled nose clashed with the fluorescent orange sweat suit she wore. She looked about fifteen years old, but upon closer examination, Susan decided that she should add at least ten years to her estimate.

"Do you want to come in?"

"Do you always open the house to complete strangers?"

"You're not a stranger. You're Mrs. Henshaw. You don't recognize me, do you?" A huge grin told Susan that she found this fact more than a little amusing.

"I'm sorry, but . . ."

"Don't worry about it. When you knew me I was a mousy brunette. Maybe you need a little hint: 'Now run along home and jump into bed.' "

Susan wondered what sleeping had to do with anything.

" 'Say your prayers and cover your head. . . .' "

And then the words rang a bell. Susan had spent two long, long years as assistant scout leader for her daughter Chrissy's troop many years ago. This woman was reciting the rhyme she had taught the girls to say at the end of each and every tedious meeting. "You were a Brownie?"

"I was the worst Brownie you ever saw. That's what you said about me!" she added happily.

"I said that to a young girl . . ." Susan suddenly remembered. "Pixie?"

"You got it!"

"You're Pixie Singer?"

"I was. I'm Pixie Newman now. I got married a couple of years ago—and moved back to Hancock. Come on in!"

Susan followed her through the arched double doors of the large clapboard Victorian home. But the well-decorated foyer she was expecting wasn't there. Nor was the stairway with mahogany newel posts, or the polished wood floors, or the shiny chandelier hanging from a high ceiling. In fact, there wasn't a foyer at all. The entire first floor of the house had been gutted, creating a space even more unusual than Pixie herself. The walls were curved, wood floors bleached, colored lights hidden in alcoves illuminated various architectural details. Stairways seemed to rise up the walls without support. Windows were swathed in exotic, eastern looking lengths of silk. Furniture was minimal, but pillows were everywhere.

"What do you think?"

"I think it's incredible. Did you do this?"

"No. But I did find the architect who designed it all and the interior decorator. I encouraged them to go ahead with their wildest fantasies. I didn't want to live in a house that was . . . you know . . . so suburban. Around here people seem to think if their home is big and expensive, it's interesting."

"I gather you don't agree?"

"God, no! I mean, when it comes right down to it, an overdecorated Victorian or Colonial is as trite in this part of the northeast as those ugly Cape Cods are at Levittown, don't you think?"

"I'd never really thought of it like that," Susan admitted, thinking of her own much loved, but not really original Colonial home. "But I do think this is spectacular."

"It should be. It cost almost as much to remodel this place as it did to buy it. Good thing I snagged a rich husband, right?"

"Uh, well, yes. . . ."

Pixie laughed. "Mrs. Henshaw, you haven't changed a bit!"

Susan got the feeling this wasn't a compliment. But she didn't have a lot of time to worry about it. Pixie may have changed her hair color and her last name, but she was one of the most energetic people Susan had run across in a while. Pixie insisted on showing Susan the entire house and they ran up and down the floating stairs and in and out of the various living spaces (apparently rooms were too suburban for Pixie) for almost fifteen minutes. Susan was relieved when she realized they were in an area with a refrigerator—this must be the kitchen.

"Could I have some water, please?" she asked.

"French, Italian, gas, or still?"

"Ah, tap water would be just fine," Susan said.

Pixie pressed on what Susan assumed had been a pillar holding up the ceiling and a door opened, revealing shelves of glasses and china. The refrigerator, a more conventional Sub-Zero, contained mostly bottles of waters; Susan wondered if the Newmans ever ate at home. Pixie poured Perrier into glasses for them both and then perched up on a three-legged stool. "Why are you here?"

"I'm . . ."

"You're investigating Amanda's murder." Pixie sounded thrilled with her own discovery. "I'll bet anything Scott did it!"

"Then they weren't getting along." In her excitement, Susan leaned forward and spilled her glass of water. "Oh. I'm sorry." She looked around—there was a sink, but nothing as prosaic as a sponge broke its elegant lines.

"Don't worry about it. I know you wouldn't approve, but my cleaning woman comes today."

Susan was surprised by that comment. "Why do you think I wouldn't approve?"

"You were always telling us we had to be responsible for our actions and clean up after ourselves."

"Oh, of course. I still believe that," Susan said, not bothering to admit that she did, however, employ someone to clean up her home—as she had back when she was leading the troop. "You were beginning to tell me about Scott and Amanda."

"Yeah, I don't really know them. I mean, I really, really try not to spend time with people as dull as the Worths. But when I heard Amanda had been killed, I did think that maybe I'd been wrong."

"You thought she was less dull because she was murdered?"

"Well, murder isn't dull, is it?"

Susan realized she was going to have to start at the beginning.

"You said you moved back to Hancock when you got married. When was that?"

"Almost two years ago. Can you believe it?" Pixie was obviously still thrilled.

Susan believed in marriage. Her "wonderful" was sincere. "Did you buy this house then?"

"Yup. We didn't move in until about a year later though— remodeling took longer than we expected."

"It always does," Susan said.

"That's why we started to hate Scott and Amanda."

"What?"

"I said that's why we started to hate Scott and Amanda— not that we would kill Amanda. After all, we won, right?"

"Pixie, I have no idea what you're talking about."

But Pixie was frowning, swinging her foot and staring at the floor. "I don't know if Beeb would think I should be telling you all this."

"Who is Beep?"

"Beeb. You know, my husband." She was uncharacteristically silent for a moment and then seemed to make up her mind. "But you know I'd never kill anyone, Mrs. Henshaw. I think I'd better tell you about it all. Just in case, you know . . . ?"

Actually, she hadn't the foggiest, but she did want to know what Pixie was talking about so she nodded and tried to put a sympathetic expression on her face. "Why don't you tell me the story from the time when you met Scott and Amanda?" she suggested.

Pixie said, "Cool." She thought for a moment. "Well, I guess we actually met them the day we moved in. But one or the other of them had been skulking around while we were looking at the house. We found the house, but we had to come back a few times before we bought it—you know, we wanted our architect to see it. And Beeb's lawyer and money manager. You know."

Susan nodded.

"Well, it was summer and every time we were here either Scott or Amanda was hanging around in their backyard. You know, pretending to dig in the garden or lounging on one of their ugly lounges. We knew they were checking us out, but, hey, what the hell?"

"Neither of them said anything to you?"

"Nope. But the real estate agent kept calling them—you're gonna love this—'important movers and shakers in the Hancock community.' She would glance over at their house and talk in this sort of hushed voice. Almost like they were royalty. Beeb and I thought it was a hoot."

Susan was beginning to remember what a chatterbox Pixie had been as a girl—apparently she hadn't outgrown it. "So you didn't meet them before you moved in?"

"Nope. But they came over the first night we were here. You'll never guess what they brought."

"A loaf of bread?"

"You got it! A homemade loaf of bread!" Pixie shrieked with laughter at the memory. "Scott kept repeating that his wife had just baked it as though her touch made it valuable or maybe weird. And they hung around. We couldn't get rid of them, for God's sake! We had to invite them in. I mean, I know that! But they sat down and started to talk about all sorts of shit—ah, stuff."

"Like what?"

"You know, the Field Club. And charities. And schools . . . Amanda kept sneaking little meaningful looks at my belly."

"You were pregnant?" Susan was astounded. There was no place to hide a child in this house. And those stairs . . .

"No way. But I was wearing a sort of smocky thing over my jeans. Anyway, I sure as shit wasn't going to get pregnant with them around."

"You were trying to get pregnant?"

"Nah. Just to get laid. Beeb and I wanted to sc—make love in every room in the house before we ripped them out. You know?"

Susan nodded.

"Anyway, we finally got rid of them. . . ."

"Did you offer them something to eat or drink?"

"God, no. They might never have gone home!"

"Is that why you don't like them? Because they spy on you and hang around?" Susan asked, having a hard time imagining the Worths hanging around anywhere, especially not with Pixie and whoever Beeb was.

"No. They're the reason we couldn't do what we wanted with the house."

Susan looked around. "I don't understand. What didn't you do?"

"The outside. Although now I think it's cool."

"What is?"

"The outside being so old fogyish and the inside so cool. You know, the contrast. Makes it interesting. Don't you think?"

"Yes, I do," Susan answered sincerely.

"Well it's not what we were planning. We were going to rip off the entire front of the house and build a new entry-way with columns and all sorts of neat little windows and angles—you should have seen the plan our architect drew up. He said it would probably get Beeb and me an article in *Architectural Digest*.

"Of course Scott and Amanda went batshit when they saw the plan."

"Why did they see it?"

"Is there anything in town that they don't see? God, they're the nosiest bastards! And I think they have something on the building inspector."

"What do you mean? Blackmail?"

"That's what I think. Beeb says the why doesn't matter. But they stopped us from doing what we wanted outside of the house."

"You know, this town has pretty strict zoning."

"Yeah, I can tell from how many houses are torn down and then others built in their place." Pixie sounded sarcastic. "But I guess the owners of those homes are lucky enough not to live next to the Worths."

"But this is good—I mean, the contrast is very dramatic."

"Yeah, I know. I just hate the fact that they won."

" 'Won'?"

"You know, stopped us from doing what we wanted to do."

"Well . . ."

"After all, they get to do whatever they want to do. . . . They have an illegal apartment, you know."

"An illegal apartment? They're renting out rooms in their house?"

"I don't know—they could be. But it's the apartment over the garage I'm talking about. I think they're renting it out."

"Why?"

"There are lights in there—late at night."

"But . . ."

"And this part of town is zoned for single family homes. I went down to the town offices and checked. They have an illegal rental. I'm sure of it."

"Have you seen anyone living there?"

"Not actually. But that's why I think it's so strange. They're hiding their tenant." Pixie's eyes were opened wide and Susan suddenly saw the young girl who had been terrified by ghost stories on the one camping trip they had been foolish enough to take their troop on.

"Are you going to turn them in?" Susan asked.

"Not yet. Beeb thinks we should just forget about it. He thinks we got what we wanted—mostly—and we should just forget about the past few years and be good neighbors."

"But you don't want to do that."

"No way! I'm still pissed! I wasn't even going to send flowers to the funeral, but Beeb insisted. He says this is a perfect opportunity to prove what good neighbors we've become. Beeb wants to put a large pool in the yard this summer," she explained.

Susan had a thought. "I don't suppose you'd help out with the reception after the funeral—it's going to be held at the house, but we need a few people to prepare in the morning.

You'd just have to dash over for a few hours. I'm going to be there," she added.

"Hell, why not? It'll prove to Beeb that I'm doing my bit. Besides, it will be an excuse to get a better look at that garage apartment. Beeb thinks we can be so nice that Scott will let us get what we want. I think we'd do a hell of a lot better if we tried a bit of neighborly blackmail!"

EIGHTEEN

SUSAN GOT INTO HER CAR, FEELING THAT SHE HAD WASTED much of the morning. Brooke had been interrupted before she could tell Susan anything interesting. And Pixie's excitement over the possibility of an illegal apartment didn't strike her as particularly significant. Lots of people had nannies and cleaning women living in their homes or on their property. It might not be exactly legal, but neighbors and town officials generally looked the other way. She started the engine and frowned. What should she do now? She had more questions than answers. She looked over her shoulder and the shooting pain in her neck suggested an answer.

Her hairdresser had recently purchased the store next to his salon, hired a masseuse or two, and created a day spa. And Susan's favorite masseuse was a notorious gossip. She pulled her phone from her purse. Maybe she could get an appointment and learn something while she relaxed that muscle in her neck. Five minutes later, she was on her way. An opportune cancellation had provided her with appointments for both a facial and a Swedish massage.

Susan knew it was self-indulgent, but she adored the spa services. She had come to facials, salt scrubs, manicures, and pedicures late in life and had almost immediately thrown caution to the winds and become addicted. She began to relax as she walked in the door.

Of course, the interior of the small spa had been designed to create just that response. The walls were painted pale blue, the carpet was the color of beach sand. Green plants sprouted in corners and hung from the ceiling. Tinkly new age music, which Susan might have found irritating in any other setting, played softly. And the scents! In the reception area there was a vague aroma of orange oil and vanilla beans. The changing room (really a locker room, but the lockers were hidden behind antique shutters equipped with shiny brass fittings, the lighting was soft, and thick sisal mats cushioned the floor) smelled of lilac, narcissus, and gardenias. The various treatment rooms were permanently redolent of the potions in use there.

She was greeted by an immaculately groomed hostess, shown to her locker, and left to undress in peace. After a few extra minutes trying on—and then washing off—the complimentary makeup displayed there, she left the room wearing the pale aqua robe and slippers the spa provided for all its guests. The hushed hallway, leading to the treatment rooms, was full of twists and corners. She didn't know her way around enough to head straight there and she was wandering aimlessly when she heard someone calling for "Ms. McCracken."

She had just found her room when an arm shot out and grabbed her from behind. Susan's scream did nothing to enhance the muted atmosphere of the spa.

"Oh, I'm sorry! I thought . . . I thought you were Ms. McCracken." The receptionist smiled, obviously embarrassed. "It happens all the time around here. It's the robes—everyone looks the same from behind."

"That's all right," Susan assured her as the door to the massage room opened and Marion the masseuse appeared.

"Mrs. Henshaw. Come on in. I'll be back in just one moment."

Susan was left alone to take off the anonymous robe and hop up on the table. The soft lighting, soft music, the warm, damp air . . .

She was asleep when Marion returned.

"Mrs. Henshaw? Susan?"

Susan woke up and stretched. "Oh, I guess I drifted off."

"Happens all the time. People come to get massages because they're stressed out—and tired—I'll bet half of my clients either fall asleep before I arrive or are asleep by the time I finish."

"Really?" Susan tried to wake up enough to ask a question about Amanda. But Marion did it for her.

"I'm so glad you're here. Now I can hear the scuttlebutt from the horse's mouth—so to speak. Everyone is talking about Amanda Worth's murder—and there's a rumor going around that you're helping the police investigate again."

"Not really. Amanda wasn't murdered in Hancock. The local police aren't involved in the investigation. They're busy keeping the press from trampling the crocuses just beginning to come up in the Worths' front yard."

"Really?"

Something in Marion's voice suggested that she knew something else. "What have you heard?" Susan asked quietly.

"You know Erika—the woman who owns Twigs and Stems?"

"Of course. We're old friends. I was at her house yesterday."

"Then you probably know about this."

"You mean about Brett?" Susan guessed.

"Exactly. I haven't seen anything about it in the paper. But I guess that makes sense, doesn't it?"

Susan was afraid a direct question would stop the flow of information. "I suppose . . ."

"I mean, if the investigation was a secret before Amanda was killed then they certainly wouldn't want it known now, would they?"

"No, I guess not." Susan was thinking furiously. What investigation? Why was it a secret? And what—if anything— did it have to do with Amanda's murder?

"Not that an investigation of the husband always has a lot to do with the wife. There are lots of couples in this town where one has no idea what the other one is doing."

"Sometimes that ignorance is what keeps them married," Susan commented.

"Damn right!" Marion punctuated her comment with a particularly strong kneading of a tight muscle in Susan's back and their conversation stopped for a moment.

Susan wondered if she was going to hear about another possible affair. Perhaps Amanda had been murdered by someone romantically—or just sexually—involved with Scott? It was something she hadn't considered. But Marion's next words suggested a completely different complication.

"From what Erika says, it sounds like the Worths' finances were a real mess—I mean, how often does the IRA come to the local police for help?"

"The IRA? Scott was involved with the Irish Republican Army? Amanda's death was an act of terrorism?"

"Oh no, I must have the initials wrong! I mean the tax guys."

"The IRS?"

"Yeah, that's right. Although I think Erika mentioned the people who run the stock market, too," she added hesitantly.

"The SEC? The Securities and Exchange Commission?"

"Yeah. Maybe that's what she said. They have to do with money, right?"

"Yes." Both the IRS and the SEC had to do with money— sometimes big money—the kind of money she had thought the Worths had before she began looking into their lives. Money seemed to be the key to everything. She turned her head to the other side so Marion could concentrate on her left shoulder and considered how the Worths' financial situation might lead to murder.

A few minutes later she was jerked awake by an energetic pounding at the muscles in her lower back. Marion was still chatting, now speaking of someone named—of all things— Crystal.

". . . other women go to her, of course. Many of them Amanda's friends."

"Is she good?" Susan asked, assuming that Crystal was a masseuse or a hairdresser.

"It's always hard to tell, isn't it? I mean most of her clients swear by her. But they would, wouldn't they? Not many people would admit spending all that money on a lousy psychic."

"How much mon—a what?"

"A psychic."

Susan put her head up. "Are you telling me this woman named Crystal is a psychic?"

"Yes. . . . I gather you don't go to her?"

"No. . . . I can't imagine going to a psychic."

"Why not? Sometimes it seems as if half the women who

come in here go to Crystal—and the others are thinking about it."

"You're kidding. Why?"

"From what they tell me, it makes their lives easier."

"Why?" Susan realized she was beginning to sound a bit like an echo of herself.

"This Crystal tells them what to do."

"What does she tell them?"

"Who to marry. Where to go on vacation. What to do with the rest of their lives."

"Sounds like a nosy mother-in-law."

Marion hooted. "Crystal's like no mother-in-law I've ever met."

"Does she come in for massages?"

"No. And, frankly, I'm not sure she'd fit on the table."

"Is she fat?"

"Nope, tall. Very tall. But that's not the most interesting thing about her. She wears the most fabulous wigs—in all colors. You know, red and brunette and blond (the standards) and then she has pink—shocking pink—and violet and turquoise. And they're all huge."

"You mean she has a big head?"

"I mean she believes in big hair—really big hair."

"Puffy."

"Puffy and fluffy and curly and whirly—that's what she says."

"So she does come in."

"Only to drop off a wig for a wash and styling."

"And Amanda went to this Crystal for . . . for what? Predictions? Reading tea leaves or something?"

"Palms. Crystal reads palms. And cards. I think she works with a tarot deck sometimes."

"And Amanda went to her for . . . for readings?" Susan asked, remembering the term she had seen on signs on windows in the less desirable neighborhoods of New York City.

"Sure did. And lots of Amanda Worth's friends ended up making appointments to see Crystal, too."

"So she must have been good."

"How so?"

"Her predictions must have come true."

"I suppose . . ."

Susan heard the reluctance in Marion's voice. "Why would anyone go to her if she couldn't predict the future?"

"I don't know that that's all people go to a psychic for."

"What do you mean?"

"Well, I'd bet most women just want someone to listen to them. I know that's why a lot of women go to the hairdresser—or even come here for some of our services. We work on their hair, or skin, or body, and they get a captive audience."

"Like a psychiatrist," Susan suggested.

"Nope. Those psychiatrists sometimes tell their patients things they don't want to hear. But someone giving you a facial or blowing out your hair or whatever, just listens."

"So you think this Crystal is an uncritical listener."

"And probably very interested. You know, the more she picks up about the women who come to her, the more she can predict their future. You know, if someone keeps complaining about her husband, she might be inclined to predict a separation."

"Do you think her predictions are that . . . that specific? I mean, would she say something like, 'I predict that you're going to get divorced'? Or would she just mutter on about a significant change in your personal life?"

"I hear she tells these women what is going to happen in their lives—and what to do about it."

Reading tarot cards had been a popular late-night activity in the dorm when Susan was in college, but nothing anyone had predicted had ever come true. She had never considered going to a psychic. And she was surprised that it seemed to be an accepted activity among women she knew.

For a moment, despite the fact that her body was beginning to feel absolutely wonderful and relaxed, Susan frowned. Was she being a snob? Was she surprised to learn that affluent, educated, middle-aged women would listen to someone claiming to foresee the future? Why would she think psychics were the sole property of the poor and uneducated? President's wives and royal princesses were known to rely on people claiming to have psychic powers. Why not Amanda?

"You know though, now that I think about it . . ."

"What?"

"I think Crystal gives séances."

Susan was stunned. This was substantially different than talking about the length of someone's life line. "Crystal talks with the dead?"

"Yeah. But only for special clients. I . . . I once overheard Amanda Worth talking about going to a séance—with Mrs. Critchley. But I mentioned it—not using Mrs. Worth's name or Mrs. Critchley's, of course—and the woman I told about it was surprised because she had just spent half an hour telling me how her visits to Crystal had changed her life!"

"Interesting," Susan muttered.

"It is. And you know what I wonder?"

"What?"

"I wonder if now, instead of talking to Amanda's dead relatives and such, Crystal will just talk with Amanda herself. You know, you should look into that. Maybe you can talk to Amanda and she'll tell you who killed her."

NINETEEN

LATER, SUSAN REALIZED THAT EVERYTHING CHANGED ONCE Crystal was in the picture. Of course, Crystal was hard to ignore. Marion's description—a tall woman in the habit of wearing flamboyant wigs—was woefully inadequate. Crystal exceeded all of Susan's expectations.

Susan was surprised to learn that Crystal worked—if that was the word—out of a small restaurant. She had been told this by the young woman who appeared after Marion to give her a facial.

"This is Cookie," Marion introduced them. "She might be able to tell you more about Crystal." This last was said while stashing Susan's generous tip into the pocket of her uniform.

"I sure can. Crystal saved my life!"

"Really? Do you mind telling me about it?" Susan asked, sitting back in the comfortable lounge, her long robe wrapped around her legs, each hand tucked into the opposite sleeve.

"Not at all. Have you ever been read by Crystal?"

"No, I . . ."

"Well, you're in for the experience of your life," Cookie announced.

"She's that good?"

"Didn't I just tell you that she saved my life? She's not just good. She's great."

"How did she save your life?"

"Well, first you gotta know that I am not a superstitious person. No way! I like to see things before I believe them. You know what I mean?"

"Sort of."

"Just so you know I don't believe just anyone can see into the future. So when I kept hearing about this woman Crystal from my clients, well, I can tell you I was more than a little skeptical. You understand what I'm saying?"

"Yes. But you did go to her for a . . . a consultation."

"Sure did. But more because I was desperate than because I believed in her spooky powers."

"Why were you desperate?" Susan asked.

"See, I was dating this guy—a real bum, but sexy. You know the type."

"I guess." She didn't, but, to be honest, there were days when she wished she did.

"Well, what finally drove me to Crystal was the big question. You know—the big question for any woman."

Cookie was smoothing a slightly stinging lotion over Susan's face and massaging it into the lines around her mouth. "The big question" could be lots of things—whether Cookie was pregnant came to mind, but just as Susan was considering why someone would ask a psychic this when there was a drugstore selling home pregnancy kits right across the street from the salon, she realized that wasn't the question.

"So, I asked whether or not I should marry this bum, right?"

"And?" Susan managed to pronounce the word with her cream-covered lips.

"And this Crystal was real sure. No ifs, ands, or buts, as they say. She told me to dump him."

"And oo dip?"

"Yup, I sure did. And it saved my life."

"Eeely?"

"Really! You'll never guess what happened," Cookie added and then continued without giving Susan time to do so. "In the first place, this guy had a real temper. I knew that. But I never saw him as mad as he was the night I told him to get lost. He flipped. Know what I mean?"

"Hm . . ."

"Well, he had this Mustang—red and really hot—he'd souped it up with his friends. And that night—you won't believe this!—that very night he was so upset that he smashed it right into the front of a 7-Eleven where he'd stopped to get some beer. And you know what?"

"H . . ."

"If I had been sitting in the passenger seat, which I would have been if we hadn't broken up, I could have been killed!"

Susan sat up and spoke clearly. "He died?"

"Nah! He just got some bruises and broke his fingers— but that was after he got out of the car and got angry and smashed his fist into a phone pole. But it was an accident. I could've been killed! That's how good Crystal is! Amazing, you know what I mean?"

"Yes. Amazing." Susan lay back down and closed her eyes. In any spa she'd been in this was the universal sign that said "Leave me alone."

Apparently Cookie didn't read sign language. For the next twenty-five minutes Susan learned nothing more about Amanda or Crystal, but she left the room with a pretty good idea of what was on Cookie's mind.

More important, she had Crystal's address in her purse. She had left the spa determined to meet with the psychic immediately. She found the address easily—and a nearby spot to park. But she hadn't counted on Crystal being busy with a client.

Susan had been greeted at the door of the tea shop by a young woman with hair almost down to her waist. She wore a long green dress styled like a monk's robe and a pentagram on a ribbon hung around her neck. "I'm a pagan," she murmured breathily, noticing Susan looking at her jewelry.

"Oh." She had no idea what else to say.

"Tea?"

"Excuse me?"

"Are you here for tea?"

"Yes, of course. And . . . and you have a sign outside. . . . It says psychic."

"It means that we have a psychic in residence," Susan's hostess explained seriously as she guided Susan to a small table near the back of the room. "Her name is Crystal. She's busy with a client. Over there." She pointed to a tiny alcove across the room. Susan had just gotten over the fact that each fingernail on that hand sported a little gold star when, spying Crystal, she turned abruptly and ran into a table, knocking a little vase of dried flowers onto the floor. "Oh, I . . . I'm so sorry. Your flowers . . ."

"Herbs. They are aromatic herbs congenial to the spirits."

"Oh." Susan was trying to walk to her table and spy on Crystal and her client at the same time. Crystal was truly incredible. A huge woman smeared with flamboyant makeup, her pale blue wig matched her baby blue gown. A few scarves were wrapped around her neck and waist, and large stones dotted the rings that covered her knuckles and dangled from her ears. Susan was as astounded by Crystal's client as she was by Crystal herself. Lauren Crone was having her palm read!

The table Susan was led to was for two people; Susan chose to sit where she could watch Crystal and Lauren.

"Herbal, black, or green?"

"Ah . . . green, I guess."

"Anything with it? We have biscotti, scones, muffins . . ."

"I'll have a scone."

"Honey or jam?"

"Jam."

"Strawberry, cherry, or apricot?"

"Cherry."

"Butter or margarine or . . ."

Susan had ordered full dinners and answered fewer questions. "Butter. And artificial sweetener, please."

"It's on the table for those who use it."

Apparently her lack of taste finally drove off the young woman to the kitchen and Susan was left alone to watch Crystal and Lauren. Both women were staring intently at Lauren's hand. Susan could see Crystal's lips (stained a deep red) moving constantly, but was too far away to hear anything. Lauren was silent; the expression on her face serious. Every once in a while Crystal would pause and Lauren would say something. This went on for almost fifteen minutes. Susan's tea was served and she had discovered that dipping a rock-hard scone into green tea was a less than satisfying gustatory experience when Lauren suddenly flung herself back into her seat and covered her face with her hands. Susan leaned forward, but she couldn't tell whether Lauren was laughing or crying. A few minutes went by. Crystal sat silently, her hands still on the table, staring at something on the ceiling over her client's head. Suddenly, Lauren put her hands down, looked up, smiled, reached out to shake Crystal's hand, and left the table.

It was such an abrupt change that Susan didn't have time to even consider turning around to conceal her identity.

"Susan! How wonderful to see you." Lauren was heading in her direction, a smile on her face. "You're eating here? No one comes here for the food—it's dreadful. We all come here to see Crystal. Oh, of course, you're having a reading."

"I wasn't . . ."

"This is Susan Henshaw?" a voice said.

Susan, stunned, looked up at the psychic who seemed to have morphed across the room and to their side. "I . . . Yes, I'm Susan Henshaw."

"And you are here to see me."

"Well, I don't have an appointment."

"You are here to see me."

"I . . ."

"You are here because here is where I work."

That was true. "Yes."

"Crystal knows everything!" Lauren announced. "You would not believe what she told me."

"You agreed not to share your future." Crystal's spoke in a tone of voice which brooked no argument.

Lauren shut her mouth immediately and pursed her lips.

Crystal turned her attention to Susan. "And you want to see me." Her deep voice commanded attention.

"Yes, if you have the time."

"You pay for my time. Ninety dollars a session."

Susan was a little stunned by this flat statement. "I'm not sure I have that much cash."

"I take Visa. Come."

Susan went. She followed Crystal back to her little alcove

and sat down in the seat Lauren had just vacated. Crystal seated herself across the table and whisked a credit card swiper from under the window. Susan scrounged around in her purse for her wallet and placed her card in the psychic's outstretched hand. The business took a few minutes. Susan noticed Crystal didn't check her credit—perhaps she already knew the Henshaws were solvent? Chalk it up to some sort of mystical divination or because Crystal realized the sweater Susan was wearing was a Donna Karan? But she'd paid her money and apparently Crystal wasn't inclined to waste time.

"Your hand." Crystal put out her own and Susan laid her hand in it palm up as she had seen Lauren do.

"You are right-handed?"

"Yes."

Crystal stared at Susan's palm for a few moments before speaking again. "You don't believe in my powers, so why do you pay to see me?"

"I—how do you know I don't believe in your powers?"

"Most of the people who sit there are anxious. Some actually hold their breath. They want me to look into their palms and tell them flattering things, help them solve whatever problem life has dropped in their laps. They don't, mind you, want me to see too much. They don't want me to see how mean-spirited they are, whom they are cheating on, what is wrong with them spiritually or personally. The combination of expectations, hopes, and fears makes many of them quite nervous."

"Understandably," Susan said. She was surprised to find Crystal so well spoken.

"I'm not what you expected."

"I . . . I'm not sure what I expected. I've never been to

a psychic before. I don't think I've ever even seen one."
Crystal was staring at her intently and Susan, not wanting
to meet those eyes, found herself examining the woman's
jewelry.

"Most psychics don't look as I do. Many are quite dull!—
demure even. There are some who still cling to the ersatz
gypsy look—so passé, in my opinion. I like to think that I
am unique."

"You are," Susan said sincerely.

"So what do you want?"

"To ask you some questions."

"But not about yourself?"

"No, about Amanda Worth."

"Why do you think I know anything about this Amanda
Worth?"

"I understand she's been coming to see you for years."

"And how do you know that?"

"Someone told me." Susan wondered, fleetingly, if Crystal could read the name of that someone on her palm.

"Amanda Worth is dead."

"I know."

"If I spoke about one client to another, no one would
come to me. I am discreet. Everyone knows that. What I see,
I do not talk about, but . . ."

Something outside of their alcove seemed to attract Crystal's attention and she stopped speaking.

"But what?" Susan asked, looking around and not noticing any changes in the room.

"But I think I will make an exception here. I think I will
help you find out who killed Amanda Worth."

TWENTY

"WE NEED PRIVACY." WITHOUT STANDING, CRYSTAL REACHED up and swung a heavy purple satin curtain across the entrance to their alcove. Suddenly they were alone; even sounds from outside seemed to be muffled.

Crystal dropped Susan's hand and, putting her own elbows on the table, she focused intense eyes on Susan's face. "Who told you that Amanda came to me? That woman who just left? Lauren Crone?"

"No. . . ."

"I should not ask you. You will not answer."

"A lot of women come to you," Susan said, determined not to be tricked into saying something she might regret.

"You find it strange that people need help in making difficult decisions?"

"No, of course not."

"Then you believe in my powers?"

"Well, I don't know anything about psychics really. I've never been to one or even met one before now."

"And you judge me from how I choose to look."

Susan was becoming uncomfortable. "I am not here to find out about you," she protested. "I want to find out about Amanda—and who killed her."

Crystal cradled her chin in her hand and closed her eyes. Susan wondered if it was possible that she was communing with Amanda's spirit. She remained quiet, just in case. Susan began to wonder if she could possibly prod her into some sort of response when Crystal opened her eyes and looked up. "I said I would help. I will. But you must understand . . . must try to understand . . . this has nothing to do with my powers—which are real—but rather my profession."

"Your profession? You mean being a psychic?"

"You may not consider it a profession, but it is how I earn my living."

Susan thought for a moment. "This is getting us no-where," she started slowly. "I don't mean to insult you. I guess I do have a certain prejudice against what you do. Per-haps the thought of someone—anyone—knowing what I'm thinking is threatening to me."

Crystal chuckled. "You're not the only one. I can't tell you how many people who plunk themselves down in that chair are more worried that I can see what they're thinking about my clothing than about what might or might not hap-pen in their lives."

Susan decided it was time to get back to the subject. "So I'm right. You knew Amanda Worth?"

"Amanda has been coming to see me for years—heavens, over a decade."

"You've been here for a decade?" Susan was astounded. So much for her powers of observation.

"No. I practiced in the city for years. I moved here slowly. I started out here—in Hancock—one day a week and, when I'd attracted enough clients, I added days. I've been working here exclusively for almost five years now."

"Was Amanda your first client in the area?"

"Yes."

"So she started seeing you while you were in the city."

"Yes."

"How did she find you? Did she just walk in off the street or were you recommended by someone?"

Crystal seemed to consider this question for a bit. "Most of my clients appear because someone has told them about me, but, once in a while, people do just wander in off the street. Not surprisingly many of the latter become some of my best clients."

"Why?"

"Many of them are superstitious. They believe they were somehow led to me and that I will be able to answer their questions."

"What do you believe?" Susan realized she was having a difficult time sticking to the subject, but it was all so fascinating.

"I need clients. I don't care if they walk in off the street, if they are recommended by another client, or if they come to me because they've read my book."

"You wrote a book?"

"You don't have to sound quite so shocked. I am literate and I have a college degree to prove it."

"I'm sorry."

"You must be upset about the murder of your friend," Crystal said kindly.

"Amanda wasn't really a good friend," Susan explained, discovering herself in the same position as all those other clients who had sat in this chair and wondered if Crystal knew what they were thinking. "But I had known her—and her husband—for years. Since we moved to town, in fact."

"And you are investigating her murder . . . as you have

many others. I am not reading your mind. I read the paper, like everyone else in town."

Susan smiled. "Yes, but, you see, it's because I have known her for so long that I am puzzled about this. I mean, I never knew Amanda had been coming to you for all these years."

"Did you ever go to her with a personal problem?"

"No. We didn't have that sort of relationship."

"Do you remember being part of a conversation about psychics when she was around?"

"No."

"Then why would you know about me? I don't believe Amanda was embarrassed to be seeing me—and I have more than a few clients who are—but she took our sessions very seriously. I don't believe she would bring it up in casual conversation."

Susan thought for a moment. "If I had gone to Amanda with a personal problem . . . if we had had that sort of relationship . . . would she have recommended that I come see you?"

"Possibly."

"Did Amanda tell Lauren about you?"

"That is what Lauren told me, yes. But then she is certainly a woman who wants everyone to know how important she is—or, rather, how important she *thinks* she is. She dropped many names—even yours."

"Really?" Susan was surprised that Lauren would consider knowing her to be a social coup.

"In truth, she warned me about you. She is concerned about your investigation."

"She told you that?"

"It's a feeling I got."

Susan leaned forward. "You said Lauren was concerned? Do you mean worried? Do you know why? Did you get the impression that she might be involved in some way?"

Crystal paused before answering. "You know nothing about what I do. . . . I don't read words in the air about my client's head. Sometimes I hear things, but mostly I get feelings about what is going on in the person's life and what may— or may not—happen."

"Do you know what's going to happen in this instance? Am I going to find out who killed Amanda?" And is the reception I'm organizing for after her funeral going to be a success? She didn't ask the last question aloud.

"You have always been successful in the past, haven't you? Why are you questioning your abilities now?"

"I'm not really. I just wondered."

"Then you believe in my powers?"

"I . . . I . . . Probably not."

"Honesty doesn't get you any points here. Although you're better than your friend."

"You mean Lauren?"

"Yes. She came here to find out about Amanda, too. She just pretended to be interested in other things."

"You said she was concerned about my investigation. . . . Do you think she was afraid I'd find out that she killed Amanda?"

"She is afraid of something." Crystal appeared to consider her own words. "Yes. But I find it hard to believe that she murdered Amanda. Amanda was not standing in the way of something she wanted. And that woman—she has many, many wants."

"Really? I can't imagine what Lauren could possibly want. She has more than almost anyone I know. . . . One of the biggest houses in town, cars, boats, a large mansion on Long Island, furs . . ."

"Maybe what she wants is what cannot be bought. . . ."

"Oh, I know that most important things are impossible to buy. . . . It's just that the things Lauren wants can usually be acquired with cash—large amounts of cash."

"You may misjudge this woman."

"You mean she wants something more from life."

"You say she only wants material possessions. And you admit she has a wealth of these. I don't know what she wants, but I can tell you that she is unhappy. Very unhappy."

"Is this the first time you've seen her?"

"No. Lauren has been coming to me for months, but because she thinks it is the thing to do. Among a certain group in Hancock, being a client of mine is chic."

"Friends of Amanda's?"

"Many of these women are friends of Amanda. Yes."

Susan had a thought. "Did Amanda recommend them? Is that how your business grew in Hancock?"

She got the impression that Crystal relaxed a bit after she heard this question. "Yes. I think I can say that Amanda has been happy with the work we've done together and has been generous enough to recommend me to her many friends." Crystal smiled. "And if you are wondering if I give her a discount because of that, you would be correct. I do. That is, I have in the past."

Susan realized Crystal wasn't infallible. She hadn't even considered that possibility. But it made sense. "The Worths seem to have had financial problems."

"I usually don't talk about my clients, but since Amanda is dead . . . Yes, I had been aware of that for some time."

"Could you—did you—help her with that?"

"I do not give stock tips. I cannot give stock tips. I know there are people who claim to be psychic who claim to be able to predict the market, but I am not one of them."

"Really?"

Crystal's broad shoulders allowed her to shrug rather dramatically. "I don't judge others. As I prefer them not to judge me."

"Why did Amanda come to you for so many years? She couldn't have had problems that entire time, could she?"

"Not pressing immediate problems, no. Not the 'should I leave my husband or stay with him' type of thing—and I'm not saying that she ever asked me that, it is only an example," Crystal added quickly.

"Then why?"

Crystal thought for a moment before answering. "I will try to explain. My clients come to me sometimes because they are in a crisis. They do not know who to turn to and many of them have done all the traditional things. They have spoken with their friends, some have gone to their priests, ministers, rabbis, and many have talked things over with a therapist. When these people fail them, they come to me. And I try to help."

"How? By looking into the future?"

"If you will. But it is not as you imagine it. I don't get a vision of what will happen. I work with feelings—my own—and I interpret those feelings into something concrete."

"You mean, you don't see a tall, dark stranger?"

"Sometimes I know that a big change is coming. And sometimes I know that change will come about because someone new enters the picture. But, generally speaking, the only hair color I worry about is my own."

"You have a sense of humor."

"And that surprises you."

"I . . . I guess so. I don't mean to insult you."

"And I am not insulted. Ignorance is an excuse. If you learned more, you might come to appreciate."

"I guess. So you have feelings about the future which you interpret for them."

"That is oversimplified, but yes."

"How would that help someone like Amanda? Her problem with not having enough money, for instance?"

"I cannot tell people how to make money, but I can tell them how they can best live their life. That is what I do for most of my long-term clients. That is what they come to depend upon me for."

"What did you tell Amanda to do?"

"I told her to be true to herself. I told her she knew what to do and that she would have all the answers if she would trust her instincts."

"You told her that for ten years?"

"Well, I was more specific, of course. And her situation changed over the years. She did not ask the same questions."

Susan realized she was getting very little information. Perhaps this was the way psychics worked—offering only suggestions which could be interpreted as the client wished.

"Our time is up," Crystal said.

"Excuse me?"

"Our time. I have other clients waiting." She reached up to pull back the curtain and Susan hurried to get in one last question.

"Did you know that Amanda was going to be killed? That she was going to die?"

Crystal paused for a moment, a sad expression passing over her face. "I thought . . . I thought something was going to happen. But I misinterpreted it. The change I saw was for the good. . . . At least, that is what I thought. I made a mistake. And I am as sad as anyone as a result." Then she straightened up, put a brisk businesslike expression on her face, and, smiling politely, ripped back the curtain, exposing them to the room.

Susan got up, murmured a thank-you that she didn't feel and walked right into Kimberly Critchley.

TWENTY-ONE

CRYSTAL MIGHT DESCRIBE HER WORK AS MAKING THINGS clearer for her clients, but she had sure confused Susan. While she had verified that Amanda needed money—and suggested that the need had been there for a considerable time, Susan realized Crystal had told her nothing about Amanda herself. And, after what she admitted was over a decade of seeing this particular client, she certainly must know a lot about her. Perhaps, Susan thought, Crystal would be asked to speak at Amanda's funeral.

Thinking of the funeral, Susan suddenly realized that she and Jed should send flowers. As luck would have it, she was driving past one of Erika's shops. She might as well give her business to a friend, she decided, finding a parking spot and getting out of her car.

As CEO and CFO of the company, Erika was about as far from a saleswoman as she could be. So Susan was surprised to see her standing behind the shop counter.

"Erika! What on earth are you doing here?"

"Hi, Susan. I might ask you the same question. I would have thought you'd be busy organizing a reception for Amanda's funeral."

"And you'd be right. Scott's credit with the local caterer is zilch—just like you said—and I couldn't seem to get out of doing it."

"Sounds like Scott. So, how's it going? Have you gotten enough donations to feed the hungry masses?"

"How did you know?"

"No big deal. I've been here since eight this morning and at least three different customers have been in complaining that you and Kathleen have turned one of the social events of the season into a covered-dish supper."

"We didn't!" Susan protested. "Scott did. In fact, Kathleen shouldn't be blamed for any of this. I was the person stupid enough to volunteer to help Scott. She's just helping me."

"Typical of Scott. . . ."

"That he's too cheap to pay for his beloved wife's funeral reception?"

"Yes. And that he expects you—and Amanda's other friends—to help out. The man is what used to be known as a male chauvinist pig."

"You mean he has women doing things for him."

"Exactly. And, just like Amanda, most women seem to do what he expects."

Susan decided to ignore the fact that right now at least she fell nicely into that category. After all, it was Amanda's death she was investigating. "Amanda did that?"

"Oh, Susan, you didn't think Amanda enjoyed all the time she spent baking loaves of bread to bring to new neighbors, turning out those little pâtés they used to offer with cocktails and such, do you?"

"Actually, I did."

"Susan, think about it. You're domestic. You love cooking. You even make wildly elaborate dishes—which impresses the hell out of me. But you don't do it all the time, like Amanda did. I'll bet that poor woman made every bit of food ever served in her home—and every hostess gift they ever gave away."

Susan thought about Erika's words. "I have made pâté, but most of the time, I just buy it," Susan admitted.

"And when you make your own, you enjoy it because you want to do it. But unless I'm completely wrong, Amanda did it because she didn't have any choice—not because it was fun to do."

"What do you mean?"

"Well, once I overheard Scott and Amanda fighting."

Susan waited for Erika to continue.

"It happened a few months ago at a party in New York City actually. I was invited by a man who was interested in buying Twigs and Stems—although I didn't know that at the time. It was a very eighties event—showy, expensive food and drink, and too much of both. It was held in a huge penthouse apartment and the host kept taking his guests from room to room, pointing out various luxurious objects— paintings, French enamels, handwoven rugs, views from numerous patios—all to prove just how much he was worth. It was catered, of course, and the food was typical of the apartment—rich, expensive, rare, and lavish. A lot of people brought hostess gifts, of course. You know the type of thing— a bottle of vintage Burgundy, an imported and unusual after-dinner cordial, French chocolates."

Just hearing the list made Susan hungry.

"The Worths were invited, too, and when Scott and Amanda showed up, the host rushed to get us together—his three guests from Hancock. He probably assumed we were good friends."

"So?"

"Amanda and Scott brought a small jar of strawberry jam. She had made it from their own berries and had even embroidered the little cloth covering the metal top. Scott explained all that very loudly and proudly. But when I looked at Amanda, I saw that she was embarrassed."

"Did Scott have his 'look what my little wife did all by herself' expression on his face?" Susan asked.

"Of course. But what I really noticed was the look of fury he gave his wife when she started to apologize for not bringing something more appropriate."

"Really?"

"Yes. It was strange—or maybe inappropriate would be a better word. After all, our host didn't give a damn what they brought. The point of the party was what he could afford to buy, not what gifts were brought to him. But Scott was quite obviously furious at Amanda—and later I realized she was pretty angry at him."

"Later? When?"

"Right before we all gathered to go into the dining room. Amanda and Scott were both in the foyer arguing. I had gone upstairs to the bathroom and they didn't realize I could hear them. To be honest, I stepped out of the way to see what was going on."

"What was?"

"They were furious with each other. To tell the truth, I was pleased to hear her defend herself. But what she was saying surprised me. I had assumed that she was upset because of what they had brought. But from what she was saying, I realized that they brought these little homemade gifts—which she made—because Scott insisted on it. And that she hated doing it as much as bringing them."

"You're kidding."

"Nope. She was quite definite. I don't remember her words exactly, but she was specific. She hated baking the bread, raising the berries, and then turning them into jam. She referred to those things as 'cheap offerings'—at least I think those are the words she used."

"What did Scott say?"

"Frankly, I thought he was going to hit her."

"Erika!" Susan was horrified. "You could see them!"

"Yes. I was shocked."

"And did he? What happened?"

"He grabbed her arm, pulled her close to him, and said something."

"What did you hear?"

"He said something about an agreement they had made. And that she had better live up to her side of their bargain."

"What else?" Susan asked, hoping there was more.

"I . . . I mentioned it to Brett while we were talking about the evening on the way home."

"And?"

"And he said something about there having been questions about Scott and Amanda and their marriage. But that's all he said," Erika added quickly.

"But it seemed significant to you?"

"Not at the time."

"But now? Now that Amanda is dead?"

"Actually, I was thinking about it before Amanda was murdered."

"When?"

"A few weeks . . . maybe a month . . . before the murder. When Brett told me—" She stopped speaking.

"Erika, I know you're discreet, but she was murdered."

"Oh, Brett's not investigating the murder. I'd never tell you what he had said if it involved an ongoing murder investigation. He knows that."

"Oh, well . . ." Susan was surprised. Had Erika kept things from her in the past?

"But this is different," Erika continued. "And I'm not sure Brett would care. Since neither one of us has all day, I'll tell you. I'd appreciate it if you wouldn't let Brett know I told you."

"Of course."

"There's a big investigation going on—the SEC and some other government agency are involved. They're looking into Scott Worth's company."

Susan was disappointed. She knew all that, but Erika's next words were more interesting.

"Brett's involved because the investigation is looking into the investments of some very important people in Hancock. Brett is nervous about this getting out, Susan."

"But you think it might have something to do with Amanda's murder?"

"I have no idea. In fact, I don't know much."

"But what do you know?"

"I know there's an allegation that Scott has been draining off money from his funds for his own personal use—illegally—and that it involves money some important people have placed with him."

"Who?"

"There's more than one person—Susan, you really won't tell how you learned about this?"

"Yes. I promise. Who?"

"Edgar Finch is one of them."

"Really?" Susan remembered Jed's suggestion that Edgar

Finch was allowing the Worths to put off paying their club dues because he didn't want anyone to suspect the problems Worthington Securities was having. "Actually, I had heard something about Edgar and Worthington Securities," she admitted.

The expression on Erika's face changed from concern to relief. "Then you already know about Edgar. You've heard about the town council, too?"

"Not everything, I'm sure. The mayor is an investor. . . ."

"And a bunch of council members, as I understand it."

"That's interesting," Susan said slowly. "No wonder Brett is concerned about news of the investigation getting out."

"Exactly. You won't tell anyone."

"No, of course not." Susan needed to think. She decided it was time to change the subject. "Has Brett ever spoken to you about psychics?"

Erika seemed taken aback by the abrupt change of subject. "Psychics? No, why?"

"Well, I've heard that lots of police departments hire—or at least use—psychics in their investigations. I was wondering if the Hancock police had ever used one to help them out."

"They may have, but Brett has never mentioned it to me. And I can't imagine that he would use one."

"Why not?"

"Brett doesn't believe that people possess psychic powers."

"Are you sure?"

"Yes, I'm sure. We've argued about it, in fact."

Susan realized what Erika was saying. "Then you believe some people actually have psychic powers?"

"Absolutely."

"Have you ever gone to one?" Susan asked reluctantly.

Apparently Erika had no such reluctance in answering. "For years and years," she said emphatically.

"You've been seeing Crystal for years?"

"Crystal? I don't know anyone called Crystal. I see a psychic named Ellen . . . Ellen Anderson."

"Ellen Anderson?"

"Yes, do you think all psychics are gypsies with weird names and even weirder clothing?"

Except for the gypsy part, it sounded pretty accurate to her. "Of course not," she lied. "Do you mind telling me about Ellen? I have a reason for asking."

"Not at all. She's wonderful. And seeing her has changed my life. Ellen was the reason I had the courage to branch out from this store and create my own company."

"She gives you business advice?"

"Of course. And she's never been wrong. She predicted the economic boom in the early eighties—and knew that the time was right for me to expand my business. There was an almost unlimited demand for luxury products for a while—and the demand came from newly affluent baby boomers who wanted to impress their friends with their well-decorated homes. On the other hand, these people had roots in the environmental movement. Thousand-dollar handwoven baskets of organic flowers just fit the bill."

"And Ellen told you all this?"

"Not in those words, no. But I could interpret what she said and that's what I did. And, Susan, I know what you're thinking. You're thinking that Ellen says a bunch of vague things—like I see success in your future—and I fill in the long blanks and actually come up with the solutions to my problems myself."

"That is what I was thinking," Susan admitted.

"It's not like that at all."

"Would you tell me about it? If you have the time."

"I have a few minutes. I'm waiting for a supplier to contact me. If the phone rings, I'll have to answer."

"Great. Tell me how it works then. Does she read your palm? Tea leaves?"

"No, Ellen reads tarot cards. And she doesn't just babble on and on. I ask specific questions and she interprets the cards to find specific answers."

"So when she suggested that you expand your business, she was answering a question? Something like 'should I expand my business?'"

"Not exactly. I was thinking of expanding. This store was successful and I had been considering it for a while, as I recall. When I went to see Ellen, I don't remember exactly what I asked her, but I probably asked if I should buy another store or something like that. I don't remember the question exactly. But I do remember her answer."

"What was it?"

"She said she saw success for me—near water—on both coasts. You can imagine my surprise. I was considering buying a second shop up in Greenwich at that time. I figured I could manage two stores and maybe start selling plant-related items in both stores over time. And here's Ellen suggesting a bicoastal business in my future. I wasn't even considering anything that would move me in that direction."

Susan frowned. "I didn't know you had a store in Greenwich. Where is it?"

"It isn't. I took Ellen's advice and ran with it. I used the small loan I'd gotten to buy that store, along with a larger loan to buy new merchandise and opened a place in New York City—in Soho. It turned out to be a smart move. A store in the city gives a business something of a national presence. I got lots of free publicity and even more credit as a result. And that led directly to the success of my other places."

"And you credit Ellen with all this."

"I would never have considered expanding like that if it hadn't been for her," Erika said flatly.

"What about personal decisions—decisions about your personal life—isn't that what most people go to psychics for?" Susan asked the second question quickly as a frown appeared on Erika's face.

"I guess you're right. Probably most people ask questions about their personal lives."

Susan waited for Erika to continue and asked another question when she didn't. "Have you been to other psychics? Do they all work the same way?"

Erika laughed. "Yes and no. Yes, I've been to others and no, they don't all work the same way. Most of them, in fact, are frauds with no more special powers than your average person."

"Did—do the other psychics live here in Hancock?"

"No. There probably are psychics here, but I can't say I've ever heard of them. Ellen lives—and works—in New Haven. The other psychics I saw lived in the city."

"New York?"

"Yes."

"I gather you didn't like the first one."

"No. She suggested that we contact the dead for answers."

"She wanted to give a séance with tables jumping up and down? That type of thing?"

"I don't know what she planned to do or how she planned on contacting the dead. I turned her down without asking any questions." Erika looked up at Susan. "I didn't answer your question when you wanted to know if I asked Ellen about my personal life."

"I'm sorry. I wasn't trying to pry."

Erika's next statement surprised Susan. "I don't know what to do about Brett," she said suddenly.

Susan waited for her to continue.

She did. "Sometimes I think we should just break up and go our separate directions and other days I'm sure we should get married."

Susan knew what her opinion was—she had been waiting to give an engagement party for Brett and Erika for years. "What does Ellen say?"

"According to Ellen, the cards say we should marry."

Thank goodness! "Don't you agree?"

"It's not me. It's Brett. He doesn't want to get married. And, Susan, you know Brett. He's not the type of man to resist commitment. I just don't understand what's going on."

"Have you ever thought of seeing Ellen with him. . . ."

"Oh, Susan! Please don't tell him I see a psychic—he'd be appalled! He thinks they're all frauds and the people who go to them are gullible fools."

"I won't say anything. Don't worry."

Erika's phone rang before Susan could assure her that Brett would never think she was a gullible fool, no matter who she saw about what.

Susan waved good-bye.

She was almost at the town hall before she realized she hadn't ordered flowers for Amanda's funeral.

TWENTY-TWO

Jed was the political member of the family. He had run for local office a few years ago. Although his term on the town council had ended, he still kept in touch with local politicians and issues. She was fairly sure he would have mentioned it if any of Hancock's officeholders had an extra million or two to invest in high risk securities. And Edgar Finch—he was wealthy, of course—but a man who would invest his money in Worthington Securities? Susan thought it highly unlikely. And the mayor—well, that was an interesting question.

Susan didn't consider herself a close friend of Mayor Pierson. But they did have something in common. They had been class mothers together when their older children were in first grade. She hoped that provided a bond because she needed answers to some pretty personal questions.

The drive to the municipal center was short and Susan easily found a parking place in the large lot that served both the municipal offices and the police department. The building had been remodeled recently by an architect who apparently believed impressive entrances demanded double doors handmade of black cherry with stained glass inserts. Susan pulled hard on the forged brass handles.

And fell flat on her butt as a young man pushed his way out.

"Mrs. Henshaw!"

"Tom!"

"Are you hurt?"

"I don't think so. . . . Aren't you going to help me up?"

"Of course. I'm sorry. I'm in a hurry. I didn't see you—Why are you here?" Tom Davidson asked, offering her his hand.

Susan, having regained her footing, brushed off her clothes and checked for runs in her stockings. "I'm here to see the mayor."

"Mayor Pierson? Why? What's up?"

"Why should something be up? Maybe we just have a lunch date."

"I'm not buying that. I spoke with Scott Worth this morning. He just happened to mention that you were organizing a dinner for five hundred people to take place right after Amanda's funeral."

"Five hundred? Dinner? I . . . Well, that doesn't matter now. Why were you talking with Scott anyway?"

"I didn't say. . . . Well, yes, of course, I did." He looked at her and seemed to make up his mind. "Listen, is there someplace we can talk? Privately."

"I suppose."

"I know—come with me."

Susan followed Tom Davidson down the long hallway, past open doors where various departments were located, staffed mainly by middle-aged women chatting together without enthusiasm, and into the elegant city council chambers. Tom carefully closed the doors behind them. "No one will find us in here."

She looked around. The council chambers had been copied from the design of a town hall in New England. They were elegant and austere. "Well, it's better than the men's room," she muttered.

"Excuse me?"

Apparently, he didn't remember their meeting place just a few days ago. "Nothing. Why are we here?" she asked.

"Why are you here? What do you want to see the mayor about?" There was an earnest expression on his face. "What do you know?"

"I'm here to ask Mary questions. Does that sound like I know anything?"

"Questions about the Worths or about Worthington Securities?"

"It sounds like you know more than I do."

Tom Davidson looked uncomfortable. "This story could make my career."

"And you don't want anyone to know what is happening before you do," Susan guessed.

"Yes, but . . ."

"But?"

"Mayor Pierson refuses to talk to the press. You called her Mary. Do you know her well?"

"Not well." She watched his face fall. "We were class mothers together years and years ago."

"That's wonderful. She'll talk to you. Let me tell you what I need to know."

"I have questions myself. . . ."

"Maybe they're the same as mine. Mine are right here. Where are yours?" Tom pulled a printed sheet from his jacket pocket. Susan could see it was a numbered list of questions.

"In my head," she answered, not admitting that they were, as yet, completely unformed.

He glanced at her messy hair and seemed about to say

something, but apparently, changed his mind. "Maybe you would just look at my questions."

She accepted his list. His first question came as such a surprise that she didn't read further. "The town has money invested in Worthington Securities?"

"You didn't know that?"

"I heard that Mary and some of the council members had invested money with Scott," she answered.

"I don't know about that, but there is a lot of public money invested in Worthington Securities."

"Is that legal?"

"Of course it is. Did you think cities, municipalities, and various governments kept their funds in the bank getting three percent interest? That would be like stashing it in a shoe box in the back of the closet."

"I never thought about it, frankly."

"You don't go to town council meetings?"

"Sometimes."

"And doesn't the treasurer read a financial report?"

"To tell the truth, I don't listen. In fact, I don't even know who the town treasurer is."

Tom Davidson glanced down at his notes. "Someone called Edgar Finch."

"You're kidding. Edgar runs the financial affairs down at the Club—and he's treasurer of Hancock as well?"

"What club?"

"The Hancock Field Club."

"Oh, that country club down by the water. . . . That's probably not significant here."

He sounded so unimpressed that Susan decided not to enlighten him further. "So Edgar invested the town's assets. . . . How does a town get assets anyway?"

"Are you telling me that you don't pay high property taxes?"

"Monstrous," she answered. "And they get higher all the time. When we moved in the taxes seemed reasonable, but for the past ten years or so . . ." She recognized the impatient expression on Tom's face and returned to the original subject. "So Edgar Finch invested the town's tax receipts in Worthington Securities—surely not all of the money."

"No, not all of it." Tom pulled another sheet of paper from his pocket and thrust it at her. It turned out to be a current statement of the town's financial situation. Susan studied it long enough to realize it made little sense to her—except she could see that millions had been turned over to Scott Worth. "How long has this been true? How long has all this money been invested like this?"

"I'm not sure. Financial records have to be public, of course, but it would take a fair amount of time to dig up that information. I was hoping to ask a few questions and find out a bit more about that or . . ."

"Or what?"

"Or you could ask for me."

"Why would I want to do that?"

"Because it's more efficient. You talk to the mayor—your buddy—and I'll go see Edgar Finch. I have an appointment with him in about ten minutes. I hope I make it in time." He stood up. "How about it? I'll ask my questions. You ask—" He glanced at the lists he still held. "—and you ask my questions. Then we'll meet and compare notes."

"When do you want to meet?"

"About an hour. That will give us both plenty of time."

"Where?" she asked, preceding him out of the room.

"The . . ." Tom started down the hall while speaking and she missed his words.

"Where?"

"The Nutmeg Motel. One hour." His words echoed down the hallway behind him.

"You must be kidding," Susan said to an empty hallway.

At least she'd thought it was empty . . . "Susan, you're meeting that hunky young man at the Nutmeg? Good for you!"

Susan turned and found Mary Pierson walking toward her. Mary's hair was a richer shade of brown than she recalled, her eyes were larger, and her skin had fewer wrinkles than Susan remembered. She looked wonderful, better—and younger—than she had years ago. "I'm not . . . we're not meeting at the motel for . . . for sex," Susan explained with an awkward chuckle.

"I doubt if anyone meets at the Nutmeg for the ambience— or the food, but feel free to keep your secret if you wish. Unless you're telling the truth, then maybe you'd like to introduce me to him, too."

"He's Tom Davidson. He's a reporter and your secretary just refused to let him in to see you."

"My secretary turned him down? The girl must be nuts." Mary shrugged silk-clad shoulders. "That's the trouble with volunteers—they're impossible to fire."

"Your secretary is a volunteer?"

"She's a vacation substitute and an intern—which is the same thing. Maybe you know her—Lissa Bradley—she went to school with our girls."

"I don't remember her, but that doesn't mean anything," Susan said, remembering Pixie.

"Why are you here?"

"I wanted to see you. To ask you something." Susan suddenly remembered that Mary Pierson was as smart as she was attractive. The mayor's eyes narrowed and she was silent for a moment. "Come into my office," she suggested, turning and walking down the hallway, her elegant Manolo Blahnik pumps clicking on the tile floor. She looked, Susan thought, more like the senior editor of a major fashion magazine than the mayor of a suburb of New York City. The office she followed her into fit the fashion image.

Charcoal wall-to-wall carpeting created a neutral background for luxurious raw silk upholstered pieces surrounding an elegant inlaid desk that could only be Louis XVI— Susan could have sworn she'd seen a similar piece on a tour of Versailles a few summers ago.

"Sit down." Mary pointed to a seat in front of the desk as she slid into her own comfortable chair.

Susan sat. "This is very impressive."

"Thanks."

"It must have cost a fortune. Did you use a local decorator?"

"Heavens no. I did it myself. I'd never use a decorator. A complete waste of money."

Susan happened to have heard the rumor that a famous— and expensive—New York decorator had spent months working on the Piersons' house, but she wasn't here to alienate the mayor.

"But you're not here to talk about decorating. . . ."

"I am, in a way."

Mary was obviously startled. "You want to talk about decorating?"

"No, about money. The town's money. Not yours," she hastened to add. In Hancock, money wasn't talked about; it was displayed by purchasing the right cars to place in the driveways of perfect and luxurious homes, by buying designer clothes and wearing them to French restaurants where high-priced food was accompanied by astronomically expensive wines, by going on vacations abroad or to chic spas at home.

Mary leaned back in her chair, crossed her legs, picked up a pen and began to tap it on the Prada notebook centered on her desktop. "What about it?"

"Well, where it goes, where it's invested. Who makes the decisions."

"We have a treasurer. Edgar Finch. I assume you know him." There was no mistaking the coolness in her voice.

"Yes, of course. I was just at his house yesterday. . . ."

"And you don't believe what Edgar told you?"

"I—no, you don't understand. Of course I would believe whatever he told me. I'm not suggesting that he's not honest," Susan said, while wondering if it were true. "But I didn't know he was Hancock's treasurer when I was there," she explained, hoping Mary wouldn't want to know why she had been at his house. Her wish was granted. Mary—as self-centered as Susan remembered her being—was interested in only one thing: herself.

"I'm afraid I don't know why you're here. I'm the mayor, not the town's financial expert."

"I know that, but . . . but everyone knows how thorough you are. How you always keep your finger on what's going on. You're known to be superresponsible." Flattery, Susan hoped, would get her somewhere.

Not this time. Mary Pierson was becoming less friendly as every moment passed. "Susan, I'm afraid I don't see why you're here. All Hancock's financial dealings are reported

biannually. Now, if you have trouble reading financial statements, I suggest you find someone who has more time than I
do to help you out."

Susan tried to think of something to say that would keep
Mary interested. "I . . . I was talking with Erika."

The frown on Mary's face deepened in a way her plastic
surgeon wouldn't have appreciated.

"And she said that Brett . . ."

The frown vanished. "Brett Fortesque? Chief Fortesque?"

"Yes. Erika and he . . ." The frown was back. "They've
been dating for years and she says . . ." How could she get
out of this? She had just promised Erika she wouldn't let
anyone know about the investigation of Scott's company and
here she was babbling on and on.

"You aren't here to talk about a silly flirtation between
Brett and some woman."

"No, of course not. I wanted to ask about the money
Hancock has invested in Worthington Securities and the investigation of Worthington Securities—"

"What investigation?"

Susan hadn't seen this woman so upset since a seven-
year-old boy had rested his head on her shoulder during a
particularly bumpy bus ride at the end of a long class trip
and proceeded to throw up in her Anne Klein–clad lap.
"Well, I heard that Scott Worth is being investigated. . . ."

"For Amanda's murder?"

"I don't think so. Scott was in New York City when his
wife was killed. There were lots of witnesses. He couldn't
be the murderer." She wondered briefly how many times she
had said this.

"I suppose that's too bad. It would save a lot of people a
lot of trouble." She looked at Susan, apparently having re-

gained some self-control. "Not that we have a problem. I would call this more of a situation. Yes, that's what I would call it. A situation."

"Mary, you're talking to me as though I'm reporting for *60 Minutes*." Susan decided to ignore the list of questions crumpled up in her pocket.

Mary took a deep breath and leaned across her desk. "How well do you know Scott Worth?"

"I . . ."

"I heard you were hosting the reception following Amanda's funeral."

"Not actually . . ."

"He wouldn't have asked you to do that if you weren't close."

"That's not true. In fact, I'm not quite sure how I ended up doing it," Susan admitted.

"Has he invested money for you?"

"No. I didn't even know about Worthington Securities until recently. Honestly!" She added the last word when Mary looked skeptical.

"But you've known the Worths for a long time. . . ."

"I knew Scott was involved in the stock market in some way, but not what he did specifically. Like I know your husband is a doctor, but I don't know what his speciality is."

"Pediatric surgeon."

"Oh, I didn't know. . . . Well, that's the point, isn't it? I have a lot of women friends, but I don't know that much about their husbands. And I doubt if Jed and I would invest with a friend anyway. We have our assets in Goldman Sachs." She hoped she sounded as though they were a major client of that company with a couple of million to invest. "Anyway, not knowing what Scott did isn't at all unusual."

She suddenly realized she was doing all the talking. "How long have you known about Worthington Securities?"

"Since I was elected mayor. I—the money was invested before I attained office. No one can blame me for this, Susan, no one."

"I don't think anyone is blaming you for anything."

"Then what is going on? Reporters are calling. And Brett won't return my calls."

"Perhaps he's just too busy with Amanda's murder and all." Susan was trying to pacify Mary, apparently unsuccessfully.

"Damn that Amanda! If she weren't dead, I'd kill her myself."

Susan was shocked, but not too shocked to ask the obvious question. "Why?"

"She really screwed everything up for this town."

"How? By dying?"

"No, the dying was fine. But her timing was rotten. She should have died before she could prevent Once In a Blue Moon from being built within the town's boundaries."

Susan was astounded. "Mary, you campaigned against that mall coming to Hancock. You thought it would ruin our small-town character."

"No, I didn't think that at all. I didn't give a damn one way or another, to be frank. But it was a hot issue. I couldn't ignore it and I thought I'd get the most votes if I came out against it—and I did."

"It worked. You were elected."

"Yes. But what I didn't know is that I ran against a candidate who knew a hell of a lot more about the situation than I did."

"I have no idea what you're talking about."

"It's a long gruesome story, but I can leave out the dry details and vicious personalities if you're interested."

"Please."

"First, I don't know if Scott has been breaking the law or what's wrong with Worthington Securities, but that doesn't matter. All that matters is that in a decade where it's almost impossible to lose money in the stock market, Worthington Securities is rumored to be losing money and lots of it. And that sometime—around five or six years ago as I recall—a large portion of Hancock's assets were invested in Worthington Securities."

"Do you know who made that decision?"

"No. But if you're interested, you can spend some time looking at our financial statements. What you'll learn is that investing money in town businesses or citizens' interests isn't an exception. And it's a practice that has worked damn well as a matter of fact. Until now." Mary frowned.

"What does this have to do with the mall, or Amanda?"

"Once in a Blue Moon mall was going to be a lifesaver. The taxes in the first year after it was built would have compensated for much of what may have been lost in Worthington Securities."

"And Amanda?"

"Amanda? You know 'don't get it for me wholesale Amanda'—she campaigned so efficiently against the mall that to vote for anyone who supported it was pretty much voting against your own place in Hancock society. If it hadn't been for Amanda, Hancock would be solvent by this time next year. Of course, if it hadn't been for her husband and his stupid fund, Hancock's solvency wouldn't be in doubt."

TWENTY-THREE

$\int$USAN LEFT THE MUNICIPAL BUILDING AMAZED BY ALL SHE
had learned—and late for her appointment with Tom Davidson at the Nutmeg Motel. There was a lot of traffic on the
road but, apparently, none of it shared her destination. Only
two cars stood in front of the Nutmeg's coffee shop. Susan
parked next to the one with the New York plates and walked
to the door.

Tom Davidson was waiting for her in a booth at the back
of the room. She hurried over to him and slid on to the
bench across from him.

"Did you find out anything?" he asked, not bothering to
greet her.

"Yes. What about you?"

"Well, Edgar just left. . . ."

"He ate here?" She looked around at the tacky plastic
furnishing, the tattered and hideous wallpaper which she
had thought was improbably decorated with rats until, on
closer examination, the animals turned out to be badly
drawn chipmunks. She couldn't imagine the impeccable Edgar Finch here.

"He didn't actually eat. He ordered tea. With boiled bottled
water. When they brought it—in a small metal pitcher—he

threw away the bag the waitress brought and got out his own. Chamomile from France. I think he took two sips before deciding the water was from a tap. No, I don't think you could say that he actually ate here."

"But you have," Susan said, seeing the pile of plates pushed up against the standard collection of condiments and a Test Your IQ game.

"Pie and coffee. The pie's pretty good. Especially the homemade lemon meringue and blueberry."

"I'll have coffee and a piece of lemon meringue pie," Susan told the waitress who had appeared at their table.

"Cream?"

"No, thanks."

"What did you find out?"

"You won't believe it."

"Tell me everything," he ordered, pulling a notebook from his jacket pocket.

"Well, you know Amanda Worth didn't want the new mall located within Hancock's city limits. . . ."

"The mall where she was murdered? Does that have something to do with this?"

"Maybe. What would you think if I told you that the taxes from that mall would have made up for the losses from Worthington Securities?"

"That's interesting. You're saying the Worths screwed Hancock twice, so to speak."

"I . . . I guess." Susan looked doubtfully at the gummy concoction the waitress had just placed on the table before her. If this pie was homemade, it had been made in the home of someone who had bought a mix.

"Are you talking about the woman who was murdered at the mall?" their waitress asked enthusiastically.

"Yes."

"All of our customers have been talking about her."

Susan couldn't resist glancing around at the empty tables and booths.

"Oh, we never have a crowd for lunch. Mostly our customers come for breakfast and dinner. Do you want more iced tea?" she asked, noticing Tom's empty glass.

"Please."

"I'll be right back."

"Customers? There aren't any customers here," Susan commented. "And I don't think there are ever. At least, I never see their cars when I drive by."

Tom picked up the corner of a faded denim café curtain and pointed through a flyspecked windowpane. "Out there."

Susan stretched her neck to peer through the filthy glass—at about a dozen cars. "You're kidding. Why is everyone parked out back?" she asked before the obvious answer occurred to her. "Does everyone in town come here to have affairs?"

Tom counted the cars out loud. "Eleven. And how many people live in Hancock? About eighteen thousand? No, I think we can safely conclude that some of the affairs indulged in in your fair city take place at other locations. But the Nutmeg Motel does seem to be popular, doesn't it? I take it you didn't know about this place?"

"I had no idea." She plunged her fork into her pie and popped the end triangle in her mouth. She had been right—a mix, but a good one, she decided. "I feel a bit like a fool not knowing," she admitted, chewing and talking at the same time.

"Why?"

"Frankly, I like to think I know what's going on in Hancock."

"But you're finding out that you're just like everyone else," he suggested.

"What do you mean?"

"You only know your own bit of the world."

"I guess," Susan agreed reluctantly.

"It's like me and Bloomingdale's," he said, nodding at the waitress who had brought him more tea.

"What do you mean?"

"I'm subletting a place right around the corner from Bloomingdale's, but I'm not a shopper. I've never been in the place."

"You're saying that proximity and familiarity are two different things."

"Got it."

Susan looked around the small café and took another bite of her pie. "Guess I'm in no position to argue with you about that."

"Where's the list?"

"The list? Oh, you mean your list of questions?"

"You were going to ask those questions to your friend the mayor."

"That's what I was starting to tell you about."

"You said Amanda was one of the reasons that Once in a Blue Moon ended up out on the highway. And that tax money from that would have made up some of the losses of Worthington Securities."

"Exactly. What did you learn?" Susan asked him, hoping to head off any more questions—questions she couldn't answer.

"That's all you learned? What about the rest of my questions? Did you find out if the Worths supported the mayor during her campaign for office? And who appointed the finance committee? And what sort of—"

"I didn't ask your questions. I—Mary was too busy to spend more time with me. Tell me what Edgar told you," she added quickly before he started to complain about her research.

"That man's had a lot of practice dealing with the press. He talked and talked and told me almost nothing."

"Oh."

"But he's worried. He couldn't hide it from me."

"About the money?"

"You know, I don't think so. . . . I think I made a mistake there," he added almost to himself.

"What did you do?"

"I asked him a bunch of general, nonthreatening questions. It's a well-known interviewing technique. And he was talking happily—and fussing with that damn cup of tea—about himself and his time in Hancock and his house. You know that his house is famous, don't you? There's actually an architect's model in the collection of the Museum of Modern Art in New York."

"That's what I've heard. What did you talk about besides his house?"

"Not much. I thought I had him relaxed. You know, feeling comfortable with me. Then I asked him about Worthington Securities and, well, it was almost like I had accused him of Amanda Worth's murder. He really overreacted."

"What did he do?"

"He accused me of hounding him."

"I thought you'd never met him before."

"Well, apparently other members of the New York City press corps have been calling him and leaving messages."

Susan tried not to smile. Tom Davidson was so obviously thrilled to be a member of this illustrious group. "And what happened then?"

"He got up and left without another word. No, that's not right. He actually said something about you."

"About me? What?"

"He said that if I wanted to find out who killed Amanda Worth I should ask some of the . . . the . . . ah, nosy women in town. Like you," Tom added reluctantly.

"He mentioned me by name?"

"Yes."

"And he said I was nosy."

"Yes."

"And then what?"

"Then he walked out the door, got in his car, and drove off."

"Was he angry?"

"Yes. I got the impression he was angry before I asked him anything at all. I mean, he was upset when the water wasn't boiled the way he liked it."

"Isn't water either boiling or not boiling?"

Tom shrugged. "Don't ask me. You're the one with the reputation as a gourmet cook."

"A nosy gourmet cook," Susan said ruefully.

"So who killed her?"

"I have no idea."

"Then why would Edgar Finch say you do?"

Susan frowned. "I don't know. I can't imagine him saying something like that if he didn't believe it."

"So he believes you know who killed Amanda."

"But I don't."

"Then maybe the question is why does he think you do. Mrs. Henshaw, what does he think you know?"

"I haven't the foggiest."

"How well do you know him?"

"Not very. In fact, I was in his home for the first time yesterday."

"And has he been in your house?"

"Sure. We've invited him to parties and he's come. In return he gives dinners at the Club and invites us. Edgar is very active at the Club. . . ."

"The country club."

"The Field Club. Edgar is on the finance committee there. And Jed's on the membership committee and has access to the finance committee notes this year." She looked up at Tom. "You see, the other day, I was at Jed's desk and there was this folder with the financial records of members of the Field Club. And I read them. Scott Worth is behind with his dues—years behind. And he's the only member of the Club who has been allowed to get so far behind. When I talked to Jed about it, he explained that Edgar is in charge of those things—that it is Edgar's decision to allow someone to retain their membership if they don't pay their dues. That's why I went to see him, in fact."

"And why would knowing that the Worths weren't paying their dues indicate the identity of Amanda's murderer?"

Susan polished off the last of her pie as she considered the question. "It doesn't. At least as far as I can tell. But I have an idea."

"What?"

"Why don't we ask him who the murderer is."

"He says he doesn't know."

"Then why does he think that I do?"

"I don't know. But he seemed pretty sure of his statement." Tom hesitated. "You know, it's possible you're not safe. If you know the identity of the murderer—even if you don't know you know—the person who killed Amanda could come after you. To protect his—or her—own identity."

For the sake of his career, Susan hoped Tom Davidson wrote more clearly than he spoke. "So . . ."

"But if I knew what you know . . ."

"But—you want to see the Club's financial records?"

"To protect you—" His serious expression turned into a charming grin. "—and to get the story, of course."

"Fine. But if you run into Jed, you have to promise not to tell him about it."

"No problem." He reached in his pocket and pulled out some money, which he tossed on the table.

"I should pay . . ."

"No way. You're a source. The station can pick up the entire tab."

They were on their way out of the restaurant as Brett Fortesque was entering it.

"Hi, Brett." Susan's greeting was enthusiastic.

"Huh, Susan." His response was not.

"Brett, this is—" She began to introduce Tom, but Brett interrupted.

"I'm in a hurry right now," he said. "I'll talk with you later."

"I . . . Fine."

Why would Brett be at the Nutmeg Hotel?

TWENTY-FOUR

"There are other people on this list. The Worths aren't the only members who are behind with their dues."

"They're the most behind, but there are reasons for the others. Illness, death of a family member. Some personal crisis."

"Maybe Scott killed his wife so he wouldn't have to pay dues at the country club?"

"He didn't pay while she was alive, so I doubt it."

"Do you want some coffee? Or something to eat?" They were sitting on the couch in Jed's study. Tom was going through the Club's papers. Susan was trying desperately to keep them in some sort of order so Jed wouldn't have a fit the next time he opened his desk.

"Sure. But I'd rather have a Coke than coffee."

"Diet?"

"If it's all there is."

Susan went off to the kitchen to get them something to eat as he continued his search. She realized he firmly believed himself capable of picking out clues she had missed, but Susan was doubtful. She took the dog for a quick run around the backyard and returned to the kitchen to get their snack.

When she entered Jed's study, she was carrying a tray

with two Diet Cokes, a bowl of potato chips, olives, water crackers, and a slab of Brie. Tom Davidson was sitting at Jed's desk writing furiously in his notebook.

"You figured it out?"

"No, I was working on possible leads for my article about all this. Once all the facts are known, there will be a big rush to get the story in on time."

"Really?" One of the most appealing things about this young man was his enthusiasm for his work. Susan was beginning to realize that it could also be one of the most irritating. But the phone rang and she had no time to say anything more.

"Hello? I . . . Sure, I . . . Well, I . . . Right away." She hung up, looked at Tom, and made a decision. "If I tell you what that call was about you have to promise me you won't publish a word until Brett says you can." As soon as the words were out of her mouth, she realized her mistake. Mentioning the chief of police was a red flag—one an enthusiastic young journalist couldn't ignore.

"What's happened?"

"You have to promise."

"Okay. I promise."

"There's been another murder."

"A mur—Who? When? Where's the body?"

He must have done well in his elementary journalism class, Susan decided. "You promised you wouldn't write anything until Brett says it's okay," she reminded him.

"I won't. You can trust me."

Susan wasn't quite so sure, but she didn't have a lot of choice. Brett had called and asked her to come back to the Nutmeg Motel. If she drove over there alone, Tom was sure to follow, get some information, and do with it what he wanted.

If they stayed together, maybe, just maybe, she could prevent him from filing a story. "Then let's go," she said reluctantly.

"I'll drive . . . If you'll tell me where we're going."

"Back to the Nutmeg Motel," Susan said. "Brett is waiting for me in room eleven."

"The Nutmeg Motel. A murder took place at the Nutmeg Motel while this reporter was speaking with an unidentified witness—or do you want to be identified?" he interrupted his own muttering to ask her.

"I just want to get to the Nutmeg as fast as possible," she answered.

Never again, she decided, would she tell anyone under the age of thirty that she wanted to get someplace as quickly as possible. She was still gasping for breath as Tom Davidson turned into the parking lot.

As at Once in a Blue Moon, spaces were at a premium. Here, however, a young policeman recognized Susan and waved the car she was in to an open spot by the front door.

"Chief Fortesque is waiting for you, ma'am," the young man said, peering at her driver. "Room twelve."

"I thought," Susan began, getting out of the car. "I thought he said eleven."

"Body's in eleven. Chief Fortesque is in twelve—Excuse me, sir, but who are you?"

"Press."

"Press are in the luncheonette. The chief will make a statement ASAP."

"Susan—" Tom began.

"Tom, I promise I'll get Brett to talk to you before everyone else." Without waiting for a reply, Susan turned and, feeling guilty, but not too guilty, took off in the direction the young officer had indicated.

They had parked next to the flickering neon OFFICE sign. The motel units seemed to be numbered starting there. Susan walked down the covered cement sidewalk, past more police officers, past room number eleven, and stopped right outside number twelve. The door was closed and she was reluctant to knock. The drive here had been short and her main concern had been whether or not Tom Davidson would keep his car on the road. Now, for the first time, she wondered who had been killed. And why Brett had called her. And not someone else.

She might have stood there longer if the door hadn't opened and Brett walked out the door.

"Susan, you're here."

"Yes—" She didn't have time to say anything else as he pulled her through the door.

"Are you alone?"

"Brett . . ."

"Susan, thanks for coming right away. The press are going to have a field day with this. I don't want anything to get out before we know the entire story. What are you looking at?"

"This room. It's hideous."

"Really? I'm told many of the patrons consider it—what's the expression? Grungy chic?"

"Shabby chic," she corrected him. "But I think this is just worn-out and junky."

The color scheme was gold and avocado and probably had benefited from years of fading and ground in dirt—the effect, at least, was muted. The carpet was spotted brown. Glitter was embedded in the ceiling's acoustic tiles. The lumpy double bed sagged in the middle. The lamps were amazing:

those on nightstands were decorated with gilded horses apparently racing around globe-shaped china. Over a broken table hung the pièce de résistance—a humongous plastic imitation lightbulb that would have given Thomas Edison nightmares.

"It's awful," she said.

"Wait until you see it covered with blood."

Susan immediately returned to the situation at hand. "Who died? Why did you call me here?" She started to speak the one word she didn't want to hear. "Je—"

"Oh, Susan, I'm sorry. Jed's fine. Your family is fine. I don't even know if you're acquainted with the dead . . . the dead person. But your name was . . . was nearby."

Susan sighed. "That's good to know. I had thought—You don't know the identity of the victim?"

"Well, we thought we knew, but things have come to our attention that . . . well, we don't really know the victim's identity. No."

"I don't understand what you're saying. Did you call me here to identify the body?"

"No. The body belongs to someone called Crystal."

"Crystal? The psychic?"

"Susan, do you go to psychics?"

"Not usually, but I saw Crystal yesterday."

"You're kidding. Does every woman in this town waste money on psychics?"

"I didn't go to her to talk about myself. I went because Amanda was one of her clients." She looked down at the floor. "I'm . . . uh, looking into Amanda's death . . . just a bit."

"You don't believe people have psychic powers then?"

Susan looked up, glad to discover that Brett didn't seem

to mind her investigation. "I really don't, no." Then she remembered Erika. "I know an awful lot of smart people who believe in psychics and consult them regularly. I've even heard that police departments—"

"Use psychics to find missing people. Yeah, I watch the news, too, Susan. And all I can say is if these psychics are so good how come so many people are missing?"

"I spoke with Erika yesterday, too," Susan said. "She told me how you feel about this."

"I think they're con men—or women—who bamboozle people into parting with their money for no good reason at all. And I'm not the only person. I've been getting calls about this Crystal person for years."

"From whom?"

"Mainly husbands—generally they're angry that their wives are wasting money going to Crystal for advice. But we can't do a damn thing about that. Although there was a mother who called concerned about Crystal's influence on her daughter. I thought maybe we had something there, but it turned out the daughter was in her early thirties; she could do whatever she wanted with her own money, no matter how foolish."

"You mean there are people who believe it's criminal to claim to be a psychic?"

"There are lots of people who think so. But it is a felony to manipulate people for your own personal gain."

"Really?"

"Sure. But again it's almost impossible to prove."

Susan thought for a moment. "Is Crystal the only psychic you get complaints about?"

"Nope. But I think Crystal may be the only one who . . . who claims to be able to predict the future out of a Hancock location."

"That tea shop."

"Yes."

"Did any of those complaints come from Scott Worth?"

"I can't name names, but . . . well, no. I wouldn't even have known that Amanda sought advice from a psychic if you hadn't just mentioned it."

"Do you think the two women's deaths are related?" Susan asked quietly.

"Two . . . oh, you mean Amanda Scott and this Crystal person."

"Who else?"

"I'm sorry, Susan. It's just that I know something apparently you don't know."

"What?"

"Crystal is—was—a man."

TWENTY-FIVE

"CRYSTAL WAS ... A TRANSVESTITE? A DRAG QUEEN? What?"

"I have no idea, but she definitely is a he." Brett put a hand gently on her arm. "Susan, would you mind taking a quick look in the room next door? My men have covered up the body, but ... well, I think this is something you should see."

"Without telling me what I'm supposed to be looking at."

"Exactly. I have to warn you—it's bloody, Susan. He was shot twice and one bullet went through an artery in his neck."

"Then let's get it over with," she said, starting toward the door.

"We can go through this way," Brett suggested, pointing to a door she hadn't noticed before. "These are connecting rooms."

Susan walked through the door he held open and stopped, gasping.

Brett grabbed her shoulders firmly, but gently. "Are you all right?"

"I ..." She didn't know what to say. There was blood everywhere—literally everywhere, even splashed on the ceiling. Mercifully, a large canvas sheet covered what must have been the remains of Crystal lying on the floor. She was ready to leave and had taken a step backward when she noticed her name—written on the flyspecked mirror over the particleboard dresser. "Is that . . . Is it blood?"

"Lipstick."

"I don't suppose you know who wrote it? I mean, the tube of lipstick wasn't found in her . . . in his hand?"

"No. In fact, we're pretty sure Crystal was already dead when it was written."

"How do you know that?"

"If you look closely, you'll see that there is blood underneath the writing." Brett noticed her looking down at the body, which lay between the doorway they stood in and the mirror. "No need for you to go inside. I just wanted you to see it." He pushed her gently and she backed from the room.

"You mean the murderer wrote it."

Brett nodded. "Probably."

"Why?"

"I can't think of a single good reason, Susan."

"Perhaps . . . perhaps it isn't my name. Maybe it refers to someone else named Susan."

"You may be right." Brett closed the connecting door behind them. "But you may be wrong and the murderer—who may have murdered Amanda as well as Crystal, remember—may be warning you to stay away from this one."

Susan closed her eyes for a moment, knowing the image of the room next door wasn't going to vanish any time soon. "You think I should just go home and forget all . . . all that?"

"It might be wise."

She took a deep breath and pushed her hair off her forehead. "I can't. Whatever the person who wrote that wanted to accomplish, he or she isn't going to keep me from getting involved in this—or staying involved in Amanda's murder investigation."

"I was hoping you'd say that. In fact, I was depending on it. My car is right outside."

"What do you want me to do?"

"I'd like you to go to Crystal's apartment with me."

Susan's eyes widened. "You're kidding. I'd love to. . . . How do you know where she . . . or he . . . lived?"

"The address on his driver's license."

"What . . . ?"

"Male," Brett said, anticipating her question. "And apparently his legal name really is Crystal."

"Someone named a baby boy Crystal?"

"He could have had his name changed legally. It only takes a few minutes and doesn't cost much money. Will you come with me?"

"Definitely. But, Brett, I came here with Tom Davidson. . . . That reporter from New York."

"I thought I recognized him earlier," Brett said. "You brought him back here?"

"Actually, he brought me. He was at the house when you called," she hastened to explain.

"Where is he now?"

"The police officer who directed me here insisted that he wait with the other reporters in the luncheonette."

Brett frowned. "Tell you what, I'll talk to him in private as soon as we get back. He'll be happy if he gets the information even a few minutes before the competition."

"That would be wonderful," Susan said, following Brett out of room twelve into surprisingly fresh air. "I didn't realize how stuffy it was in there," she commented.

"It's a dump. The windows don't open and I'll bet the air-conditioning hardly works. Why amorous couples choose to go there is beyond me. I . . ." He paused as he opened the door to the passenger seat of his police cruiser for her. "I gather you and Tom Davidson . . . ?"

Susan realized what he was asking. "Brett! I'd never be unfaithful to Jed. You know that."

"I'm a police officer. What I know is that the most unlikely people do the most unlikely things. And sometimes they get caught, and most of the time they don't. What I'm saying is that I would never, ever swear that I know what someone will or won't do."

"Well, I never set foot in the Nutmeg Motel until after Amanda was killed. . . ."

"And why is that?"

"Because it's a dump—oh, you mean what does Amanda's murder have to do with the motel."

"Exactly."

"I heard she was having an affair with someone there—well, that's not exactly what I heard."

"Tell me," Brett ordered, starting the car.

Susan explained what Lauren had told her just a few days ago.

"She didn't recognize the man?"

"No. I think she said—or I may have just gotten the impression—that she only saw the back of his head. Of course just because they were eating here doesn't mean that they were sleeping together."

"Susan, the food at the Nutmeg Motel is so bad that even the cops don't stop in for coffee."

"But that doesn't mean Amanda was having an affair. After all, as you said, no one goes there for the ambience. They

go because it's private. So, if Amanda wanted to meet someone in private, the Nutmeg is one of the best places in town."

"Good thinking," Brett agreed.

Susan peered out the window. "Are we heading downtown?"

"Yes. I don't recognize the address, but I think it's in the
same block as the drugstore."

"What are you expecting to find?"

"I don't know. I . . . well, I haven't been keeping track of
the investigation of Amanda's death. I've been worried
about other things frankly."

"The SEC's investigation of Scott?" The moment the words
were out of her mouth, she regretted them.

But Brett didn't seem interested in how—or that—she
knew about it. "Exactly. Not only didn't the murder happen
in Hancock, but we've had a hard time keeping the press
from annoying Scott Worth—not that he doesn't have a lot
to be annoyed about. And now this." He shook his head as
he pulled his car into an empty spot directly underneath a
NO PARKING sign. "I don't know how our payroll is going to
stretch to meet all the needed overtime."

"I guess the problems at Worthington Securities aren't
helping."

"True. And if Worthington Securities fails . . . well, it
won't be the first time a municipality has been forced to declare bankruptcy, but the implications are enormous. The
school system alone . . . Well, this isn't the time or place to
worry about that." He looked down at the index card he'd
pulled from the pocket of his uniform. "It's 77½ South Main
Street. Right up there." He pointed to second-floor windows
above street-level shops.

"How do we get up?"

"There should be a door here somewhere . . . Here it is."

Susan noticed the dark green painted metal door for the first time. "You know," she said, as Brett pulled it open and they entered a small dark foyer with a stairway leading upward, "I had no idea there were apartments here."

"There are apartments tucked away all over Hancock. They're an economic necessity."

"What do you mean?"

"Do you think the golf pro down at the Club can afford to live in one of those new condos on the river or to buy a home in town?"

"I guess not."

"Well, if he lives in town he probably lives someplace similar to this—or in an illegal apartment on one of the larger estates. Most of my officers can't afford to live anywhere around here."

"I guess," Susan said, mounting the stairs slowly. There had been four wall-mounted mailboxes in the foyer. C. STAR had been printed in number three. "How are we going to get in?"

Brett held out his hand.

"Keys. How did you get keys?"

"They were in Crystal's purse. I thought, under the circumstances . . ."

"Is this legal?"

"It will be once I get a court order."

She decided to shut up.

It took only a few minutes for Brett to choose the correct key and unlock the door. Susan took a deep breath and followed him in, not knowing what she might find.

It certainly wasn't the charming apartment she found herself in. "This is amazing," she said as Brett closed the door behind them.

"What were you expecting?"

"I don't know," she answered, looking around.

They stood in a large living room with an old Oriental carpet on a parquet floor. The furniture was well worn, but attractive. Prints hung on the walls between three windows that looked out on the street below. There was a Pullman kitchen at one end of the room. A doorway at the other presumably led to the bedroom. Susan headed to the kitchen, Brett in the opposite direction.

Crystal hadn't been much of a cook, she decided, peeking in the refrigerator and opening cupboards and drawers. Prepackaged meals filled the freezer and microwave dishes seemed the best-used utensils. There was a good selection of single malt Scotch and a couple of bottles of gin, but nothing else of note. She headed to the bedroom.

The room was dominated by a king-size bed and a big screen TV. Susan glanced at the shelves of videos, most of which were various sporting events and movies of the cops-car chase variety. For a man who made a living predicting the future while wearing women's clothing, Crystal seemed to lead a remarkably ordinary life. She walked over and looked in the drawer of his nightstand, left open, apparently by Brett. It was almost empty except for a package of tissues and an unopened bottle of Tylenol.

"Brett?"

"Here. In the closet."

Susan followed the sound of his voice through another door and into what turned out to be a good-sized walk-in closet.

"Not bad for an apartment," he commented.

"Are you kidding? This closet is as big as the first place

Jed and I rented after we were married. It's damn near as large as Amanda Worth's closet."

Brett was looking into the toes of the large women's shoes lining the floor almost around the entire room. Susan started going through the clothing. It seemed to be divided into three sections. The women's clothing that Crystal wore for work—exotic, colorful, dramatic, was the largest group, filling two-thirds of the space allotted for things on hangers. Then there was casual clothing—jeans, shirts, sweaters, and the like. Although appropriate for a woman, a man could wear anything here without feeling effeminate. Susan wondered if, perhaps, Crystal had a life as a man and wore this clothing then. The other group was made up of fewer than a half dozen items—women's clothing like any woman wore—any exceedingly large woman.

Susan opened a long cupboard running around the top of the room and found six brightly colored wigs on their stands. She frowned. "You know what? I'll bet the wigs and exotic clothes and makeup were put on so that no one would ever guess Crystal was a man."

"It's possible." Brett didn't sound very interested.

"But there is something else. Crystal didn't have to dress up like a woman. He could put on other clothing and resume a male role. He could, in fact, have been the man that Lauren saw with Amanda at the Nutmeg Motel."

TWENTY-SIX

BRETT WAS LOCKING UP CRYSTAL'S APARTMENT WHEN Susan realized they were being watched. "Brett." She stabbed him in the back with her fingernail as she spoke.

"What?"

"Shhh. There's someone looking out the door over there . . . Oh, my goodness, it's . . ." She snapped her mouth shut. Damn! Why was she so bad at names? It was Kathleen's cleaning woman, the sister of the man who owned that wonderful restaurant they'd eaten at the day Amanda was killed. "It's . . ."

"It's Mrs. Henshaw. Yes?" The words came through the half-closed door.

"Brett, this is . . ."

"Carla. You may call me Carla," she introduced herself, opening the door and coming out into the hallway. "I see you and wonder if something is wrong with Crystal. If there is something I can do to help."

"Do you know Crystal well?" Brett asked in his best police officer voice.

"We neighbors for many years." Carla pursed her lips and Susan realized she wasn't going to say much more. "Why you here? Has something happened to Crystal?"

"Crystal's dead," Brett answered bluntly.

"There was a car accident?"

"We think Crystal may have been murdered," Susan said, trying to be gentle. Brett had not hinted at Crystal's sexual identity and she carefully followed suit. Brett's beeper went off, preventing him from saying anything more.

"I have to go right away," he announced.

"I . . ."

"Mrs. Henshaw need ride home?"

"Brett brought me here . . ."

"I take you. I pick up my daughter at high school in about one hour—she play forward on girls' basketball team—I drop Mrs. Henshaw off on way."

"Well, that settles everything," Brett said, apparently choosing to ignore the annoyed expression on Susan's face.

"I—"

"I'll call you." Brett interrupted Susan one last time before disappearing down the stairway to the street.

Susan glanced at Carla.

"If you not want to look more at Crystal's apartment, you come with me. We have coffee and snack."

"I—"

"And we talk about my good friend Crystal."

Susan hurried after Carla into an apartment that looked as though it had been decorated with rejects from El Toro Nero.

"You sit at table. I must stir while we talk."

Susan plopped herself down at the table, moving a geometry text and a pile of construction paper and crayons out of the way. "Smells good," she commented, realizing that Carla was making dinner.

"Chicken mole. I make once a week, put in microwave

plastics and my girls heat up for their own dinner when they come home."

"You have daughters?"

"Six girls. Fourteen. Fifteen. Sixteen. Seventeen. Nineteen. Twenty. The two oldest are away at college."

"Six children?" Susan hoped this apartment was larger than the one across the hall. "You and your husband must have your hands full."

"My husband gone. He left over a dozen years ago. He wanted sons." Carla shrugged. "I raise my girls by myself."

"You're raising six children by cleaning homes?" Susan realized immediately how rude that sounded and started to apologize. But Carla didn't seem offended. In fact, her next words indicated pride in her accomplishments.

"We all work. I clean. My girls baby-sit and work either at El Toro or in one of stores downstairs on weekends and during summer. They all good girls and smart, too. The ones at college on full scholarship."

"That's wonderful!" Susan's enthusiasm was sincere.

Carla poured out a mug of coffee and passed it to Susan. "Now you tell me about my good friend Crystal."

"He was murdered, Carla. There really is no doubt about it."

"At that silly tea shop?"

"No, at a motel out on the highway. The Nutmeg Motel."

Carla continued to stir and Susan could only see her back. "When?"

"I'm not sure. This afternoon I guess." Susan paused. "You knew he was a man."

"Yes. I not know for always. But we good friends. He help me and I help him—you know when he sick and all. I find out that he man. I worry some—you know, my girls—there a lot of strange people out there. I can't risk them being hurt. But Crystal a good person. I don't know why he choose to dress as woman, but it not make him less good.

"You not go to Crystal?"

"No. I hadn't even heard of her—him—until a few days ago."

"I know you investigate murders."

"I have."

"You investigate Crystal's murder."

"Well, I'm actually trying to discover who killed Amanda Worth."

"You investigate Crystal's murder."

Susan was beginning to understand the strength of character that was raising six successful children in difficult circumstances. "I don't know anything about him. We just met yesterday for the first time." She had no intention of telling Carla about the writing on the mirror in the room where Crystal was killed.

"All you need to know about Crystal, I tell you. You find the person who killed Crystal."

"I don't know if—"

"You try."

Susan picked up her cup and took a sip of the dark chocolate-flavored beverage. "Yes. Okay. I'll do my best."

"His powers were real." Carla stopped stirring, turned the heat down to simmer, poured herself a cup of coffee, and sat down at the table across from Susan.

"You're saying he really was a psychic."

"Yes. He tell us he was born that way. Like you or I have brown hair. His power was that real."

"Had he always made a living as a psychic?"

"No. He was an actor. He even went to college to be one,

but that no way to make a living. He say not many people make living like that. He always tell my girls to go to college and learn something practical. And they listen. My Mellie going to be a doctor and Annie, she want to be a scientist. A scientist," she repeated.

"That's wonderful," Susan said sincerely. "But Crystal couldn't make a living as an actor?"

"No. Very hard job. And he say he always knew he must work to help people. If he cannot do that by making them happy with his acting talent, he do it by helping them to live their lives better."

"So he just put a sign in his window and offered to give psychic readings?" Susan was intrigued. How, in fact, did a beginning psychic find clients?

"No. He hired as an actor to tell fortunes—by a person who not believe in psychics, he say."

"In New York City?"

"Yes."

"At a restaurant?"

"No. For parties. People hire him to amuse their guests at their parties."

Susan nodded. "And that's how he started his career?"

"Yes. Crystal tell my daughters that you never know what sort of hike you go on when you make your first step."

"That's true. But he was . . . dressed like a man when he started."

"I don't know. I do know Crystal said most of the people whose fortunes he tell are women and they trust another woman more. That not surprise me."

"Me either. Did you know him before he came to Hancock?"

"No. I not know him when he first get here either."

"Were you living here then?"

"No. I move into my sister-in-law's apartment when I move here. And Crystal live with those Worths . . ."

"What?"

"He live in apartment over their garage."

"You're kidding."

"Mrs. Worth bring him to town and he live there until he move in here."

"Why did he leave the Worths?"

For the first time, Carla hesitated. "I not know. I got impression that maybe his being there not please Mr. Worth."

"Did the Worths—both of them—know that he was . . . well, was a he?"

"Mrs. Worth, she know. She come over here when he not wearing his hair. But I not know about Mr. Worth."

"Did they get along? Scott and Crystal?"

"I think . . . No, they not get along. Like Mr. and Mrs."

"You're saying that Amanda Worth and her husband didn't get along."

"They hate each other."

"Are you sure?"

"I sure. He—Mr. Worth—use his wife to get what he want. Crystal worried about her and say more than once that he would like to kill that man for the way he treat his friend."

"Did Crystal think Scott murdered his wife?"

For the first time in their conversation, Carla seemed to have trouble answering. "Crystal been very upset since Mrs. Worth's murder. He say he not see Mr. Worth as killer, but he think maybe Mr. Worth cause his wife's death. You not know him, but I do and I believe him."

Susan remembered Brooke's suggestion that Scott had hired a hit man to kill Amanda. "What did he mean?"

"He say Mr. Worth had put Amanda in what Crystal called 'a bad place'—a place where bad things can happen. He worried about it. He talk to me about it. He talk to Mrs. Worth about it. I know he talk to her, but he say she not listen, that she never listen when he warn her about the man she married."

"That's interesting. Carla, what was the relationship between Amanda Worth and Crystal?"

"I not know about Amanda, but I tell you about Crystal. He loved Amanda. He loved her for years, for always."

"Are you sure? Did he tell you that?"

"Yes. He say that over and over to me. And he always acted like a man in love when she was around."

"Amanda came here?" Susan hoped she didn't sound too surprised; she didn't want to be offensive.

"She here all the time. They very close. And . . . and he help her." Apparently the dinner needed more attention; Carla got up and resumed stirring.

"Carla . . ."

"I tell you things I should not tell anyone because you Mrs. Gordon's friend. I have much respect for Mrs. Gordon. She not born rich. She work as police officer. She good person."

Susan got the impression that she might not live up to the same standard, but she could only agree. "Kathleen is a wonderful person."

"And you will work hard to find out who kill Mrs. Worth and Crystal."

"Of course."

"So you need to know truth. Even if truth not so nice."

"Yes, I do."

Carla put down her spoon and resumed her seat. "I help Crystal in his work."

The change of topic caught Susan off guard. "How?"

"He need to know things about people."

Son of a gun! Susan made an effort to sound calm. "About the women who came to him for advice."

"Yes. I work for many people and I hear about even more. You need more coffee."

"No. No, I'm fine. Please go on. It could lead to the person who killed Crystal and I . . . I don't gossip—really." She knew she would have to tell Brett about this conversation, but she also knew he would be discreet.

"I cannot get work if people think I talk about them."

"But you did talk about them with Crystal."

"Yes. To help him."

"But you don't work for all that many people." Susan knew there was always a long list of people looking for a competent and honest cleaning woman, but still . . . even if Carla changed jobs a few times a year, how much help could she be to Crystal?

"But the people I work for know many people and I learn about them, too. Like I know you and what you do."

"And you passed that information on to Crystal so he could use it when he told them their fortunes."

"Yes. He not pay me. I do it to help out a friend. It's not easy being a single mother. Crystal help me with money, with baby-sitting, with being my very good friend."

Susan nodded. "I understand. And you wanted to do what you could in return."

"Yes. Exactly. I do what I can in return. I tell him what I know about the people who he talk to. And he use this to predict their future. Sometimes."

"And other times?"

"Other times I help Crystal help Mrs. Worth."

Susan leaned forward. This was getting more interesting every minute. "And how did you do that?"

Carla suddenly became shy, getting up and stirring the bubbling mixture on the stove, her face carefully hidden from Susan. She started with a question. "How well you know the Worths?"

"Apparently not as well as I thought I did."

"They always need money."

"That's one of the things I've learned since Amanda's death," Susan admitted.

"Amanda's husband want her to make money for him."

"I don't understand."

"I do not either. I have a small bank account. And I insist each of my girls have bank account. We have good home, food, my girls get education, do well in this country with many opportunities." She turned around and faced Susan again. "We busy and not eat together every night the way my family do when I growing up. But every Sunday we get up early, go to church, come home to meal at this table and I tell them same thing over and over. We are rich. We have what is important."

"You do and you are," Susan said sincerely.

"But I work for many people who not know what they have. They not know when they are rich. They have much, but they always want more. I think Scott Worth like that. He has that big house, fancy cars, job in city, but all he worry about, all he think about is money."

Susan refrained from explaining that worrying about money was what Scott did for a living, the same way Carla washed floors, but she understood what Carla was saying and remained quiet. "But Amanda didn't work for her husband. How did he expect her to make money for him?"

"He always need more and more money, more and more rich people to give it to him. Sometimes Amanda find those people. Sometimes I hear about them and tell Crystal who they are. And Crystal help convince them to give Scott Worth their money."

TWENTY-SEVEN

SUSAN LOOKED AROUND HER CLEAN KITCHEN. SHE HAD NO idea what to do first. Jed would be home in two hours, hungry and expecting something to eat. Clue, tail thumping, was looking at the back door with a pleading expression on her furry face. The light on the answering machine was flashing the number sixteen; sixteen messages would certainly take some time to deal with. She was exhausted. Crystal had been killed and what she had just learned at Carla's apartment might have something to do with it. She needed to call Brett. . . .

But first she'd see who was pounding on the front door. She left her kitchen and walked through the large hallway to the door. She always told people that she felt safe living in the suburbs. But what she found on her front stoop was a lesson: always look through the peephole before opening the door. The door wasn't even fully open when lights blinded her and she detected the whir of video cameras underneath questions shouted by complete strangers.

Clue proved her worth as a guard dog, dashing out the door and into the center of the group, barking joyously.

"Clue!" Susan screamed. There was more traffic in front of her house than she'd ever seen before; her dog could be killed.

"She has a clue! She knows who did it!"

"Listen, lady, tell us. I can get you on CNN. Tomorrow morning the whole world could be watching you talk on television with the lawyers who got O.J. Simpson off."

"Mrs. Henshaw—"

"Do you know about your name at the murder scene?"

"Did you go see this psychic on a regular basis?"

"Did Crystal tell you the names of the murderers you've been given credit for discovering in the past?"

"Who—"

"My dog," Susan wailed to the wall of humanity. "Does anyone see my dog? I—"

"Susan! Susan! I have Clue. Back door!"

Susan recognized Kathleen's voice. She scowled one last time at the group before spinning and reentering her home, slamming the front door behind her. She slipped the dead bolt and flipped the switch to turn off the light over the doorway. As much as she believed in freedom of the press as a general principle, she didn't think they should be free to stamp all over her lawn and damage the budding azaleas which she had planted only last fall.

Kathleen, younger and in wonderful shape, had zipped around the garage, through the backyard, and was entering her kitchen, Clue by her side, as Susan pushed open the door from the hallway. "Oh, Kathleen, I can't tell you how relieved I was when I heard your voice," Susan said, kneeling down to hug her dog. "For a moment, I thought I'd lost Clue." She buried her face in the dog's golden ruff.

"Susan, we have a problem."

Susan stood up, stretching out her back. "I assume you're referring to something other than those idiots out front."

"Have you seen today's *Hancock Herald*?"

"Kathleen, I've been too busy to read the paper. You won't believe what's happened. . . ."

"Look at this." Kathleen pulled two crumpled sheets of paper from her jacket pocket and placed them on the kitchen table.

The headline said it all: HANCOCK'S FUTURE JEOPARDIZED. SCOTT WORTH AND WORTHINGTON SECURITIES IN DIRE FINANCIAL SITUATION.

"I know all of this," Susan said, heading for the refrigerator. She could use a Coke.

"Then have you thought about how angry people are going to be when they hear about this? This article implies that Scott is personally responsible for putting Hancock at risk. There's even a mention of municipalities who have been forced to declare bankruptcy over less than this. Susan, we pay huge taxes. This type of thing isn't supposed to happen here. Everyone is furious."

"How do you know?" She opened the can and pulled two glasses from the cupboard.

"I've been getting calls all afternoon. Haven't you?"

"I was out. But why would anyone call me about this?"

"Because they're refusing to bake or cook or bring food to help Scott entertain after Amanda's funeral."

Susan put down the Coke can and reached back in the refrigerator. When she turned around again there was a bottle of white wine in her hand. "Want some?"

"Definitely."

"How many people have quit on us?"

"A half dozen before I left home."

"I have lots of messages on my machine. They could be calling about the same thing."

"They probably are. Thanks." Kathleen accepted a glass of wine.

"On the other hand, fewer people will be coming to the funeral and to the reception afterward. . . ."

"I wouldn't count on that. Everyone I talked with is furious, but they're curious at the same time. They are determined not to help Scott out, but they have no intention of missing what might turn out to be the oddest social event of the season—and maybe the largest."

"You're telling me fewer people are going to bring food, but more may be coming."

"The press alone—" Kathleen began.

"We have to feed those monsters who are squashing my garden right now?"

"We don't have to. Scott has to," Kathleen reminded her quietly. "Why are the press hounding you all of a sudden?"

"Probably because my name was written on the mirror in the room where Crystal's body was found."

"What?"

There was only one way to interpret that shriek. "I gather you didn't know that Crystal was killed at the Nutmeg Motel today."

"I had no idea."

"Did you know that Crystal lives next door to Carla? And that Carla has been helping her—or him—by supplying background information about some of the people who come to him to have their fortunes told."

Kathleen looked at her friend. "Her or him?"

"Crystal is a man. In drag. Or a transvestite. Or a cross-dresser."

"You're saying he wears women's clothing—for whatever reason."

"Yes."

"And he lives near Carla—the Carla who cleans my house once a week."

"Yes."

"And she tells him things about people that she finds out while cleaning their homes."

"Yes, but not just things about the people she works for, also about their friends and acquaintances. I mean, think of the phone calls you make that she overhears. She . . . she does it to help Crystal."

Kathleen was silent for a moment.

"Kathleen, I don't think you should be mad at her. She's a good person and she wouldn't have done anything if she thought it might hurt someone."

"I'm not mad at Carla. I know how hard she works—on my house and bringing up her girls. I was just remembering how shocked I was when I first came to Hancock at the way all you people had so many strangers working on—and in— your homes. I thought it was odd because you all seemed completely unaware of how much these people knew about you, and your families and your lives. Now I've become the same way."

"I know what you mean. But—for better or worse—we need all these people to maintain our lifestyles."

"I guess."

Susan realized she had more explaining to do. "Carla didn't just help Crystal with background information about his clients. She also helped Crystal help Amanda get clients for Scott."

"How did she do that? And why?"

"I'm telling this story backward. You see, it turns out that Crystal came to Hancock at Amanda's invitation. In fact,

Crystal lived in an apartment above the Worths' garage when she first came to town."

"Really?"

"Yes. Carla didn't know a whole lot about that. But she said something that really struck me as odd."

"What?"

"She said that Crystal hated Scott because of what he forced his wife to do."

"What? Baking all that bread? Being the perfect little shopper?"

"No, he depended on her to get him new clients—is that what they're called?"

"The people who invest in Worthington Securities? I suppose. But how did he do that? I mean, besides the social schmoozing that goes on all over town incessantly."

"What Carla told me goes way beyond giving gourmet dinners for potential clients."

"What?"

"Carla heard rumors about who had money—either some sort of financial windfall, a promotion, or an inheritance. The example she gave—without mentioning names—is a someone who had invested in an IPO that boomed in just weeks. She told Crystal and Crystal told Amanda and then . . ."

"And then?" Kathleen prompted as Susan stopped to take another sip of wine.

"And then Amanda got the wife of the person to start seeing Crystal and Crystal convinced her to invest in Worthington Securities."

"Sounds like a lot of work."

"Not for a couple of million dollars."

"That's true. . . ."

"The strange thing is that Carla got the impression that

Amanda didn't want to do this for Scott. That he somehow pressured her into doing it. And that Crystal helped out because he knew that."

"Did she say anything more specific?"

"She didn't know anything more specific. I told her to give me a call if she could think of anything concrete, something for me to check out, but I got the impression that she told me all she knew."

"How about names of people?"

"I asked. I asked and asked. She hated to tell me. But then, finally, she did. The Critchleys—Dr. Critchley, I should say. Apparently she worked for them. . . ."

"Sure. Kimberly and her ex. I actually got their day when Carla stopped working for them."

"Do you know why they no longer needed her?"

"Well, they left their house when they got divorced. Dr. Critchley and his new wife moved into a mansion. I heard that they were going to get a live-in housekeeper. And Kimberly moved into an apartment, didn't she? She probably decided that, living alone in a smaller place, she could do her own cleaning."

"She probably couldn't afford one either," Susan suggested. "But, apparently, Carla knew that the doctor was looking for someplace to invest his money; she told Crystal and Crystal told Kimberly . . . or maybe the new wife. And Worthington Securities got another big investor," she added, frowning.

"What's wrong?"

"Dr. Critchley's new wife is a scientist. Would a scientist see a psychic?"

"Good question. Is there a list of Crystal's clients somewhere?"

"Brett and I looked around his apartment and I didn't see one. I don't think Brett took anything with him. If there's a list, it would be there."

"Crystal didn't have an office, did she? Or he."

"Not unless there's one at that tea shop downtown where he did his readings." Susan put down her wineglass. "I wonder if there is one."

"It would be interesting to find out."

They exchanged looks.

"Jed will be home, but I could leave a note for him."

"Jerry's already home."

"What?"

"He came home early. He says he gets more done at home. I suppose I could give him a call and see if he would feed the kids."

"The only problem is how are we going to get past that crowd out front?"

"Are they still there?"

"You call Jerry and I'll go look."

"Don't open the door!"

"I'll use the peephole," Susan assured her.

But the press corps had left, her smashed azaleas the only sign that they had ever been there. And Jerry, apparently, was more than happy to quit work and drive the kids to McDonald's for a fat-filled Happy Meal.

Susan and Kathleen went to the tea shop, stopping their investigation long enough to wonder at the ability of males to completely ignore nutrition when feeding their young.

TWENTY-EIGHT

THE TEA ROOM WAS STILL OPEN AND A WAKE WAS IN PROGRESS. Susan didn't know whether the place had a liquor license, but she and Kathleen were offered glasses of wine as they walked in the door. The waitress who had waited on her the other day was wandering around, in tears, talking about the pagan concept of an afterlife to anyone who would listen.

Susan and Kathleen were not interested. Many of Crystal's clients were sitting around, drinking and talking about what her death would mean to them. Susan and Kathleen sat at an empty table and listened in as they sipped dreadful, sweet wine from not terribly clean glasses.

"They all seem to be referring to Crystal as her," Kathleen whispered, leaning toward Susan.

Susan nodded. "Interesting, isn't it? I think these people were mainly clients. I sure wish I could ask one of them if he had an office here."

"Maybe you should just look around."

"Good thinking. I think I'll try to find the ladies' room," Susan said loudly, standing up.

Kathleen, who had an idea of what Susan was really planning to do, nodded. "I'll see what I can find out here." She smiled across the room at an elderly woman sitting alone sniffling into her teacup.

"Great." Susan slung her purse over her shoulder and walked toward the back of the room, past the alcove where Crystal had worked. Someone had hung black crepe paper around the curtains. It had apparently been used before. Susan noticed a scrap of tape decorated with a perky jack-o'-lantern still attached to one end of the crepe. There was a sign on the wall nearby directing patrons to the rest rooms, but Susan, choosing to ignore it, kept on in the direction she had been heading. Opposite the rest rooms, there were two unmarked doors. She opened the first one she came to.

An office! Glancing over her shoulder to check if she was being observed, she slipped in and closed the door behind her. Now to find out whose office. It was a tiny room, almost filled by an old, ratty metal desk and a newer, but still ratty, chair. There was also a two-drawer file cabinet with a much used Mr. Coffee on top. Susan was about to open the desk drawer when she realized she wasn't alone.

"May I help you?" The voice of the woman standing in the doorway was definitely more than a little cool.

"I . . ." When in doubt, try honesty, Susan decided. "I was looking for Crystal's office."

"Why?"

"He left something in there for me." Susan bit her tongue, realizing she had used the wrong pronoun for this environment.

Or perhaps she hadn't. A weak smile flickered over the woman's face. "So you know our Crystal well. Then you might as well see if what he left you is in his office. Next door. On the right."

And Susan was left alone, heart beating furiously, but

pleased with herself. Maybe telling the truth was as good an idea as she had always insisted it was when talking with her children. She hurried into the office next door.

This one reflected more of Crystal's professional image. The walls were covered with posters of astrological signs. A bentwood coatrack displayed capes and shawls in various exotic silky fabrics. Instead of a desk and chair, a rose-colored velvet chaise longue stood in the middle of the room, embroidered pillows piled luxuriously against its back. Susan frowned. A brass samovar stood on a tiny inlaid teak table. If Crystal had paperwork, she didn't have it here. On the other hand, Crystal had taken a credit card in payment from her. Certainly she wasn't the only person who hadn't paid cash. There must be records. . . .

"Can't find what Crystal left for you?" The woman who had directed her here had returned. Her smile had turned into a frown in the minutes since they last met.

"I . . . He . . ." Well, it had worked once, she might as well try again. "I'm looking for credit card receipts, records of clients, that sort of thing," she ended, realizing she'd better figure out a reason why she would need such things.

"Oh, my God, you're his accountant. He told me he was going to be audited by the IRS and that he was hiring someone to help him out."

Truth would only get her so far. "Yes, I am." She looked around the room again. "I gather I'm in the wrong place for such things?"

"You sure as shit are! Crystal used this place to talk privately to his clients—you know, some of the hoity-toity people in this town don't want it known that they see a psychic."

"Where are those records?" Susan asked, not interested in the opinions of this woman.

"You were in the right place when I first ran into you. My office. Come on back."

Susan sighed. She would have liked more time to look around, but she had to follow through with her own lies.

"I should introduce myself. Joyce Patterson. I own this dump."

"If you don't mind my saying it, you don't seem like the type of person who would own a tea shop. I mean, I think of them as being owned by English gentlewomen and the like."

"And what the hell is like an English gentlewoman?" Joyce Patterson growled. "But if you're looking for one of them wilting flower types, you better look somewhere else. I ain't her."

"No, I—" She retreated to her former lie. "I'm just looking for Crystal's financial records."

"They're gonna audit a dead guy?"

"You know the IRS," Susan replied, hoping that Joyce didn't.

"Yeah. I dated one of them auditors once. And only once. If you know what I mean."

Susan didn't, but she didn't argue either. If Joyce wasn't a wilting flower, she wasn't the chatty type either. She went straight to the file cabinets on the wall and pulled out three manila folders. "This is what you're looking for."

"Thank you." Susan flipped open the one on top and pretended to study the documents inside. "How long did Crystal work here?" she asked, as though making casual conversation.

"A few years."

"Have you owned this place a long time?"

"Listen, you may be an accountant." She narrowed her eyes. "Or you may not be. I can't say that I care. But I ain't the one getting audited and I ain't answering any more questions."

"I . . . I'm sorry. I'll just take these with me and . . ."

"Now, I don't know that you should be taking things off the premises. . . ."

Kathleen appeared in the doorway. "Do you have the records? We need to return to the office," she announced in her most professional tone of voice.

"Yeah, she got her stuff. Good luck with those IRS bastards."

"I never let them get the best of me," Susan assured her, clutching the papers to her chest. The two women wove their way between tables. The wine seemed to have numbed some of the pain of the patrons and there were giggles as well as tears.

"What is that stuff?"

"All Crystal's financial records."

"You didn't claim to be employed by the IRS, did you? It's a felony to claim to be an officer of the United States government."

"I said I was Crystal's accountant."

"Oh, well, I think anyone can say they're an accountant. What was the office like?"

"Crystal's office was really a private place to meet clients. The owner's office was as run-down and sloppy as the owner herself."

They got into Kathleen's car. Susan tried to go through the papers, but it was too dark.

"You know, neither of us has any responsibilities for the evening. . . ."

"Except for figuring out how we're going to feed all those

people coming to Scott's home the day after tomorrow," Susan reminded her.

"I was going to suggest we go to the Inn, get dinner, and go through those papers."

"And maybe sit down and try to figure out what's missing from this puzzle," Susan said, nodding vigorously. "But I have a better idea."

"What."

"Dinner at the Nutmeg Motel."

"Susan . . ."

"I know. The food is dreadful, but I have a lot of questions to ask."

"The police have probably finished their work and left by now," Kathleen reminded her.

"I wasn't thinking of them. In fact, I'd rather avoid Brett right now. There are things I probably should tell him. Like what Carla told me."

"Are you protecting Carla?"

"I guess."

Kathleen chuckled. "So you have decided you'll figure out who killed Amanda and Crystal, and Brett will never have to know what Carla was doing to help out Crystal."

"Exactly," Susan answered.

"I understand and I'm sure Carla would, too."

"Do you think there are two different murderers here?" Susan asked.

"I don't know," Kathleen answered. "What do you think?"

"Somehow I think so."

"Why?"

"Well, the locations where they took place are so different. The dressing room was a pretty public place. Anyone could have pushed aside that curtain and seen what was go-

ing on. Heavens, if Amanda had fallen in a different direction, she might have landed in the aisle and the murderer
probably would have been caught immediately."

"And you think Crystal's murder was planned?"

"Yes. That motel is known—among its clients—as a
place to find privacy. A place where illicit affairs take place
with, apparently, no fear of discovery is a pretty smart place
to kill someone."

"So you think that Amanda's murderer took advantage of
finding Amanda at a vulnerable moment in a private spot,
but Crystal's killer lured him there."

"Exactly!" Susan said.

"It's also possible that the same person killed them both,
but the second killing was less urgent."

"What do you mean?"

"Well, the first murder was riskier—there was a greater
chance that the killer would be seen and caught. But, for some
reason or another, it was important that Amanda die as soon
as possible so it was worth taking a risk. The same person
could have wanted Crystal dead, but it wasn't as urgent. So
he—or she—arranged for Crystal to be in a private place."
Kathleen turned the steering wheel sharply and, looking out
the window, Susan realized they were in the Nutmeg Motel's
parking lot. "We're here," Kathleen announced.

"Good thing. I'm starving. . . . Or maybe that's a bad
thing," Susan said, remembering the food she had been
served here.

"Possibly," Kathleen agreed. "Look on the floor of the
seat behind you. I think there's some paper back there."

Susan felt around and came up with a puffy plastic Hello
Kitty notebook. "This okay to use?" she asked, waving it in
the air.

"Sure is. Someone gave it to Alex. He hates it, but won't let his sister have it. If we take it over, it will end their argument."

"Nothing like sibling rivalry," Susan commented waiting for Kathleen to set the car alarm.

"It gets better as they get older, right?"

"Nope," Susan assured her friend.

The restaurant at the Nutmeg Motel seemed to be enjoying a surge in popularity. Four tables were full.

"These people don't look like couples enjoying an illicit evening together," Susan whispered to Kathleen.

"Maybe ménage à trois has become popular in Hancock," she suggested, looking around.

"You can seat yourself," came the call from the woman behind the cash register.

"Over there." Susan pointed to a table in the far corner of the room. "We're less likely to be overheard."

"Fine." For the second time in less than an hour the women wove their way across a table-strewn room.

"You know, I don't remember ever before spending so much time in restaurants and actually losing weight," Kathleen said, picking up the spoon before her and wiping it on a paper napkin.

"True. You know, considering the fact that we started out investigating the murder of a woman I assumed was one of the wealthiest in town, we've been hanging out at a lot of real dives. . . . You know, maybe it's time to find out what we would discover if we asked a few questions in Amanda's regular hangouts."

TWENTY-NINE

"Susan, we are hanging out in the places Amanda hung out in. They're just not the same places she and Scott talked about going to," Kathleen said, picking up one of the menus the waitress had rather casually tossed on their table.

"She didn't live the life we all thought she lived, did she?" Susan commented, doing the same thing. "And she's not the only one," she added.

"Who are you thinking about?"

"Kimberly. I keep remembering what she said to me about living in Hancock without a considerable income."

"It can't be a new idea, Susan. You're not naive. You know most of our friends and neighbors have more money than . . . well, than necessary."

"Yes, but for something so important, we sure don't like to talk about it."

"What do you mean?"

"Well, look at us. We're good friends. Jerry and Jed have worked together for decades. We probably know pretty much what Jerry makes, and you and Jerry could make a pretty accurate guess about Jed's income. And we talk about most everything—except our incomes."

"True."

Their waitress had returned and they focused their attention on the menu.

"What is the dinner special?" Kathleen asked.

"Same as the lunch special. New England Clam Chowder. Corn bread muffins. Green salad with house dressing."

"Is the clam chowder canned?" Susan asked.

"Yup."

"I'll have the special then."

"I'll have the turkey dinner. With gravy on the side, please," Kathleen said.

"I'll see if I can do that. What do you want to drink?"

"I'll have decaf coffee," Susan answered.

"Just water, please."

"Ours comes out of the tap, not a bottle."

"That's fine."

"Just thought I'd warn you. You wouldn't believe how fussy some of our customers are. Act as though they think they're at the Ritz."

Susan and Kathleen exchanged looks.

"Have you worked here long?" Susan asked.

Any inclination the woman had to stop and chat vanished immediately. "You two aren't reporters, are you? Because I told them and I'll tell you. I take your order to the kitchen. I bring back your food when it's ready. I don't answer questions."

"Just making conversation," Susan lied. Apparently it was getting to be a habit.

"Yeah, right, I've heard that before." And their waitress vanished.

"How the hell does this place stay in business?" Kathleen asked when they were alone again. "There can't be that many people in Hancock having affairs—and want to have them in a fleabag motel as well."

"Good point. Hey, look who's here."

Susan turned around as Erika backed out of the doorway. "Erika! Erika!" She lowered her voice and turned to Kathleen. "Do you mind if she joins us?"

"Sounds like a good idea to me. Maybe Brett has told her something we don't know."

Erika hurried over to their table. "I don't suppose you've seen Brett," she said after greeting them.

"Not for hours. Were you meeting him here?"

"No, we had dinner plans, but he canceled. The message on my machine said something about an investigation at the Nutmeg Motel. I was hoping to catch him and talk him into a quick bite to eat. Guess I'm too late."

"We haven't seen him."

"He's probably with that woman."

"What woman?"

"Our esteemed mayor. She has a crush on him."

"Mary Pierson? You're kidding."

"Nope . . . she calls and calls. About things that are only vaguely business."

"Maybe she isn't interested in Brett," Susan suggested. "Maybe she just wants to know what he knows—about Worthington Securities."

"Maybe. Mind if I join you?"

"Of course not. But the food here is dreadful."

"Doesn't matter to me. I need to lose a few pounds." She picked up the menu and ordered a turkey dinner when their waitress reappeared with drinks for the table. "Brett's message was also about Crystal's death. So, do you think there is one murderer or two?" Erika asked when the three women were alone again.

"We were just discussing that," Susan explained, flipping open the notebook she had retrieved from Kathleen's backseat. "In fact, we're trying to get our thoughts organized. Maybe you can help."

"I'll try, but, frankly I'm not thinking all that well these days." Erika turned to Kathleen. "Brett and I are having problems. I want to get married and he wants to be married to someone who doesn't make more money than he does," she added in her typically blunt fashion.

"It's a male thing," Susan added.

"Not necessarily," Kathleen said. "I was hesitant about marrying Jerry. . . ."

"And you were a cop, too. Did that have anything to do with it?" Erika leaned across the table.

"Not really. Don't get me wrong. It's like coming from a different world. The police have a culture all their own. But that wasn't it. Jerry is a good person and he didn't need to be married to a reflection of himself. What got to me and made me hesitate was the money."

"Really?"

"Sure. In the first place, people with money are different. But I figured I was smart and I could blend in with Jerry's world. But money is power. And status. And as a society, we believe that the more money you have the smarter you are. The difference between Jerry's earning capabilities and mine was so great. I didn't want to end up the lesser person in the relationship. It didn't have anything to do with male and female differences. In the long run, it had to do with pride. My pride in my own worth."

Erika frowned. "Sounds like Brett."

"But not like Scott Worth," Susan commented. She had been writing as the other two women talked.

"Are you taking notes about our conversation?"

"No, just scribbling and thinking about Scott Worth and Amanda. I wonder if one of them married into money."

"Oh, Scott did," Erika explained.

"How do you know that?" Susan asked.

"Brett told me. Apparently Amanda's family had tons of money. Her father developed whole blocks of New York City," Erika answered.

"That was in Amanda's obituary," Kathleen said.

"But Brett said that Scott's family was involved in New York real estate, too. His father was actually the super in one of the buildings Amanda's father owned—and this was back in the days when superintendent was a long name for janitor."

"Wow. Amanda's parents must not have been thrilled about that marriage," Kathleen said.

"According to her obituary, they certainly sprung for a fabulous wedding," Susan reminded her.

"Oh, my God . . . I wonder if Carla was talking about Amanda when she told me—" Kathleen stopped.

"Told you what?"

"About a wealthy woman who was pregnant by one man and married another."

"Why—?" Susan began to ask the obvious question.

"Let me explain. See if you think it fits the facts here.

"The only reason I know about this is that Carla was worried about one of her nieces who was dating a young man Carla referred to as scum. Anyway, she started talking about a woman she . . . let me think for a minute. She said someone had told her about this woman."

"Could that mean it was someone she worked for?"

"I have no idea. Anyway, listen to this story and see if it fits. Oh, and the woman lives in Hancock. She did say that."

"So tell the story," Susan insisted.

"To begin with, the woman Carla told me about was the pampered and much loved daughter—an only child—of two wealthy and well-known parents. She fell in love with an unsuitable young man from the wrong side of the tracks, and her parents were not thrilled. They insisted she stop seeing the unsuitable young man and she did. They probably thought all was well; their daughter went on with her life and they did, too. Until a year or so later when their daughter again put them in a panic by explaining that she was pregnant."

"The unsuitable young man?" Susan asked.

"Nope. Someone else. Carla didn't tell me who he was, or even if he's a significant part of the story, but this young woman explained that she would not or could not marry the father of her child. Her parents were upset; no one had any idea what to do. Until the unsuitable young man reappeared and offered to marry their pregnant daughter."

"Could he have been the father?" Susan asked.

"Maybe. The parents of the girl were thrilled. They gave her a huge wedding. They paid for a lavish honeymoon. And then they retired to the sun belt somewhere and the happy young couple moved into their house."

"Does that fit what you know about Scott and Amanda?" Erika asked.

"Up until the baby is born. The Worths don't have any children," Susan said.

"The baby only lived two days," Katherine explained. "Carla thought perhaps it was a sign that the couple should not have married. She said it was not a love match."

"But she loved him once," Erika said.

"He did not love her. He married her because he wanted her family's money. And, of course, he got some of it—an expensive trip, a fabulous house. But, for a greedy person, it wasn't enough. And—and this is where it sounds even more like Amanda and Scott—in her grief, the young wife began to see psychics. She was trying to talk with her dead child apparently."

"That could be how Amanda met Crystal," Susan said, writing furiously.

"It could be. And, you know, it's possible that Crystal told Carla this story. She would protect Amanda's identity."

"True. They were close. In fact," Susan continued, "it would explain why Crystal came here from New York City. She moved into an apartment over the Worths' garage. Amanda would have wanted her nearby if she was helping her commune with her dead child."

"That's possible." Erika nodded vigorously.

"And Scott was around to see the effect Crystal's psychic powers had on his wife. Let's assume he married Amanda to get her parents' money. A man like that would always have his eyes open, hoping for an opportunity to make more money."

"What do you mean?"

"Well, we do know that Scott used Crystal's connection with Amanda for his own purposes."

"True."

"And you know what else we know?" Susan added.

"What?"

"We know that Crystal loved Amanda. That's what Carla said. And apparently she would know."

"So?"

"So suppose Scott sees that Amanda would do anything for Crystal hoping, sadly, to stay in touch with her dead child. And he sees that Crystal cares for Amanda and will do anything for her."

"Wait a second," Erika said. "Wouldn't Scott be jealous of Amanda and Crystal's relationship?"

"Possibly not. He didn't care about Amanda's relationship with the father of her child. And it's entirely possibly Scott didn't even know Crystal was male."

"Good point. Go on."

"There really isn't anything else. Crystal helped Amanda, and Amanda and Crystal helped Scott search out new investors for Worthington Securities. Everyone got what they wanted from this situation."

"Okay. Let's assume that you're right. What does that have to do with—" Erika shut her mouth and waited for their waitress to plunk their plates down on the table before them.

"What does it have to do with the murders?" She finished her question and peered down at her plate. "What is this yellow stuff? Mustard sauce?"

"I think it's turkey gravy. Kathleen asked for hers on the side."

"A request which was ignored," Kathleen said. "But that doesn't matter now. Answer Erika's question. What does this all have to do with the murders?"

"Damned if I know," Susan said and tasted her soup. It was awful.

"How is everything?" Their waitress reappeared by their table.

"Is this Campbell's soup?"

"No. Cook ran out. So she added some water and milk to

some clam dip she found in the back of the freezer. How is it?"

"I . . . Dreadful, to be honest."

"Told her it was a stupid idea," the waitress announced in a "don't blame me" tone of voice and turned and left.

The women looked at one another, almost identical expressions of astonishment on their faces.

Kathleen scraped the gravy off her turkey. "Ugh. Turkey loaf. I haven't seen this stuff since I was in grammar school."

"You know, I'll bet we could get a table at the Hancock Inn," Erika suggested quietly. "I could leave a message for Brett to meet me there."

Susan stood up. "You two go on ahead. I have an idea."

"What is it?"

"Tonight is the first night viewing at the funeral home, isn't it?"

"Yes, but I don't particularly want to go on an empty stomach," Kathleen said.

"I don't want to go. I just want to make sure Scott isn't home."

THIRTY

AMANDA'S VIEWING WAS PROVIDING MANY EXCELLENT opportunities for an enterprising burglar. The block the Worths lived on appeared deserted. Neighbors were probably busy comforting the bereaved husband, Susan decided, dashing up the driveway to the garage. She had parked around the corner. Right now she was wishing she was in better shape. Her heart was pounding. Of course, as she was going to break into a house for the first time in her long life, a jump in blood pressure wasn't terribly unusual.

Well, not a house, she reminded herself. The apartment above the garage was her goal. There was an outside stairway and she ran up it, her feet pounding on each step. The door at the top was locked. Damn! She spun around. Tripped. Reached out to catch herself. And put her hand through a pane of glass.

"Shit!" She had pulled her hand back out before realizing that she was risking a bad cut. She peered at her wrist. Not a scratch.

Well, as long as the glass was already broken . . . Carefully this time, she reached in, found the doorknob, and turned. The door opened. Susan slipped inside, closing the door behind her.

She was glad to detect the musty smell of a space long closed up. Perhaps no one had visited for years. Perhaps there was some sign of Crystal's habitation. Two small dormer windows admitted some light and she peered about her.

The large room had been divided into a sitting area and a sleeping area. Couches and chairs were arranged in one, a bed and dresser in the other. Everything was covered with dust. But only one thing interested Susan. Along the far wall, on the other side of the bed, old torn bedsheets covered large rectangular objects.

If only she had thought to bring . . . Before she had formed the thought, she saw the flashlight lying on top of the dresser. Bingo. Her luck held, the batteries were fresh. She picked up the sheets and discovered long racks of women's clothing—clothing too small for Crystal.

Susan sighed and plopped down on the bed. She had found the overflow from Amanda's closet. Big deal. Lots of women had a place like this where they stored clothing they had loved in the past and were hoping to fit into again in the distant future. She leaned back and thought. She'd been running around for three days. There had been a second murder. She had learned a lot and accomplished nothing. As well, plans for Amanda's reception were falling apart. The thought of finding more people to bring food was exhausting.

So much so that she fell asleep.

Her first thought upon waking was earthquake. The bed was shaking. The walls of her—and then, of course, she realized she wasn't in her bedroom. And the reason for the shaking was the garage door opening. No, closing, she decided, hearing the smack of wood hitting cement. She struggled into a sitting position, stiff, cold, and nervous. The flashlight was lying by her side, batteries dead. As she got up, light came through the dormer windows and she realized someone had illuminated the porch. She peered out the window. Scott Worth was entering his house. And he wasn't alone.

She tiptoed to the door and climbed down the stairway, wondering why it hadn't seemed as creaky on the way up. She was cold and stiff. But, mostly, she was curious. Who had accompanied Scott home from the viewing? Staying in the shadow of the garage, she ran to the house and tiptoed up the stairs to the porch. Only to realize that Scott and his guest were standing just inside the back door. They were arguing. She leaned closer.

"I was her best friend. . . ."

Lauren!

". . . and I brought big money clients to Worthington Securities. You might want to remember that. Amanda knew how much you both owed me."

"In the past few years, my wife and I spoke as little as possible. But whenever Amanda spoke about you it was with undisguised disdain. My wife, dear Lauren, couldn't stand you."

"I—"

"You are everything Amanda claimed she hated: shallow, interested only in money and social position; she despised you and avoided you. Of course, I am, as you undoubtedly know, exactly the same. And it was not quite as easy for Amanda to avoid me."

Susan held her breath, not wanting to miss a word of Lauren's response. Lauren was always talking about how close she and Amanda were. . . .

"I didn't like Amanda any more than she liked me!"

"I wouldn't say that in public, my dear. You don't want anyone to think you might have had a motive for murder."

"I don't kill everyone I hate. Otherwise, you wouldn't be walking around."

Susan swung back around a corner, barely avoiding being caught by Lauren as, pulling open the ornate screen door, she stomped out of the house and started down the driveway. Only to stop dead.

Susan realized what the problem was.

"Lauren!"

"What—?"

"Shhh. Lauren, I'm over here."

"Who's calling me?"

She gave up. Lauren was incapable of being quiet. Susan ran out of her hiding place and hurried down the drive, away from the house, grabbing Lauren as she passed. "It's Susan Henshaw. And I have a car," she hissed.

"Why didn't you just say so, for heaven's sake?"

"It's parked around the corner," Susan explained in a normal voice.

"Why did you park so far away? Why are you here?"

"I—"

"It doesn't matter. Just as long as you can give me a ride."

"Sure. Where do you want to go?"

"My car is at the funeral home, but I can't stand the idea of going back there. Such a depressing place. Just drive me home, why don't you?"

"Of course."

The activity level on the street had picked up. Couples were arriving home, lights were being turned on. Dogs barked greetings to their owners. Pixie, waving happily, roared by in a bright red Porsche. The man driving was wearing a baseball cap over long, silvery hair. Susan waved back and unlocked her car.

"Who was that?" Lauren asked, getting in the passenger's seat. "And who's the hippie driving?"

"Pixie Newman. I guess she's with her husband. He's called something like Beep. . . ."

"Beeb Newman! Pixie and Beeb Newman. Don't tell me you know them."

"Pixie was in my Brownie troop when I was a scout leader. Why?"

"Susan, everyone knows about them. Beeb is famous. He's on MTV all the time."

"Why?"

"He's a singer. He has his own rock group. You didn't know?"

"No. Pixie didn't mention that."

"I'd love to be introduced to them," Lauren said. "They're not involved in anything around here. They don't mix much with their neighbors is what I heard. But you know Pixie."

"Maybe we could all have lunch together sometime," Susan suggested knowing that, like many of these things, this particular event would never happen.

"Fabulous idea. We should go someplace interesting. You know, not something standard like the Hancock Inn, someplace sort of . . . uh . . . funky."

"I don't think I know—actually, I do know a place that's interesting, unusual—and the food is fabulous." And Carla's family could use the business.

"Great. Why don't you call her and suggest next week sometime. Monday would be best for me."

Susan sighed. So much for getting out of it. "I'll call Pixie after the funeral. Or maybe I'll talk to her at the Worths'. She said she would help me set up in the morning before the church service. . . ."

"I will too. Susan, don't tell me you have all the people you need," Lauren pleaded.

"I don't. In fact, I still need a volunteer to bring salads and bread," she added, striking while the iron was hot.

"I'll do it. My cook can make big bowls of tortellini salad—her recipe is wonderful—little tomatoes, peppers, dill, peas, olives, sweet pickles, all sorts of stuff. Everyone loves it! And I'll go to the bakery and buy bread. Croissants, baguettes, those little Italian rolls—for how many people?"

"Say four hundred," Susan answered slowly.

"Fine. Now, what time is Pixie going to be at the house?"

"Nine A.M.," Susan answered quickly, hoping she remembered to call Pixie and relay this information to her.

"Great. I'm getting my hair done at eight. And I'll pick up the bakery order on the way to the house. Oh, Susan, I don't know how I can thank you. I've been dying to meet Pixie and Beeb Newman. Who would have thought you would turn out to know them."

"Oh, stop. Turn there. Not left. Turn right."

"Where are we going?"

"My house. . . . Oh, I guess you didn't know. We moved. Over a year ago. We live on Weston Road now. At the top."

The lots got larger and the houses bigger as they approached what Lauren had referred to as "the top." Susan looked around as she drove. She hadn't been in this section of town for a while and she hardly recognized it. House after house had been torn down, replaced with modern extravaganzas. All sorts of colors had been used and facades were wood, stone, stucco, or brick. There was a large variety of styles and shapes. But there was one common denominator: all the buildings had been designed to impress.

Susan glanced over at Lauren. She couldn't see any sign

that Scott Worth's anger had upset her. "How was the viewing?" she asked.

"Standing room only. Amanda would have loved it! Everyone who is anyone in Hancock was there. I saw the mayor. And Brett Fortesque—our hunky police chief—of course, he may only have been there because Amanda was murdered."

"Why did you come home with Scott?" Susan asked.

"He was so upset. I didn't think he should be alone."

"That's nice of you," Susan said, putting her foot on the brake. She was coming to the end of the road.

"Number eight is mine," Lauren announced, pointing to a particularly hideous mansion set in the middle of a fabulously manicured large lawn.

"You have daffodils. So early! What kind are they?"

"I have no idea. The gardener planted them a few days ago."

"Fall bulbs in the spring—You mean they were planted in bloom?"

"Sure. We're having a few people in after Amanda's funeral. I wanted everything to look nice."

"Of course. . . ." Susan had no idea what else to say. She wondered if Lauren would invite her in to see her new home.

Apparently the thought had never occurred to her. "Thanks for the ride, Susan. Don't forget about lunch with Pixie Newman!"

"I won't," Susan assured her. And, in fact, she wouldn't. She wouldn't arrange it. But she wouldn't forget it, either.

Despite her short nap, Susan arrived home exhausted. It was late and she had missed dinner. But, on the plus side, Clue had been fed and walked, and was keeping a sleeping Jed company in front of the TV. And she happened to know there was a small crock of Stilton cheese in the back of the refrigerator—and a nice bottle of Merlot in the basement.

She dumped her purse on the kitchen counter and reached for the refrigerator door, remembering when she had bought this crock of imported cheese. She had been planning a lazy evening after a day of productive shopping at Once in a Blue Moon. This was to have been a treat for herself and her cholesterol conscious husband. They would sit in front of the fireplace and snack while she modeled the clothing she had bought that day.

Susan frowned, putting down the cheese. So much had happened that she hadn't even tried on her purchases. Her full shopping bags were still on the window seat in her bedroom where she had left them the day of Amanda's murder. Well, no time like the present.

A few minutes later, she was standing in front of a full-length mirror wearing a swimsuit, T-shirt, and a pair of Cole-Haan fur-lined boots. She looked foolish, but she wasn't thinking about the way she looked. She had just realized that she might know who had killed Amanda.

Tomorrow she would check it all out.

The next morning, early, Susan was sitting in her car, parked behind the Dansk outlet at Once in a Blue Moon, talking on her cell phone.

"I'm early, but I couldn't wait to get here," she explained to Kathleen. "What do you think about my idea?" She didn't listen to Kathleen's answer. "Kath . . . I think the stores are opening. I'd better get going. I'll give you a call when I have some answers." She flicked the phone shut and hopped out of the car.

Once in a Blue Moon seemed as popular as it had been on

opening day. Susan slipped into the crowd of early bird shoppers. She carried a small Anne Klein shopping bag and headed to that store first.

"I need to return this shirt," she explained to the woman at the cash register.

"Customer service. Other register."

Susan interpreted that to mean that the blond woman standing next to the other cash register was the only person capable of taking back her shirt and giving her a refund.

Perhaps customer service was her job description, but she sure didn't interpret the words the way Susan would have.

"Do you have a receipt?" she asked, examining the price tag suspiciously.

"In my purse." In fact, Susan had a whole pile of receipts in her purse. The problem was finding the correct one. "I know it's in here somewhere . . . You know, this shirt only cost sixteen dollars."

"I follow the rules. No receipt, no tags, no returns. You wouldn't believe the stuff people pull. We go through the dressing rooms at night and find more of our customers' property than ours."

Susan stopped searching through the little pieces of paper and looked up. "Do you try to return their property to them?"

"They don't want the stuff they leave. That's why they leave it. They want the stuff they exchange for it. They're stealing."

"How?"

The woman sighed at Susan's ignorance. "They take off their clothing, put on our things and walk right out of here."

Susan nodded. Exactly what she had been thinking. "Do all the stores have the same problem?"

"All of them that I know about."

"You know what? I think I'll keep this shirt," Susan said.

"Was it something I said?" the customer service representative asked, a knowing expression on her face.

Susan didn't bother to answer. She tucked everything—T-shirt included—in her capacious handbag, turned, and left the store. She had one more thing to do. It was time to return to the scene of the crime.

The Saks outlet was jammed and Susan, listening to the shoppers, realized many of them were more interested in seeing the spot where Amanda had been killed than in shopping for bargains. Susan understood exactly what motivated them. She was here for the same reason.

"Can I help you?"

Déjà vu! Susan recognized that voice and turned to find the store security person at her side.

"I remember you. You claimed to have found the woman who was killed."

"I did find her!" Susan protested.

"So you say. I happen to know the police are still investigating her murder and that they have ruled out no one."

Susan realized what was being implied, but chose to ignore it. "Actually, I'm here to see the place where I found her."

"Why?"

"The police want me to look around and see if there's anything I missed the first time. Anything that might be significant," she lied.

"Then you better come with me. We'll look around together."

It didn't make any difference to Susan whether she was alone or not. She shrugged and followed the store detective through the milling crowd to the small dressing room. It was strange to be there again and she found herself remembering the afternoon Amanda was killed. She was sure she knew who the murderer was. It couldn't be anyone else. Not so much because there weren't other people around with a motive. Or even an opportunity. But because only one person had worked so hard at covering up.

From the minute Amanda was found, Susan had been looking in the wrong direction and at the wrong people. But that wasn't because there was no place else to look or no one else to look at. And it wasn't because she had eliminated all the other possibilities. She had been looking in the wrong place because she had been sent there—by the murderer.

THIRTY-ONE

KATHLEEN SANK DOWN IN A PLUSH CHAIR AND WAVED TO A hovering, attentive waiter. "I'll have a martini. Dry. Two olives, please."

"Yes, ma'am. Right away." He hurried off.

"I don't usually drink martinis, but it's been a trying day," Kathleen said.

"It turned out to be a nice funeral though, and it's great to be back here." Susan put down her drink and glanced around the flower-filled bar of the Hancock Inn.

"Amanda's reception was sensational—unique and so-phisticated at the same time. She would have loved it," Kathleen said.

"Thanks to Carla's uncle and El Toro Nero. They really came through at the last minute."

"I've been worrying about that ever since I realized El Toro Nero was catering. They are going to be paid, aren't they?" Kathleen asked.

"They already were paid," Susan assured her. "Scott gave them a money order this morning, before the church service. I was there."

"How did you manage to get a man who never pays his bills to pay ahead of time?" Kathleen asked.

"I blackmailed him."

"Are you saying he killed . . . ?"

Susan realized exactly what Kathleen was going to ask. "No, he's not the murderer."

"Susan, I've been waiting all day to hear this story. Has there been an arrest?"

"Yes."

"Who?"

"Lauren Crone."

"Lauren murdered Amanda?"

"Yes. She was arrested last night, but the public announcement was put off. Brett believed it was appropriate to wait until after Amanda's funeral and apparently whoever is in charge of the other police department involved agreed with him."

Kathleen's drink had been delivered. She thanked the waiter and took her first sip before asking another question. "Why?"

"Because when everyone finds out about Lauren, they're also going to discover some pretty unappealing things about Amanda."

"Like what? That she shopped at outlet malls?"

"She wasn't shopping. She was shoplifting," Susan explained.

Kathleen took another sip and frowned. "Are you sure? I don't remember any bags of clothing at the crime scene."

"There weren't. But she was wearing new Ferragamos. Brand-new. She had walked from the Ferragamo outlet to the Saks outlet in them—leaving her old shoes behind."

"You're kidding."

"Nope. According to the salespeople at Once in a Blue Moon, it happens all the time. Of course, it happens in other places, too. My guess is that Amanda has been stealing from some of the best stores in New York City for years. In one way or another, she ended up with much of her extensive, expensive wardrobe for free. What with the stuff she stole and the stuff she returned after wearing once or twice . . ."

"Amanda did that?"

"You should see her closet. And, when I suggested to Scott Worth that he return an outfit I found in there with tags still attached, he went nuts. I didn't understand at the time, but later I realized he was afraid I'd stumbled onto information about the way Amanda obtained her elegant wardrobe."

"Did you?"

"Nope. I just thought she had died before she could wear those things. I don't bother to take tags off clothing until I'm ready to wear it sometimes. I assumed she had done the same. I had no idea why Scott was so upset."

"Did she steal all those Hermes scarves?"

"Maybe some. But I think a few may have been her mother's. Hermes has been around for generations. There's lots of old stuff in the house. She may have been selling off what she didn't want to wear."

"Funny how much of this had to do with clothing."

"Are you two talking about going shopping again?" Erika stood by their table. "I would have thought that your last shopping trip put you off new clothes for a while."

"Susan is telling me about Lauren's arrest," Kathleen explained.

"Would you like to join us?" Susan asked.

"I was hoping you'd ask. Brett was supposed to be meeting me here, but with all the press trying to interview Scott Worth again, who knows when he'll be free."

"You mean they're all interested in the arrest?" Kathleen asked.

"Nope. What interests them is Scott Worth and his financial scams."

"That did turn out to be interesting," Susan said.

"Susan, don't change the subject," Kathleen ordered. "You were about to tell me how you knew Lauren killed Amanda."

"I realized it the night before last when I was trying on the clothes I bought the day Amanda was killed."

"The mind works in mysterious ways," Erika commented to Kathleen.

"Susan's mind especially," Kathleen agreed.

"Do you want to hear how I came to my conclusion or don't you?"

"Yes, we do."

"Please go on."

"Well, it wasn't until I started trying on my new clothes that I realized I hadn't even considered going back to the mall and looking around. And, when I started wondering why I hadn't done something so obvious, I realized something else. From the minute I found Amanda, I was led in the wrong direction. Not because there was no place else to look. I was looking in the wrong place because Lauren sent me there.

"Like the Nutmeg Motel," she explained when neither woman responded. "The Nutmeg Motel had nothing to do with Amanda. She wasn't having an affair. She wasn't meeting a man there. But I got so caught up in the lie Lauren told that I didn't even consider anything else. Of course, Lauren also kept me so busy that I didn't have a lot of time to think."

"How did she do that?" Erika asked.

"She's the one who decided I should organize the reception today."

"But I thought Scott—"

"I know what you're going to say," Susan interrupted Kathleen, "and it was Scott who asked me to run the reception, but the idea was Lauren's. I should have realized that at the time.

"Scott didn't like the fact that I found Amanda. He knew I had investigated murders in the past and he was afraid I might discover unsavory things about his wife—such as the fact that she stole clothing. He called me at home the evening of the murder and threatened me. Lauren was at his house and may have overheard that conversation. Anyway, she suggested to him that I be put to work doing something else. When I saw Scott, he thought Lauren had already asked me to run Amanda's reception. I assumed he was confused by the shock of his wife's murder, but, in fact, Lauren and he had already discussed it.

"Of course, later, when I realized how odd it was that I had ended up involved like that, I just thought it had to do with Scott Worth's inability—or disinclination—to spend money. And everyone else thought the same thing."

"That's what I thought," Erika agreed.

"But I was so stupid! I did talk with the Worths' neighbors and with Kimberly, but I wasted so much time in the wrong place looking at the wrong things. I knew perfectly well that Lauren was nearby when Amanda was killed. She instigated a great cover-up. Right after the murder, Lauren picked up her cell phone, called everyone she could think of and told them about it. It was brilliant! The resulting mayhem, as well as the inexperienced security people at the mall, guaranteed that the investigation would get off to a rather unusual start."

"But why? Why did Lauren kill Amanda?" Kathleen asked.

"Money. Lauren thought she was using her friendship with Amanda to climb her way up in Hancock society. But Amanda was using Lauren. After years of this supposed friendship, the Crones had invested a lot of money in Worthington Securities. Lauren thought the investment would bring them status as well as money. But Lauren's husband is on the board at the Field Club—and he probably discovered that the Worths don't pay their bills. Like everyone else, he assumed that indicated that Worthington Securities was losing money. Lauren was furious when she heard about it. She encouraged and encouraged and encouraged Amanda to go to the mall. And, when she met her there, she killed her.

"You know, Crystal told me that Lauren would only kill Amanda if Amanda was standing in the way of something she wanted," Susan continued. "And he was right. Lauren wanted to be important and she knew that in Hancock, no matter how much we may deny it, money is status. She couldn't stand the idea of losing it."

"Did Lauren kill Crystal, too?"

"I think so."

"Why?"

"Fear. You have to remember that Lauren went to Crystal because she really believed that Crystal had special powers—could see into the future or read minds. After the murder, Lauren was probably terrified that Crystal knew what she had done. And then I asked Crystal to help me investigate. Lauren was nearby when Crystal agreed to help me; she may have heard it all. She must have been afraid that her secret wasn't safe as long as Crystal was alive. So she lured Crystal to the Nutmeg and shot him there. It was another smart move. Now, not only was I looking in the wrong place, but the entire police force was looking there with me.

"The police never connected Lauren with that location. To tell the truth, I never connected her with Amanda. Lauren was always talking about what good friends the two of them were, but I doubted if Amanda felt the same way. Of course, it turned out I was right. I don't think Amanda had any friends."

"Really?"

"Except for Kimberly Critchley. They remained friends after Kimberly's divorce. A divorce that cost Kimberly her financial stability. But, of course, Amanda managed to get Kimberly's ex-husband and his new wife to invest in Worthington Securities. I guess it's just another case of Amanda trying to get new investors for her husband's business."

"I thought Worthington Securities had lost lots of money," Erika said.

"That was a lie."

"You're kidding!" Kathleen exclaimed.

"That's what I was going to tell you earlier," Susan explained. "In fact, it's probably what Scott is explaining to all those reporters right now. I'm just glad it wasn't public knowledge this morning, otherwise I'd never have gotten Scott to pay El Toro Nero before they catered Amanda's reception."

"Does this mean you're finally going to tell me how you blackmailed Scott?"

"Blackmail? How interesting. Go on, Susan, tell." Erika put her elbows on the table, cupping her chin.

"Well, I told Scott that unless he did what I told him to do . . ."

"Pay for the catering ahead of time," Kathleen explained to Erika.

"I would tell Edgar Finch what he had been up to financially."

"But I thought Edgar knew Worthington Securities was losing money."

"That's what Edgar thought, yes. But it's not true."

"What?"

"What?"

Erika and Kathleen spoke together.

"Edgar Finch thought the Worths didn't pay their bills because they didn't have the money."

"You're not saying that it's not true."

"That's exactly what I'm saying. It's what the IRS and the SEC told Brett yesterday afternoon."

"But Scott—"

"Scott created a rather bizarre double-edged charade. To many people—most people in town until just a few days ago—he was a man who spent a lot of time broadcasting his wealth."

"Like those stories about Amanda shopping," Kathleen said.

"Exactly. But everyone knew those stories were a bit over-the-top. So the people the Worths owed money to just dismissed them as lies, decided the Worths didn't have the money they claimed to have and—"

"And stopped sending them bills!" Erika said, her voice rising. "You're saying it was all a scam!"

"Yes. And Edgar Finch was, unwittingly, a big part of that scam."

"How did that work?"

"Everyone in Hancock knows Edgar and respects him. Edgar had been keeping the Worths on at the Club and not requiring them to pay their dues because he firmly believed that Worthington Securities was insolvent. As the man in charge of the town's finances, he knew how important it was that there be no hint of problems there."

"Was he responsible for how and where Hancock's money was invested?"

"Yes. So he worked very hard to make sure no one might think the Worths were having financial problems—that was why he was so upset when he heard Amanda had been murdered. He thought the Worths were insolvent and that that fact would come out immediately. Of course, it looked like it did when the *Hancock Herald* published that inaccurate story."

"So the Worths are rich and Worthington Securities is doing just fine and all the little guys around—the small businesses—have been getting stiffed by them."

"Yes."

"Not after I make a bunch of phone calls. Scott Worth is going to do some serious bill paying in the not too distant future," Erika promised them.

"Good," Kathleen commented before asking another question. "But I have one more question. Why did Amanda stay with Scott?"

"That's the saddest thing of all," Susan answered. "She married him because it was convenient. And she stayed for what he offered. The money, the status, the lifestyle were all as important to her as they were to her husband."

"You know, this entire thing never would have happened if the people involved hadn't made money such an important part of their lives," Kathleen said.

"That's true." Erika spoke up. "Brett and I were talking last night and he said that the mistake everyone made was making decisions based on money rather than on the things that matter—like love." Erika ended almost silently.

Susan and Kathleen looked at each other. "Does this mean what I think it means?" Kathleen asked.

"Are you two getting married?"

"Engaged! You're engaged!"

"Well, we haven't set a date yet. . . ."

"Can I give you an engagement party?" Susan asked.

"I don't know—" Erika began.

"Oh, it would be such fun! We could have it outside as soon as the weather gets warmer. El Toro Nero can cater. And I could use those napkins I bought at the mall. I'll go back first thing in the morning and pick up a couple dozen more. I think margaritas for drinks and maybe quesadillas— wait, let me write this down before I forget." Susan pulled a notebook from her purse and began scribbling furiously.

"Well, you and Brett have done it now," Kathleen said to Erika. "One of the few things Susan enjoys more than investigating murder is planning a party."

Susan looked up. "Funerals are so sad, and Amanda's life ended up to be so meaningless." She sighed, put down her pen, and waved at the waiter. "But two of my favorite people are going to get married—finally. I think we should order a bottle of champagne. I need to make a toast."

"To what?" Kathleen asked.

"How about friendship," Erika suggested.

"And love," Kathleen added.

"And living happily ever after," Susan ended with a smile.

In affluent, suburban Hancock, Connecticut,
murder has become an unexpected
next-door neighbor to Susan Henshaw—
mother, housewife, and amateur sleuth.

VALERIE WOLZIEN
The Susan Henshaw Mysteries

MURDER AT THE PTA LUNCHEON
THE FORTIETH BIRTHDAY BODY
WE WISH YOU A MERRY MURDER
AN OLD FAITHFUL MURDER
ALL HALLOWS' EVIL
A STAR-SPANGLED MURDER
A GOOD YEAR FOR A CORPSE
'TIS THE SEASON TO BE MURDERED
REMODELED TO DEATH
ELECTED FOR DEATH
WEDDINGS ARE MURDER
THE STUDENT BODY

"Valerie Wolzien is a superlative crime writer."
—Mary Daheim

"Stylish, witty, wicked, and pleasing."
—*Tulsa World*

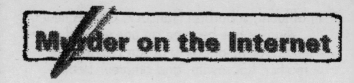